ONE STEP AHEAD

Steve Tullin

Kindle Direct Publisher KDP

Cover design by: Steve Tullin
Library of Congress Control Number: 2018675309
Printed in the United States of America

I would like to dedicate this novel to my deceased mom, Eleanor Tullin. She was not college-educated, but was one of the smartest people I've ever known. She was an avid fiction reader during much of her life. She instilled the love for books in me at a very young age. I remain a chain fiction junky to this day with way too many new books sitting on several shelves in my office.

PROLOGUE

I wriggled along the cold parquet floor of the narrow hallway like a snake. I tried to get up, but I could not. My hands were tied behind my back and my ankles were duct-taped tightly together. It was dark, but I could see a half-inch strip of yellow light between the frame and the wooden door. Whispers. I heard whispers. I tried to call out but my mouth was desert dry. More tape. More duct tape across my lips. I grunted, then screamed behind the tape. Can anyone hear me?

I was about twenty feet from the bedroom door. I heard a woman hissing, then a quick scream behind the door with the yellow strip of light. I moved my 6'4" frame forward a few more inches. My brain was swimming in a bath of dark Jello. I needed to get into that bedroom down the hall. I managed to undulate my stiff body more and then was violently halted by a giant rusty chain around my feet. Pulled back a foot or two. Gotta get into that room. Who screamed?

The bedroom door opened an inch more on squeaky hinges. More light spilled into the dark hallway. I tried to focus my eyes. Who was inside? Who screamed? I stretched my body forward again and raised my head a few inches off the floor. Huge droplets of blood splattered on the wood squares beneath me. My arms smeared the garnet fluid. Dripping. Dripping. From where? The door opened a bit more like a tree bough in a gentle breeze. More light. Another scream and more hissing. What is going on in there?

The door opened half-way. There was a man and woman standing near the queen sized bed. At first I couldn't make out who they were. More blood dripped on the floor. Dripping from my skull. I needed to see who was in that room. I stretched some more as the chain clanked on the wooden floor. I could see the man had his arm around the woman's neck. He had a gun in the other hand pointed *into her temple.*

"Del, Del, Del..." I yelled behind the duct-tape. She could not see me on the floor. I yelled again, but the man kept squeezing her neck in a choke hold. "Del, Del..."

"Corny, Corny, wake up. Corny, it's okay." Del shook him awake. Corny shot up from a prone position. The sheet fell from his upper body. There was a sheen of sweat all over his bare chest and back. "You were dreaming again, Corny. You're gonna be alright, Babe." Del explained. She jumped out of bed and ran for a towel in the bathroom. "Same nightmare?"

Corny shrugged with a slight shoulder tilt. Buster, his wire-haired terrier, raised his head in alarm.

"Here, you're all sweaty again. Wipe yourself off."

"Wow, again that freakin 'shit is tormenting me even after Joey blew Herman Girtler's brains out over a year ago," Corny muttered. "You got some cold water for me, please?"

"Sure, Babe. Be right back." Del padded barefoot into the kitchen. She took a cold Poland Springs bottle from the fridge and tossed it to Corny, sitting up in bed.

"Thanks." He unscrewed the cap and guzzled a quarter of the way down. Buster crawled over to him to make sure he was alright.

"Wanna tell me about it? Good for you to talk it out," she whispered.

"I talked enough to the department shrink, don't you think?" he replied.

"Herman's still in your head big guy. When's he gonna leave?"

"I don't know Del. Takes time I guess. The thought of losing you and I couldn't do anything about it..." Corny looked away through the window.

Del snuggled up against his back and wrapped her arms around him without saying another word. Of course, Buster joined in the group hug.

Detective Cornelius (Corny) Prince, has been with the NYPD for 18 years. He's been Detective 1st Grade in Homicide Midtown South Precinct for 9 years. He is a 6'4" bi-racial, 42 year old dedicated cop with an athletic build and an uncanny resemblance to Lester Holt, the journalist who hosts NBC's Nightly News. His mother is Linda Levine, a Caucasian music teacher who teaches in a private academy in Manhattan's upper West Side. Wendell Prince, a black retired NY City firefighter who bravely saved lives for 23 years in the South Bronx is his stoic father. In his retirement, Wendell opened a pawn shop in Harlem. Corny was once married to Eva Peters Prince who died 9 years ago in a car accident on the FDR drive. They had no children. Buster was Corny's only companion...until Del moved in with him.

Detective 3rd Grade Kristina DelVecchio (Del) began her career 7 1/2 years ago. She moved up the ranks of the NYPD by demonstrating exceptional service and valor. She has been on the Homicide Squad for over a year and partners with Corny. She is a 31 year-old attractive female detective, about 5'4", with light brown straight hair and milk chocolate eyes. She had been a gymnast since she was 5 years old. Kristina was so talented and committed that she became very close to making the the USA Olympic team at 17. Her specialty was the uneven parallel bars and the rings. She had been dating a financial analyst on Wall Street, off and on, when she began her career in law enforcement. Her parents were divorced for years and she was never married. Del's father was a cop in Staten Island and her mother was a surgical nurse. Last year her mom, Rose, was murdered by the perp they eventually hunted down, Herman Girtler. Del's hurt ran deep and she still hasn't made peace with her death.

What came out of her tragedy was the evolving relationship with her partner, Corny. He took Del under his wing and they began to get close. He lost his wife years before and she recently lost her mother. Leaning on each other, they fell in love. After several months she moved into Corny's small apartment. She loved Buster, but only tolerated Corny's mess...for now.

Their boss, Lieutenant Jesse Woods--a bear of a black man with white tufts of curly hair who came up the hard way, was not thrilled that two of his detectives got cozy enough to have a serious relationship. However, since their work did not seem to suffer and they were highly competent, he let it go with the stipulation that if he detected any conflict with their jobs, he'd separate them in a heartbeat.

CHAPTER 1

Corny figured that at this point he was supposed to take it to the next level. He wasn't getting any younger and he didn't want to waste his time and Del's. What's the expression? "Shit or get off the pot?" So it was time for her to meet his family. After all, they've been living together for over a year and everyone's been asking about her. Since Cara was throwing a party for the twins 'high school graduation, it was the perfect time for Del to get to know his only older sister, and his mom and dad.

Compared to the city, driving on the Belt Parkway was a piece of cake. There was traffic, but it was moving. Whenever they had a long drive, they took Del's bright yellow Hummer. Funny how she never minded tossing him the keys. He figured she'd never let him get behind her wheel since she's so damn independent. Guess she likes the idea of being a couple. The feeling grew in both their hearts.

It was a warm, yet cloudy August afternoon. The air was moist from last night's gentle drizzle. The wealth of green shrubbery and dense tree growth was a refreshing change from the concrete and metal montage of the cityscape. Nassau County was filled with one-family homes, retail stores, restaurants, condo developments and commercial enclaves all connected by the tentacles of the Long Island Railroad and a few overcrowded freeways. Several recreational parks, long stretches of beachfront, boardwalk and a few museums serve its residents and a host of city visitors.

Corny's sister lived in an expanded Cape Cod home in North Bellmore. It was in the middle of a long curvy street with tall elm and maple trees growing from the grassy apron near the curb. Some had been wrenched from its roots by storm Sandy and were gone. Others forced up one or two inches of sidewalk. Most of the homes were Capes, vinyl sided with one or two car garages connected, some of which were reconstructed as family rooms. It was a working class neighborhood with good schools and friendly neighbors. Perfect suburbia.

"So do you think they'll like me?" asked Del.

"Are you kidding me? What's not to like?" He replied.

"Corny, you know what I mean. You were married to someone else before. I assume they accepted Eva. And now I show up." said Del softly.

"They're gonna love ya. The girls will be thrilled to meet an Olympic gymnast."

"An *almost* Olympic gymnast. I didn't quite make it on the team. Remember?" Del shot back.

"Okay. But they will be very impressed by you. And so will the rest of the family. My mom will be crazy about you. She's warm and welcoming."

"And your dad and Cara?"

He hesitated a moment. "It takes them a little bit of time to warm up to anyone new. It'll be just fine. Promise."

As they turned the corner of Cara's block, there was a stout, bald man mowing his front lawn on the left hand side of the street. He needed to wipe the sweat and a few green blades of grass off his face. On the right, in the roadway, two adolescents with safety helmets were atop multi-speed bikes with thick tires. They were riding side by side, oblivious to our Hummer. He slowed down and gave them wide berth. Del was looking for the address numbers on each house.

"It's been awhile since I've visited Cara and Doug."

"There it is: 582. The green house on the left." Del shouted.

Corny pulled into the mouth of the driveway, backed out and shot into a spot near the curb and turned off the engine. He turned his head to face Del, staring into her gorgeous brown eyes.

"Look. I love you. That's all that counts. Everyone will accept you. Trust me. It just takes some time. Okay?"

Del brushed a small tear from her left eye. She nodded and slid off the high seat of her Hummer. They held hands as they walked up the pathway to the door. Cara met them at the screen door and a wide grin opened on her angular face.

CHAPTER 2

Angry clouds erased the pale yellow half moon. Huge rain drops splattered the windshield and rolled down in pre-determined rivulets which led to the soaked wipers. At 3:30AM, no one was on the suburban street. No one was awake to notice the navy blue van parked near the corner of Comstock and Bell. Engine was turned off. The hood was hot to the touch. It took over an hour to get to this location.

Two burly men and one slim, muscular man sat quietly in black trousers and black T-shirts. They knew their mission very well since they'd done this kind of thing before. The two big guys waited for the slim guy to give the 'Go 'sign. They had all been on this block before, but not in the van. They approached this house a week before in a silver BMW to identify and verify the address. They came during the day and simply drove down the street slowly. No one seemed to notice. Cars drove by all the time since it was a secondary roadway in an ordinary residential neighborhood.

The driver and the slim guy were in the front of the van, just watching and waiting for the right moment. Slim guy trained a small pair of Bushnell Waterproof 12x25 binoculars on the third house from the corner. The other big guy was in the rear of the van awaiting the signal and checking on some equipment they would need. The house was a small split level home with the front door two steps up from the sidewalk. It was a neat house with brick a third-of-the-way up from the foundation and yellow siding reaching up to the dark brown roof. On the left side of the door was a large bay window on the first floor. On the right side was the two-car garage with bedroom windows above. All the lights were off inside. There were two lights shining outside, one on a lamppost leading up a winding path to the front door and one above the garage doors. There was also a white four-foot PVC gate connected to the house on the garage side and to a fence reaching further into the backyard. Trimmed green shrubbery and groupings of annual flowers dressed up the entire frontage of the home.

They assumed that the two-car garage was filled, but the red Honda Civic, the car that interested them, was parked right in front of the house. Another few looks around and they got ready to approach. Each man removed black latex gloves from their pockets and shoved their hands inside. The gentle snaps of latex on flesh was only audible within the van. A large dog began to bark down the street, but no house lights came on. They listened closely and sat still. The driver remained behind the wheel. Slim guy gave the signal to burly guy in back and they simultaneously donned their black woolen balaclavas. Burly guy got out with a small canvas bag in his big mitt of a hand. He gingerly closed the door and came around to the front to join slim guy who was on the street already. They both silently ran to the house they had been studying and trotted for the side gate. In three seconds they were through the gate and worked their way to the back door of the house.

The two intruders felt confident since previous surveillance proved there was no alarm system. Slim guy produced a set of lock picks from his trousers. It took him 25 seconds to pick the top lock and about 15 seconds to pick the bottom lock within the door nob. They were both standing in the shadows of the large kitchen in under a minute. They stood still and listened carefully. Listened for any sound that could lead to a complication of their plan. They were professionals. On slim guy's command, they both moved forward, slowly, on rubber-soled shoes. Tiny creaks from the wooded joists of the floor seemed louder to them than they really were. Their target, they assumed, was in one of the smaller bedrooms on the second floor. They crept toward the carpeted staircase near the front door. Just as they began their accent, a light flicked on upstairs.

They froze in place.

CHAPTER 3

"Hey Sis, how are you?"

"Hi there little brother. Almost didn't recognize you." Cara explained sarcastically. "Been awhile, huh?"

Corny bent down and leaned in for a hug and a peck on the cheek. Cara was about 5'10" and fit. She had the body of a tennis player with sinewy arms and short auburn hair that smelled of lilac. Freckles dotted olive skin on high cheek bones. She was a very attractive woman with attitude. Cara was definitely her father's daughter.

Cara hugged back reluctantly and playfully slapped her brother a few times on his cheek. "Missed you. The girls missed you, you know?"

"I know. Just been so busy on The Job. There's never a lull in Homicide." Smiling, Del waited patiently to be introduced. She awkwardly stood a little behind Corny in faded blue jeans and a man-tailored hunter green buttoned-down blouse. The first two buttons were undone to reveal a heart shaped locket on a thin 20-inch gold chain. Her two inch high-heeled sandals clacked on the bluestone step.

Del finally took the initiative. "Hi, Cara. I'm Kristina." She scooted forward in front of Corny and extended her hand. "So nice to finally meet you. Corny won't admit it, but he talks about you, Doug and the girls all the time."

Cara shook Del's hand warmly and smiled. "So I finally meet the partner and the girlfriend all in one tightly wrapped package. So happy you were able to celebrate with us." Cara looked Del up and down and seemed to approve. "Come on in you guys. Everyone's in the backyard. You'll find the beer in the cooler on the deck."

Del and Corny exchanged glances and followed his sister into the house. Del elbowed her beau and gave him a sly smirk. He shrugged and drew her close to him by her waist. They strolled through the tastefully furnished living room, into the remodeled kitchen. Cream colored granite with rusty streaks were atop the cabinets and the small island. The wood cabinets were blond wood with brass metal pulls. Cara took up her familiar station by the sink, continuing to prepare the huge green salad. Del asked, "oh, can I help with that, Cara?"

"No, no, you go out back and meet everybody else. I'm sure they're all curious, Kristina."

"All my friends call me Del."

Recalling her last name, Cara raised her left eyebrow and pointed toward the door. "Okay, I will, **Del**. Go ahead, make yourselves comfortable."

Feeling the approval, they breezed through the rear door onto the redwood deck. Immediately the chatter of teenage girls enveloped them. Doug was manning the Weber gas grill-- seasoning the steaks, brushing the chicken thighs with a citrus marinade. Wendell, Corny's dad was in the middle of a firefighter story with Doug in a low, but animated voice. Since Doug was currently one of New York City's Bravest in a South Queens house, he listened with rapt attention. Wendell's firefighter career still had a stranglehold on his psyche even after being retired for 12 years. This was very common amongst firemen and cops, not to mention NY City teachers as well. Civil service--once in your blood, it never leaves.

Linda, Corny's mom was lovingly surrounded by the twins (fraternal), Emma and Jordan, newly minted high school graduates. Emma wore stylish glasses and wore her lush wavy black hair down on her swan-like neck. She sported a wide-mouth smile and light blue cut-off jeans and a navy blue Nike T-shirt with the logo on the upper left chest. Flip flops covered her bare feet. Emma was a budding violinist and excelled as a creative writer. Perhaps journalism was in her future. She shared a swinging love seat with her grandmother.

With dark closely-cropped hair, Jordan's piercing gray eyes were striking amidst her smooth amber skin. She was more athletic, yet more sarcastic of the two. She was a starter on the girls 'varsity volley ball team hoping a college scholarship would come through for next year. She preferred dark jeans and a floral print cotton blouse with white & blue Sketchers. They were both filling their grandmother in on their graduation gift--a ten-day teen tour of California. Linda and Wendell donated some cash for their summer adventure.

"Hey everybody. What's going on?"

All conversation abruptly stopped when Corny and Del appeared. They all stared for a quiet moment. Even the chirping sparrows remained silent.

Emma was the first to pipe up and uncurl her feet on the swing. "Uncle Corny! Hey you." She sprang up and ran to give him a tight hug. He wrapped his long muscled arms around her and gave her a peck on the left cheek.

"Been too long since I've been out here. Congratulations hon. Finally made it, huh?"

Emma took a step out of the embrace and stuck a stiff arm out toward Del in hopes of a friendly handshake. "You have to be Del. So nice to meet you. So you're the partner AND the girlfriend," She had no idea that she parroted her mother's first thought. "I'm Emma." She warmly shook hands and smiled gracefully. Del face reddened. Emma added, "welcome."

Corny jumped in and announced, "everyone, this is Del. Come over and say hi." Linda walked over to them and so did Doug. Wendell slowly ambled in their direction and Jordan got up too. Linda went right up to Del and have her a warm hug.

Linda whispered in her ear, "so now I meet the pretty woman detective who has captured my son's imagination. What a pleasure to have you with our family today. Welcome." Before she backed up she smiled and said, "we definitely need to share some stories sometime Del."

Del felt her warmth. She then shook hands with Doug, who clearly appreciated Del's gorgeous face and attractive figure.

"So glad you could make it to the girls 'graduation celebration. How do you like your steak?"

"Thanks Doug and I love a rare steak," she purred.

Wendell shuffled over to Corny and gave him a tight hug. "Very pretty girl, son. Good detective, too?"

"Yes, dad. I helped train her on the job and she is very brave, smart and intuitive. Please welcome her."

Wendell turned to Del and smiled broadly. "Hello, Kristina. I'm Corny's dad. Spent 23 years as a N.Y. City firefighter. Worked hard for the citizens of New York. Don't believe what you hear about the South Bronx. Some mighty fine folks living up there. And some...well. Nice to see you serving the city too."

"Hello sir." She tilted her head a bit and grinned. "My friends call me Del, sir."

"Okay, Del. My friends call me Del also, as in Wen-DEL." They both gazed at each other for a second and shook on it, each with a firm grip.

Jordan was the last to greet Del. She approached awkwardly and didn't quite know what to say. She was a bit embarrassed and didn't make eye contact. Corny rescued her and grabbed her playfully around the neck and pulled her close to his chest. She smiled and leaned into him. "Hi uncle C. So happy you came out to celebrate with us."

Del jumped at her chance to break the ice with Jordan. "Hey, love your blouse. I have one just like it."

"Oh, thanks. Glad you came over too," she said demurely as she looked Del up and down.

Cara carried out a huge salad bowl from the kitchen and Doug called, "I'm taking steak orders. How does everyone like it cooked?"

Linda shuffled up from behind her husband and wrapped her arms around Wendell's chest. With a grin she whispered in his ear, "this is the way I like it. We're all together." Wendell turned and gave her a kiss on her left cheek and Cara's heart skipped a beat.

CHAPTER 4

The toilet flushed in the upstairs bathroom. They could hear the water refilling the bowl. The bathroom light turned off. Only the shadow of the staircase railing appeared from the streetlamp shining through the small window at the top of the stairs. The two men remained silent and listened. Their emotions were calm because they were professionals. Bottom line was there would be hell to pay if they screwed up.

They began to climb the carpeted steps one behind the other. Reaching the second floor they listened again for any movement or sound. The fact that they discovered that this family had no dog or cat was not dumb luck. They had had quite a bit of info on this household. They knew what they were getting into. They knew that the man of the house was away on a business trip. They knew he was in Toronto at a pharmaceutical convention. They knew that the wife was alone with her son who was 12 years old and her daughter who was 16. She was the target.

Slim guy signaled burly guy to check the bedrooms. Margot Jeffries was in one of three rooms. Burly guy checked the first small room. It was the son's bedroom and he was out cold. The target was asleep in the next bedroom. Slim guy slowly and quietly opened the door. A tiny lamp with a round flowered shade was lit on her white-painted night table. Margot's iPhone was charging next to the lamp. The walls were painted powder-blue and dark blue Hunter Douglas metal blinds were drawn on the double windows behind her headboard. A white wooden desk and chair hugged the opposite wall. A gray sweatshirt was haphazardly thrown on the upholstered chair and there were school texts and a MacBook Air 13.3" scattered across the desktop. Posters of Shawn Mendes, Ed Sheeran, Bruno Mars and the Jonas Brothers dotted the blank wall space around the room. Assorted make-up, lip gloss and a lighted mirror occupied the left corner of the desk. There was a lavender scent in the room.

Margot's white and blue gingham comforter covered half of her body lengthwise. One arm was off the bed hanging in mid-air. The back of her head crushed the edge of her soft blue pillow. Several strands of straight brown hair covered her closed left eye. An occasional snore emerged from her mouth as she breathed in and out. Several stuffed animals sat on the edge of the bed abutting the wall.

Burly guy placed the canvas bag on her textbooks and opened the zipper. It opened to 180 degrees. There were six empty syringes strapped in place and a small bottle of fluid nesting in a hollowed out tight space just for its size. He removed the bottle and one syringe. He punctured the rubber top of the bottle with the syringe needle and filled it about half-way making sure that no air was mixed with the ketamine.

Margot turned in her sleep and emitted a throated groan. Slim guy gave burly guy the signal and they both approached Margot's bed silently. Slim guy shot his hand across Margot's turned head and clamped down over her mouth with a powerful gloved hand. Margot's eyes flipped open and she tried to scream and struggled to move the hand away. Burly guy grabbed her extended arm and inserted the syringe into the muscle just below the shoulder and depressed the plunger. Margot flailed her legs and torso simultaneously with muffled screams and upper body jerks. In 5-10 seconds her body relaxed and she stopped moving.

Burly guy placed the syringe back in the case and zipped it up. He gave the case to slim guy and went back to the bed. He threw the comforter off of Margot and grabbed the sweatshirt from the chair. With little effort he lifted Margot in her pink pajamas off the bed and folded her over his shoulder at the same time that a pink stuffed elephant landed on the floor. In two minutes they were out of the house and back in the van. Slim guy used duct tape to tie Margot's hands behind her and over her mouth. She was as snug as a bug in the back of the van with a blue tarp covering her with a few spaces open for her to breathe. The driver cranked the engine and slowly coasted down the block in the dark of the early morning.

CHAPTER 5

Del drove her yellow Hummer with Corny riding shotgun to their daily grind: Midtown Precinct South, Homicide Squad, Monday morning. Corny led a 4-man team with Del, Detective 2nd Grade Joey Hernandez, and a newbie Detective 3rd Grade Teddy Huong.

Joey, a muscular 5'11" cop, a marathon runner, came from Vice, where he spent seven years. While in Vice, Joey had trouble with his partner, Sammy Turpin, a cop 'on the take 'who was suspended indefinitely until a full investigation concluded. Joey wanted no part of that mess so he found a new home in Homicide and grew to appreciate his teammates. Black curly hair with flecks of gray and a thin dark mustache drove the ladies wild. However, when he was actively pursuing a case, he was laser-focused.

Joey took a bullet last year, saving Corny and Del. The lunatic serial killer, Herman Girtler, trapped them and was about to kill Del while Corny watched. Of course, at the last moment, Joey jumped in and did not hesitate to put a double tap directly into Girtler's face at the same time the killer fired. It took a good few months for Joe to heal up enough to be cleared to get back to work.

The newest member of the team is Teddy Huong. Teddy, in his late twenties, made detective pretty quickly, making a name for himself working the gangs in Chinatown. He, too, sought a different path. Once given the opportunity for Homicide, he grabbed it. Teddy is a beefy guy, 6'2", and sports a crew cut. He wears a sport coat and tie at work and studies Martial Arts in a local dojo. His young wife Maggie is also of Chinese dissent . She's a CPA for a small Manhattan firm. They had a baby boy last year, Micah, who stays with Maggie's mom and dad during the week. Nothing like family daycare.

Lieutenant Woods walked out of his office with a swagger, "never a dull moment in this city of New York, boys and girls. There's a body in the Jamaica Bay Wildlife Refuge . Some bike-riding kids found it in some tall grass. I want the four of you to take a look."

Corny asked, "why us? We're Midtown South. Where are the Queens boys?"

"They are up to their asses with murders and other shit. You know the numbers are way up this year in Brooklyn, Queens and the Bronx . They need a hand. See if you guys can work your magic. Patrol will give you the initial details."

"Ok, Lieu."

"Mount up. Time you got your feet wet Teddy."

Teddy smirked and piped up, "ain't my first rodeo boss."

"Yeah, okay, your second maybe. Why don't you guys take a bagel and cream cheese for the road. I'm getting the feeling it's gonna be a long morning." Corny advised.

"All I need is another cup of joe. Monday morning sucks," complained Del.

Joey replied, "Bullshit Del. You love the action. Get's your engine running."

"Hey, my engine's running just fine, Joe." She looked at Corny with a girlish grin.

Del's pretty face lit up. When they got outside, they split up. Joe and Teddy took the unmarked sedan. Del effortlessly hoisted herself into her Hummer and Corny got in the passenger side.

"You alright? You seem a bit off today. Didn't you love meeting my family yesterday?" he asked a bit sarcastically.

She smiled. "Actually, I did. They made me feel like I fit in. Been a while since I've done a family thing."

Corny leaned into Del and planted a gentle kiss on her cheek.

She revved the engine and placed her warm hand on

Corny's upper thigh. Two seconds later, she placed the stick in Drive and sped away looking briefly over her shoulder.

Thick clouds pushed together overhead. Light rain and wind whipped around the dozen or so uniformed officers circling the crime scene inside the police perimeter tape. The tall macabre grass danced around the partially hidden body. Some mumbling onlookers crowded behind the barriers. They pointed and shook their heads. A few tried to video the scene with their phones before a few uniforms ordered them to stop.

The four detectives arrived about the same time. Corny thought that it was time Teddy took a lead role in the initial investigation. He wanted to see how detailed Ted could be at a crime scene. Ted and Corny ambled up to the sergeant-in-charge. Corny nodded to Ted to take the initiative.

"Good morning Sergeant. I'm Detective Huong. This is Detective Prince. Detectives DelVecchio and Hernandez," swiveling his head 45 degrees to the left. "We were called in from Midtown Precinct South. Heard your detectives are up to their eyeballs with shootings." His tie began to flap in the wind.

"Detective," making eye contact. "Sergeant Meloni, Queens South."

"Okay, what do we got?"

"Young female, Caucasian. Maybe mid to late teens or early twenties. She put up a fight. Take a look at her nails, hands."

Corny and Ted each put on black latex gloves and squatted down in the grass to briefly eyeball the body. Corny held back some of the grass and carefully moved some leaves and twigs away with the eraser of a pencil from his jacket pocket. Ted saw the blood and scrapes on the victims fingernails and hands. There were duct tape residue marks around her mouth and on her wrists and evidence of ligature marks on the neck.

"Looks like strangulation was the C.O.D. (Cause of Death). Her hands were tied with duct tape. She definitely put up a fight. Four or five broken polished nails. Cuts and bruises on her hands and arms. Doesn't look like she was sexually violated at this point. Panties on, but no pajama bottoms. Pajama top—three buttons opened. Bare feet with cuts and some encrusted dirt." Ted explained.

"What do you think?" Corny asked.

Del and Joey looked over their shoulders.

Ted wrinkled his brow and thought for a moment. "Kidnapping perhaps from her own bed? Pajama top. Maybe she was murdered because she fought out of panic. Maybe a rape gone south. Fuckin 'pricks taking and attacking a pretty kid like this."

Corny shook his head up and down. "Good job, rookie. Any ID found?" He looked up at Sergeant Meloni. "No ID, no wallet, nothing," Meloni replied.

"What don't we know?" asked Corny, teaching the rookie.

"Was she murdered here or dropped off? T.O.D. (time of death)? Why was she abducted and then killed? Where is she from? Why was she wearing a pajama top? We need a forensics team to scour the immediate and surrounding areas. Was the coroner called, Sarge?"

"En route detective."

Teddy stood and so did Corny. "We have to check 'Missing Persons'. Kid like this is no prostitute and must have a family who filed a report. I'll check down at the squad."

While they were inspecting the body, Joey asked the sergeant to instruct his officers to canvass the crowd. There was an outside chance that one of the locals saw or heard something relevant to the crime. After 45 minutes, Meloni had no witness information. Del looked around the remote area. No houses, no permanent structures. Just a few fishing boats out in the gunmetal gray chop. She wondered if a boater saw anything. There were some tire tracks in the soft earth near the site. Forensics would photograph and process the entire scene. Joey studied the onlookers and searched for odd behavior or facial indications that showed stress or anxiety. Unfortunately, he believed they just came for the show.

Corny rounded up his team. "Let's head back to the squad and wait for the Coroner's report and forensic evidence."

Joey said, "I'll check the system for similar murders where young women were abducted and murdered. In this city, the scum-bags don't ever stop. It's either money or sex or both."

Teddy said he'd check the 'Missing Person 'reports. "We have to get an ID fast. If there's one out here, there might be others."

They all headed back to the squad. In the Hummer, Del asked, "so how did the rookie do at the scene? Better than me the first time I bet."

Corny answered, "it's not a competition Babe. He did pretty well. Good instincts. Now we all have to find the perps. My gut tells me this isn't the only young girl victimized. Not by a long shot."

CHAPTER 6

It took the driver of the navy blue van more than an hour to drive back to the Deer Park warehouse in the rain. None of them said a word in the vacant cavity of the van. The three operators knew there would be hell to pay once they returned empty-handed. Boris made a left into the parking lot and glided into a spot parallel to the nondescript building. Inside, the ceilings were cavernous with pipes and electrical wires hanging down. At one time the warehouse stored Ford automobile parts. One half of the warehouse was subdivided into several caged rooms, three of which contained metal army-like cots, a few toilets and a few sinks. There were rows of wooden cubby-holes against one side of each caged room for a few personal items and clothing. The other half of the interior was subdivided into offices and other storage rooms.

Boris killed the engine and sat still in the driver's seat. Alexey, the slim, muscular guy shifted in the passenger seat and spoke first as he turned around to face Egor, who was slumped in the back seat with his eyes closed shut. Sweat covered his forehead and his hands were shaking.

"What the fuck happened back there?" demanded Alexey.

Egor shook his head and kept his mouth and eyes shut. The front of his pants were urine soaked.

"Answer me, you stupid prick!" Alexey had his HS2000 semi-automatic pistol (manufactured in Croatia) pointed at Egor's chest. "You don't think I'm gonna take all the shit for this fuck-up. You know they're expecting a delivery. Each piece of merchandise is custom ordered. You had to strangle her, you fuck?"

Boris kept his eyes on Alexey in the front of the van. Egor

suddenly opened his eyes and imaginary shards of terror shot from his pupils. He held his hands up in front of his chest as if they would stop a 9x19mm Parabellum round.

"Alexey, I don't know what happened! I gave her the shot of ketamine. You saw. You were there in her room. She just woke up and started to scream," he pleaded in a Russian accent.

"But you did not have to kill her. Bringing her in damaged is better than no merchandise at all," shouted Alexey. He looked over at Boris who remained terrified and silent.

"But she somehow grabbed the handle of the back door and it opened. I thought she was going to jump out...right on the street. Other drivers would see. I had to stop her!" yelled Egor.

"You didn't give her a full needle of the drug, you idiot! I'm not taking the full hit for this. Get out of the van! Get out!" Alexey turned to Boris. "You too...get out! Time to, as the Americans say, 'face the music'. Move!"

The three of them slowly ambled to the door of the warehouse like they were going to a funeral. Not far from the truth. Alexey had his gun pointed to their backs as they entered the dark recesses of the building. They slowly made their way down a dank corridor to the main office on the right hand side. The fetid odor of stale tobacco smoke attacked their nostrils as they trudged forward. The door was open and three more men were inside.

Leonid, one of the upper bosses who was entrusted to watch over the merchandise before delivery, was sitting in a cracked black leather cushioned desk chair under a metallic office desk. An old rectangular florescent fixture floated overhead. Leonid's organization smuggled him into the U.S. via Montreal about eight years ago, originally from Moscow. He was a true Russian bear. Leonid had straight black hair. A sizable belly put a strain on the buttons of his black dress shirt from eating rich American food and drinking too much booze. A gray-black unibrow underscored the wrinkles on his white forehead. A Glock 19 was nestled in an underarm holster under his sport jacket.

Papers were organized in piles on a horizontal multi-level tray, mostly a prop. A blue crystal glass ash tray sat filled with cigar butts on the left side of the surface. A half-empty bottle of Stolichnaya Red Vodka was near his elbow. He was about to take another gulp by placing the glass between his thick wet lips when the three operators walked in. Leonid's steroid-pumped bodyguards stood erect in both corners of the room. The one on the left was tall and perpetually chewed on a toothpick. The one on the right had beady eyes and was the size of a squat refrigerator. Leonid slowly placed the glass on the desk and stared at the three men, wondering where his merchandise was. He managed to belch out one word that he used all the time. "Yeah?"

His eyes widened and snarled, "where the fuck is the merchandise?"

Alexey moved off to the side, still aiming his hand gun. "We had a problem."

Leonid's laser-gaze moved back and forth between the three operators in front of his desk. His face reddened as his blood pressure went through the roof. He waited for the explanation.

"The target woke up much too early and began to move around the van. Somehow she managed to scrape the tape off her mouth and began to scream bloody murder. She even kicked the back van door open," Alexey explained.

Egor was trembling and sweating. Boris just stood still waiting for his fate. He was keeping a cool head, his eyes darting from one bodyguard to the other.

"Then what the fuck happened? Where is she?" replied Leonid.

"She's dead! And we dumped her body in the tall grass in Queens, near Jamaica Bay. The wildlife refuge. Nobody was around."

Leonid stood up with fire in his eyes. "My question was: What the fuck happened? Why is she dead?"

"Egor was in the back seat when she woke up and started

moving around. We were on the highway heading back here. He turned around and grabbed her to shut her up. She fought like crazy. He..." Alexey explained but was interrupted.

"I want to hear it from him!" Leonid starred stone-faced at Egor. Tears dripped down Egor's cheeks.

"Ssssorry boss. I had to grab her and hold her tight. She was squirming like a fuckin 'fish on a line. She wouldn't stop moving. I guess I squeezed her throat ttttoo tight. And she stopped moving." Egor looked at the floor.

"And why the fuck did she wake up too soon?" Leonid asked.

"I guess I didn't give her enough of the drug in the needle," Egor confessed.

"So now we need another fuckin 'target 'cause we have a specific order for this kind of kid. I gotta call Sophia now and get another target for you clowns to pick up."

The three operators began to relax just a bit. Leonid's ranting seemed to subside. The two bodyguards took a step or two forward, knowing full well that Leonid was not done with them.

In the blink of an eye, he pulled his Glock out of the holster and quickly aimed it at Egor. He pumped two bullets into Egor's left knee cap, exploding the joint. Egor crumpled to the cold cement floor yelling in agony. Dark ruby blood pooled around his leg on the floor.

"Get this piece of shit out of here, now! I'll call you when we get another target," shouted Leonid.

"Do you think you and Boris can handle it this time?"

"Yes, boss. Absolutely," answered Alexey as he and Boris dragged howling Egor out of the office.

CHAPTER 7

Shades of grey clouds blanketed the entire sky. Thick raindrops continued to soak the vehicles in the parking lot of Midtown Precinct South on West 35th Street. Uniformed officers and detectives darted in and out of the glass and metal front doors, trying to duck the rain.

Once in the squad room, Teddy took the initiative to set up the white bulletin board. All the information and photos they'd gather would be displayed on it for visual investigation and discussion. Forensics already faxed over photos taken of the victim at the scene. Ted chose three shots of the deceased young lady and posted them at the top of the board with small magnets. Much more information was forthcoming.

Lieutenant Woods called from his office, "Got a 'Missing Person' report from our brothers in Suffolk County, boys and girls. Home invasion in the middle of the night. A sixteen-year-old girl was plucked from her bedroom in Bay Shore. Mother is frantic."

"Any other reports of missing kids?" asked Corny.

"Yeah, plenty, but they are mostly people of color, and a wide range of age. The abducted girl from Bay Shore is Caucasian. She matches the description."

"Lieu, Del and I can head out to the house to speak with the parents," responded Corny.

"Got a call from a Detective Morris out there. I'll text you guys the address. You can meet Morris at the house. Father's on a business trip. You can speak with the mother. But be gentle. She's a wreck. On a prescribed tranquilizer," explained Lieutenant Woods.

"Will do, Lieu."

Corny swiveled in his chair, "Joey, you and Ted head over to the coroner. See what he's got so far."

"Copy that, boss. Then we'll call forensics," Joey said.

Before they left, Del grabbed half a sesame bagel with a schmear of butter and a black coffee to go. "Let's go, boss. Want to drive so I can eat my late breakfast?"

"No problema, Babe. Let's go. Should take about an hour. Toss the Hummer keys."

Del lobbed the fob in the air and they both headed out into the rain again. She had a few photos of the dead girl on her iPhone.

"What's the kid's name?"

Corny checked his iPhone texts. He stopped for a moment in the hallway and looked. "Jeffries. Margot Jeffries. A Bay Shore senior high school 11th grader." He rubbed his forehead and rotated his neck, trying to get the kinks out. "Only sixteen, for Christ sake."

"Not looking forward to meeting the mom," Del shook her head. "A freaking nightmare."

"Let's go, Del."

The traffic on the Southern State Parkway was light, but slow due to the rain. Del dove into her bagel with relish. She always watched what she ate since her mindset was one of health and moderation. Felt a twinge of guilt consuming the carbs in the half bagel. She still viewed herself as an athlete, albeit an aging athlete. Del also loved the image of her slim, muscular body in the mirror. And so did Corny. She also relished the thought of their loving relationship and where it could go.

"Hey Corny," she said between bites. "Can you see yourself in the suburban lifestyle like your sister? Nice house, the backyard barbecue...kids?"

Corny smiled and momentarily gazed at Del's chocolate brown eyes. His eyebrows arched and he painted that image in his mind. "Maybe." He let that word simmer in the front seat of the Hummer. "When I think of you..."

Del took a sip of black coffee and her face lit up. They were definitely in love. She placed her strong warm fingers in his olive hand and gripped tightly. She thought about maybe having kids someday...with him. Suddenly the daydream broke and she refocused on the case.

"Now if this was the kid from Bay Shore, why the hell did she pop up in Queens?" Del posited.

"Good question. If the perps killed this girl, there are plenty of places on the 'Island 'to dump her. Woods, beach areas, remote sections along highways."

Del shook her head and used a finger to curl her straight hair behind her ear. She didn't need a few strands sitting in the rest of her buttered bagel.

The Hummer's navigation brought them to the Jeffries house. Morris's unmarked was parked at the curb. Through the screen door, Corny was able to see that the front door was ajar. Morris and probably his partner, a tall black woman in a beige rain coat, stood in the living room with their backs to the door. Del rang the bell out of respect. The female detective stepped to the doorway.

"Detectives Prince and DelVecchio, NYPD," Corny announced.

"Come in detectives. I'm Detective Winchester, Western Suffolk," she responded. She had unblemished mocha skin and high cheek bones. Her hair was close-cropped and curly black. They entered the room slowly. Detective Morris turned his head and nodded. He was a heavy set guy of about six feet. He's had his share of beer and booze, like quite a few guys 'on the Job'. He was definitely well into his 60's. His hair was wavy salt and pepper edged with a receding hairline. A day or two of stubble was on his chiseled face. A checkered, wrinkled sport jacket hung unbuttoned and damp from rain.

"Mrs. Jeffries," Del said softly. "We're from NYPD. Detectives Prince and DelVecchio." Corny frowned and nodded to Morris. They shook hands briefly.

Mrs. Jeffries was an attractive woman with dirty blond hair cut in a pixie bob. She was forty-ish, slim and wore a stylish red tunic sweater over fitted light-blue jeans. She sat on the edge of a beige-print upholstered sofa. Her legs were folded together and her blue eyes were watery red. She held a wad of Kleenex in her right fist. She glanced at Corny and Del and pleaded with her eyes.

"Mrs. Jeffries, I know you already told these detectives what occurred. Would you mind telling us again what happened in the house and what you think happened to your daughter, Margot?" Corny whispered.

"Detectives, did you find my baby?" She pleaded.

Del said, "Please, Mrs. Jeffries, one step at a time. What can you remember?"

"I woke up this morning to get the kids ready for school. I went into Corey's room because it's harder to get him out of bed. I woke him and told him to get dressed. I called out to Margot and walked to her room. She was gone! I called out to her several times. Thought maybe she had gone downstairs when I was in Corey's room. I ran downstairs and called out to her again. I ran to the basement. I ran into the garage. I ran out to her car." Mrs. Jeffries shook her head. She started to sob and her body shook. She dabbed her eyes with the tissues.

"Did you call any of her friends or neighbors?" asked Corny.

She nodded and mouthed the words, "no one had seen her. She was just gone."

"Have you had any arguments with her? Had she ever run off before?" asked Del.

"No, never."

"Detective Morris said you found a girl?" she began to cry again and shook her head.

"Mrs. Jeffries, where is Mr. Jeffries?" Corny asked.

"He's at a convention in Toronto. I called him to tell him Margot was gone. He said he'd take the next flight out." She was barely audible. She looked up at Corny and Del, knowing that the hard part was coming. She braced herself.

Del took her phone out and found a picture of the victim. She took a few tentative steps forward and held the phone a few feet from Mrs. Jeffries 'face. She reached out with a trembling hand to grasp the phone.

Her eyes grew big and horror registered on her ragged face.

"Oh, no, no, no, no...my baby. My baby," she cried. She rocked back and forth. "Margot, oh, no." She broke down and slipped off the couch. Del reached for her and caught her under her limp arms. Detective Morris helped to place her back on the couch. Detective Winchester went over to try to comfort her too.

Corny and Morris glared at each other, shaking their heads. They both retreated from the couch and huddled together. Detective Morris whispered, "there were some signs of a home invasion at the back door. Scrapes on the door jamb. The locks were picked. Professional job."

"Did you check out the girl's room yet?"

"No, we got here about 10 minutes before you and began conducting the interview."

"Where is the son, Corey?"

"Haven't spoken to him yet. I understand he's in his own bedroom."

Detective Morris said, "I'll call in the forensics team since it's now a crime scene."

"Okay. We'll hang out for awhile. I'd like to see the girl's bedroom after your guys do their magic."

"Copy that detective."

CHAPTER 8

The houses on Harding Street in Smithtown were large and expensive with attached two-car garages. They were well kept with neat front lawns all dotted with assorted tall trees. The properties were obviously all professionally landscaped with tons of bushes and shrubs. During the fall, most people were either in their homes or in their cars running errands or frequenting restaurants. You'd see an occasional dog walker with an upturned collar, huddled against the stiff autumn breeze.

The sun had just fallen under the horizon. This is the second time the navy blue van with dark windows slowly passed number 29. The white Jeep Grand Cherokee Limited Sport Utility was in the driveway--the target's vehicle. Alexey was planted in the passenger seat up front. He focused his Firefield Nightfall 4x50 Night Vision Monocular to double-check the license plate on the Jeep.

"Okay. This is it. Go around the block one more time and park across the street a few houses from our target. Then turn off the lights."

"I know what to do, boss. As the Americans say, 'not my first rodeo 'Alexey," Boris said quietly.

"We can't afford to fuck this one up, Boris."

Boris stared at Alexey for a few moments, letting his comment sink in. He drove around the street once again and parked silently. He killed the lights. They waited for the target to come out.

After about thirty minutes, the front door opened and a teenager appeared. She swiveled her head and shouted something inaudible to her mom and dad inside. A moment later she bounced out of the house and down the four bluestone steps. She wore a light blue windbreaker, jeans and Nike Women's Air Max 270 Casual sneakers. Her long blond hair danced around her face in the wind. She pressed the key fob to open the door to the Jeep, a promised high school graduation gift from her well-to-do parents.

Kimberly revved the engine and slowly backed out of the driveway. Simultaneously, the navy van came alive without headlights. It faced the correct direction, knowing where she was going beforehand. The radio in the Jeep woke up immediately when the engine kicked on. Her favorite was Teen Pop on Pandora. Dua Lipa was singing 'Break My Heart 'and Kimberly joined in, loud and clear.

It took Kimberly 15 minutes to get to the Smith Haven Mall. Even though her iPhone signaled several texts, she knew enough to ignore them temporarily while she was driving. Kimberly didn't have a clue that another vehicle was following her.

She pulled into a spot in the back near Chico's, a women's apparel shop. She kept the Jeep running while responding to several texts from her best friend Cindy. She explained that she had arrived at the mall since she needed a few items in Sephora. She'd also do a spin around Barnes & Noble. Cindy responded that she had promised her mom that she would help her clean out a closet so she couldn't meet her there. Next time, she wrote.

Kimberly shut off the engine and hopped out of the large vehicle. Simultaneously, Alexey exited the van several parking spots from hers. He wore dark trousers, black rubber-soled casual Sketchers and a light-weight black leather jacket. Kimberly walked through a breezeway into a small courtyard with several outdoor stores. The mall entrance was on the left and she headed toward center glass doors. Alexey followed from a safe distance. Once inside the mall, Kimberly ducked into Sephora. She was interested in buying lip gloss and other make-up items. First she sampled a few perfumes. Nearly 18 years old, her mindset was on college away from home. She was into partying and boys, friends and boys, and of course, studying. Kimberly was determined to actually make something of herself and not waste what college had to offer. Whatever that was, she wasn't sure yet.

Alexey kept a low profile in the mall corridor and kept fingering the hypodermic needle in his jacket pocket, which he prepared in the car. It was nearly filled with ketamine, much more than Egor had prepared for their last target. He was going to make sure Kimberly was out cold until they reached the Deer Park warehouse. He could not afford another fuck-up.

Kimberly pranced out of Sephora with a tiny bag swinging from her hand. She made a sharp left and went through the doors to the courtyard. Alexey followed slowly. He spied her going into Barnes and Noble. He followed again. This store was easy for him to keep an eye on her. He knew where she was parked and knew that when finished, she would exit through the same door that she entered. He browsed the music CD's and the DVD's, keeping one eye on the exit.

Ten to fifteen minutes later, she walked through the security barrier with a second purchase from the bookstore swinging in her hand. Again, he was happy to see she was alone. He exited the store as he placed a quick remote call from his pocketed smartphone to Boris. "On our way out now. Get ready."

"You got it. I'll be ready," Boris responded.

As Kimberly approached her Jeep, Alexey rushed to catch up from behind. She had earbuds in her ears and heard nothing but Dua Lipa from her iPhone library. Boris began to walk back toward the Jeep. He noticed that Alexey was very close to the target. Kimberly saw Boris approach and her antennae rose quickly of possible danger. Her sense of fear caused her pupils to dilate and she thought she might scream for help.

Boris thought fast and said gently with a thick Russian accent, "Excuse me miss. Could you tell me how to get to Barnes and Noble bookstore?"

In those brief moments in which Kimberly's fear eased, Alexey came up to her from behind. He wrapped his strong hand around her mouth and skillfully injected the ketamine in her neck. In her confused state, she lashed out with both hands and arms, dropping her small packages. Boris rushed up to her and grabbed her arms in a bear hug. Within five to ten seconds her body went limp. Alexey picked up the small bags. Each man took each side of her and carried her to the van which was open. They hoisted her into the back and Boris jumped up as well. He used duct tape to tie her hands behind her and cover her mouth. Several strands of blond hair got caught under the gray tape. He hopped out and closed and locked the back door.

It took about a half hour to reach the warehouse. This time, there was no incident or problem. The navy blue van pulled into the parking lot and the target was still sleeping in the back like a baby. The large building had white-washed exterior walls with three small windows placed high up. A dull amber glow illuminated each one. The dead-end block was quiet, barren and treeless. Both Alexey and Boris had smiles on their faces as they got out of the van and approached the back door.

CHAPTER 9

Boris carried the target into the warehouse over his shoulder. She was still unconscious. Her long blond hair hung straight down a few inches away from the back of Boris's brown jacket. Alexey led the way through the corridor on the right. Cement floor, gray cinder block on the outer wall and hastily constructed dry wall on the left. Dirty old, round glass light fixtures, dangling from the 30 foot ceiling, shed dim illumination on this half of the building. The corridor led to a very large open area with a maze of metal cyclone fencing. A female attendant unlocked one of the enclosures and opened the gate wide enough for Boris to bring his latest victim.

The female was a Russian woman of middle age and stern facial features. She wore a brown woolen sweater that had a few small holes on her elbows and loose jeans over tan high faux leather boots with low heals. She had no make-up on her face. She held a hard-wood baton in her right fist. A nasty scowl dominated her mood. "Over there. That's her space," she said as she pointed to an empty cot with the baton.

Boris dumped his charge onto the paper-thin mattress. At the end of the cot was an army green woolen blanket, folded neatly. The girl began to stir, confused and afraid. Boris and Alexey ignored the female attendant and trudged out of the enclosure. They walked back to the other side of the warehouse to report to the boss.

Suddenly, the other abducted children sat up erect on their cots and stared at the new girl. There were three others, two teenage females and one younger boy. Not knowing what was going to happen to them, fear dominated their waking thoughts. They weren't physically abused, but told they would be moving soon to other places to live. The attendant had a small wooden desk, with a dated goose-neck lamp on the right hand corner, outside their enclosure. Keeping a keen eye on them was part of her job.

"Hey, mind your own business. Get busy with something," she scolded through the fencing. They had some books, magazines and puzzles to occupy their minds until the time they were about to be moved out. They were fed twice a day with sandwiches before noon and hot meals at dinner time. There was a small make-shift bathroom in one corner of the 20'x20 'enclosure. It had a tiny sink, a white porcelain toilet and a small pre-fab stall shower. The bathroom was cleaner than a contractor's portable toilet, but not by much. Odors were alleviated by one or two hanging air fresheners in the shape of Christmas trees.

Carmen, the olive-skinned 17 year-old jumped off her cot and slowly walked over to Kimberly, who seemed to be half asleep. Carmen had warm dark-chocolate eyes, full lips and short curly hair. Her 5'4" frame was fully developed with wide hips and an ample bosom. She squatted next to Kimberly's cot and reached out to comfort her. She gently stroked her arm and grasped her left hand. Kimberly's eyelids popped open. She tried to sit up.

"What...where..." she opened her mouth, which was bone-dry. Her eyes darted around the enclosure. Fear grabbed her by the throat when she saw the cyclone fence.

"Hey, hey. Take it easy. I'm Carmen. You're safe...for now," she whispered.

"Where the hell am I?" questioned Kimberly. "What is this place?"

"You've been kidnapped by these goons," Carmen whispered in Kimberly's ear again. "We've all been taken against our will."

"I was in the mall parking lot and these two guys grabbed me and..."

"Yeah, I know. We've all been drugged and brought here,"

said Carmen.

"Where is here?" asked Kimberly as she sat up straight.

"Some kind of large building or warehouse."

"Why? What are they going to do to us?" asked Kimberly again.

Tears came to Carmen's eyes. They dripped down her face. "I think some rich people are buying us. They want to make us slaves," sobbed Carmen.

Wesley and Brianna joined Carmen at Kimberly's cot. Brianna gave Kimberly a small bottle of room temperature water. Kimberly took it and guzzled half of it. "Thank you," she said.

Brianna was a 16 year-old high school junior from Commack. Her parents were immigrants from Korea and came to the U.S. when her mom was pregnant with her. She was petite with jet-black hair and a round pretty face. She was an excellent cheerleader and a B+ student. Wesley was in his last year of middle school from Northport. He had blue eyes and longish blond hair. He was only 15 years old and suffered from a stuttering issue. His rich father owned a couple of paint stores and he was hoping they wanted a ransom for him.

"I wwwas wwwalking hhhome from school and they grrrabbed me off the street," cried Wesley. Brianna curled her arm around Wesley's shoulders.

"I was waiting for my mom to pick me up from cheerleader practice outside the school. She was late. All the other kids were gone by then. This big van pulls up and a huge guy jumps out. He grabbed me, stabbed me with a needle and threw me into the back of the van," explained Brianna.

Kimberly started to cry. "Why us?"

Carmen shook her head back and forth. "Don't know."

"The cops must be looking for us. They have to find us! They have to," exclaimed Kimberly. "Our parents are going crazy by now."

"Hey, enough chatter. Shut up and get busy. You go to sleep soon. Lights out. Quiet!" shouted the attendant. "No quiet, no food tomorrow!"

The other three youngsters went back to their cots, all with tears in their eyes. Then the overhead lights shut off with a muffled click. The only light was from a nightlight in the bathroom and the 15 watt bulb in the lamp on the attendant's desk.

CHAPTER 10

After watching the Suffolk forensic people work in Margot's room and the rest of the house, Corny took the contact information for Detectives Morris and Winchester and said they would keep in touch to exchange forensic findings.

Once back in the squad, Corny and Del updated Lieutenant Woods, confirming that the victim was, unfortunately, Margot Jeffries from Bay Shore. The laptop they found in the victim's bedroom would be analyzed by the Suffolk tech people and the detectives would get back to Corny to share what they found. While in Woods 'office, Teddy and Joey walked in to listen to the new developments.

"Our coroner harvested some DNA from under the victim's fingernails and is running it through NDIS (The National DNA Index System) and CODIS (Combined DNA Index System) as we speak. You know it could take a while," Ted explained. "If the perps have their DNA on file, we should get a match. If not...they may be foreigners."

"What about the forensics team? They find anything useful at the scene?" ask Del.

"Tire tracks, probably from a small truck or a van. They'll analyze the tire tracks and get back to us," said Joey.

The phone rang on the lieutenant's desk. "Woods. Yup, they're back in squad Captain. What do you got? No shit." Woods listened as he stared out the window at nothing in particular. "How many?" He continued to listen and rotated his neck working out the kinks.

"All four detectives initially gazed at their lieutenant. A minute later, Del looked up at the ceiling. Ted glanced at Joey. Corny paced in the small office. He desperately craved a cup of black coffee.

"Okay, Captain. Please keep me in the loop. Yes, a task force, I'm sure." Lieutenant Woods hung up the phone and turned around. He took a deep breath and said loudly, "okay boys and girls. It seems as though we are right in the middle of a shit storm! There's been a bunch of abductions in Suffolk County in the past week or so. Parents of these kids are frantic and the Suffolk boys don't have enough manpower to handle this storm."

Corny asked, "How many?"

"Four kids taken plus the poor kid found in Queens. They think they're all connected."

"Oh my God," swore Del, shaking her head.

Joey asked, "Time for the FBI? A combined task force?"

"Hopefully. But you know how the Feds play it close to the vest. They may want full control. Suffolk police force placed a call and the Feds are en route." explained Woods.

Everyone spent a few minutes in quiet thought. "I don't know how the Feds are going to play this out, but I expect that we can all contribute to the task force. The Suffolk detectives, you guys, specifically Corny and Del, with Ted and Joey as support here in the squad. And, of course, the Special Agents," said Woods.

"Once I get the call, and the task force is confirmed, you two," Woods pointed at Del and Corny, "will head out to Long Island. I'm sure their home base will be the Long Island FBI field office in Melville. You may want to go home and pack a bag."

"Copy that Lieu," said Corny.

Del quickly piped up.

"We need copies of all our information and photos to bring with us." She walked over to a desk in the corner of the squad and asked Peggy List to gather the necessary information. Peggy is a middle aged civilian secretary who did all of the photocopying. She also gathered the paperwork evidence. She's worked for Lieutenant Woods for over ten years. Peggy smiled and quickly responded by rolling her chair out and swiveling at the same time.

"No problem, detective. As soon as I have what you need, I'll let you know. It should take an hour or so."

Del nodded. "Corny, this is a good time to pack our bags at home and come back for the evidence."

"Copy that," Corny formed a huge silly grin.

CHAPTER 11

"Okay, I'm packed. You got your stuff, big guy?" asked Del.

"Yeah, almost done. I need my shaving equipment and deodorant. Gimme another minute," Corny shouted from the white-tiled bathroom.

Buster, Corny's wire-hair terrier, jumped up onto the worn brown sofa. Del sat down and gave him a tight hug. He began to lick her face and placed his front paws on her shoulders. She rubbed his sides and combed his hair with her slender fingers. "Buster gonna stay with Mrs. Cohen again?"

Corny walked out of the bathroom smiling. He loved Buster and he loved how much Buster accepted Del. Now that she was a permanent fixture in the apartment, Buster had to share Corny with Del.

"Yeah, she loves the little guy. She said, 'any time 'she'd dog-sit. Besides, she loves the company especially since Mr. Cohen passed last year. We'll bring him across the hall on the way out."

"Speaking of leaving, let's stop for a quick bite before we go back to the squad. We have at least another half hour. I'm sure Peggy is still working on the copies."

"What do you think, Babe? Chinese?" asked Corny.

"Why not. We'll go to Chen's Garden. I can go for House Special Wonton and steamed chicken with broccoli."

"Sounds like a plan, Babe." Corny stopped in the hallway, pulled her close and kissed her lips for several seconds. She kissed back as she rose up on her toes a few inches. She blushed and pushed herself away as another tenant rushed through the front lobby door.

Corny knocked on Mrs. Cohen's door as the taste of Del remained on his mouth. Buster barked. She opened the door within seconds and her face lit up. "Oh, my. Look who's here? My little buddy. Hahaha. Come on in Buster!"

"Thank you so much Mrs. Cohen. I brought his food, some treats and a few toys. Sure you don't mind? We'll be gone for several days, probably. A work thing."

"Hi Del. How are you dear?"

"Hello Mrs. Cohen. Thank you."

"Are you kidding, Cornelius? I love the company. Leave Buster for as long as you want," smiled Mrs. Cohen.

"Okay, we'll keep in touch." Corny spied Buster rubbing his back on Mrs. Cohen's easy chair in the corner of the living room. He rolled his eyes up to the ceiling. "He's a funny, funny dog."

"No problem, Cornelius. Speak to you soon, Mrs. Cohen." And she closed the door slowly.

Out the door, down the steps and in the Hummer. Del said, "Next stop, Mr. Chen's."

"Let's go, I'm starved." Corny wrapped his long right arm around Del and pulled her close.

"I thought you're hungry," said Del.

"I'm hungry for you!" Corny exclaimed.

She turned her head and stared at the side view of his face with a warm glow. At this point in time, after losing his wife several years ago, he finally knew that he was in love, too.

After the quick Chinese meal, Corny's iPhone buzzed in his pocket. He had been holding hands with Del, finishing a third cup of tea. They sat in one of the two window tables, enjoying the street scene of pedestrians strolling by. He reached in and answered the phone. "Yeah, Lieu. You got the call?" He waited a few minutes while Woods explained. "Okay. Just finishing a quick meal. Coming into the squad. Peggy finished?" He listened again with his right hand holding the phone to his right ear. He held onto Del's warm fingers with his left.

"Copy, boss."

"Check please," he called to his female server. He made a grand gesture of a check mark in the air. She saw him and nodded.

"Well?" Del asked, raising her eyebrows flecked with blond hair.

"Back to the squad and then out to Melville. We got us a bona fide task force, but you know who's taking the lead."

"Yep, I could only imagine," said Del.

Corny paid the check and followed Del out the door.

CHAPTER 12

Sheepshead Bay has a large enclave of Russian immigrants. They seemed to have spread out east along the shoreline from Coney Island and Brighton Beach. Many Russians came with plenty of cash to invest, to build and to spend. Elaborate bars, nightclubs and restaurants dotted the commercial thoroughfares of this cultural neighborhood. A tremendous number of immigrants sought a better life in America and planned to achieve citizenship like so many other ethnic groups who arrived at the shores of our country. However, along with hard-working folks, came the ones who continued or began criminal careers to increase their fortunes.

Spasibo stood on a corner lot on Emmons Ave. across from the bay, taking up a third of the block. The name of the Russian night spot was spelled out on a vertical line with separate blue neon letters in a lower case
Monaco font. The 'b 'flickered on and off. The facade of the building was a combination of brick and navy diagonal vinyl siding. The double doors were made of solid butcher block with long, ornate, golden vertical handles. There were a handful of well-dressed young men and woman smoking and chatting out in front. Some, no doubt, high on lines of coke. Muffled music floated from inside the nightclub, mixed with the clouds of cigarette smoke in the autumn night air.

The club had a dark and rich decor. On the left was an area for thick mahogany tables suitable for four or six patrons and small leather studded booths for intimate twos. A gold and burgundy print wallpaper covered the walls under gold-plated wall sconces which shed cones of dull light. Most of the tables were occupied with groups of young adults and middle-agers engaged in eating and discussion. The conversations were difficult to navigate since the noise level was so high from the pulsing music and loud intercourse.

Some traditional Russian appetizers, as well as American favorites were served in the club along with plenty of booze. Cold indigirka salad (diced frozen whitefish, onions, salt, pepper, and lemon wedges) was atop a few tables. Cold kholodets (meat with vegetables in a gelatine) served with a strong horseradish and hot Russian mustard was consumed. Stroganina--a Russian sashumi (whole fish frozen raw, skinned and cut into thin slices served with onions and scallions) was also a favorite. Many others preferred Buffalo chicken wings and pizza wedges over the Russian fare.

The center of the club had a sizable hardwood dance floor. There were couples and threesomes gyrating to the sounds of Pitbull and Beyonce. Most men wore slacks and open-collared dress shirts and many women wore very short, tight tube dresses. Stiletto heels were a must because they didn't really move much off their places on the floor. The nightclub scene was a 'tango 'of sex for one-night-stands upon leaving and perhaps more dating from there.

At the huge mahogany bar on the right side of the club stood numerous red leather four-legged stools. Most were taken by the serious drinkers, singles and mobsters. The back wall was covered with three quarter inch mirrors, decorated with gold curlicue designs. There was a latticework of shelves, which were installed against the mirrored wall, filled with name brand liquors. A huge wine rack, attached to brick, was off to the left side approaching the back of the club. The beer taps abutted the inside of the wooden bar. A glass rack overhead held a large assortment of wine and champagne glasses. On top of the bar rested several small dishes of osetra caviar and several plates of blini (Russian pancakes). Pretzels and nuts were ever-present too.

Four bartenders were in a state of perpetual motion. Shaking drinks, pouring whiskey, taking cash, opening beer taps, cleaning the bar surface, filling the nosh bowls, chatting up the singles. The fifty-year old boss, Vladimir, was bald and burly. He kept a broad smile on his face the whole night. He wore a black dress shirt under a tight three-button gunmetal gray vest. The three other bartenders wore the same uniform and were quite a bit younger, but all good looking. The two young ladies were very pretty blondes. Nikita, was 22 years old and an art history student in Brooklyn College. She had straight dirty blond long hair and was short, but muscular. The other one, Svitlana, had cobalt blue eyes, short wavy hair and was willowy tall. She studied the viola and played in a small local orchestral group from time to time. The young man behind the bar, Ivan, had dark hair and green eyes. He was also a student, but at Kingsborough Community College in the nursing program. All of them were trained in bartending and customer courtesy.

A tall, handsome Russian-American ambled into the bar area searching for a stool. Another guy got up from the middle of the bar and nodded to the tall guy who just walked in. Tall guy nodded back and slipped onto the stool. "Hey babe, Yorsh please," he said to Svitlana.

She nodded and said with a crafty smile, "of course, sir."

"And don't spare the vodka," raising one of his dark eyebrows.

Yorsh was a combination of beer and vodka.

Svitlana first poured a generous portion of Stolichnaya red vodka into a large beer glass and then filled the rest with the beer on tap. She gently placed a napkin on the bar and then the glass in front of 'tall guy'.

Svitlana leaned in smiling and asked, "how's that?" She was obviously displaying a clear view of her cleavage since her three top buttons were open.

Tall guy licked his lips and slowly moved his gaze from her breasts to her blue eyes. "That is a beautiful sight." He continued to stare at her and made no move to lift the glass.

"Hey, what's your name? Been in *Spasibo* before?"

It was hard to hear her throaty voice over the boisterous

gang of guys on his left and the loud music. He leaned in, as well. "Dmitry," he whispered.

Nikita briefly glanced over at the encounter in the center of the bar, obviously admiring 'tall guy'.

Svitlana stuck her slender alabaster arm over the bar and extended her hand in friendship. Dmitry gently took her hand in his and brought it to his full lips for a gallant kiss. She immediately blushed, but kept her hand in his for a few fleeting moments.

"Nice to meet you, Dmitry."

Vladimir cleared his throat with few coughs. He motioned to Svitlana with his eyes to get working the bar. There were plenty of thirsty patrons who needed help. Svitlana's spell had been broken. She retrieved her arm and moved down the bar toward the front door.

One of the gang turned toward Dmitry and rolled his head toward the end of the bar. "Hey buddy. She's a babe, ain't she. Her brother's a regular in here on Friday and Saturday nights. And he's connected, if you know what I mean. Watch your step, pal."

"Oh, is that right? Who is he?" asked Dmitry.

" Name is Boris and you need to be careful. He's got some serious business on the island," said the gang member.

"You mean, Long Island." Dmitry probed a bit further. "Hey, fella, my name's Dmitry. Moved into the Bay a few weeks ago."

"Hey man. I'm Victor." He whispered, "we all do a little business with Boris from time to time." Waves of a beer odor floated from Victor's mouth. He put his finger up to his mouth and made a shushing noise. Victor's inebriated state made it easier for Dmitry to pump him for more information.

"So what kind of work do you do, my friend?" Victor slurred his words and swayed on the barstool.

"I worked on the docks of Jersey City. I waited tables in a few diners," said Dmitry. "Actually, looking for work closer to home now."

Two of Victor's gang yelled in unison, "Victor, what the fuck, man? Who the fuck you talking to?"

Victor turned on his stool and shouted back, "he's a good friend of mine. This is Dmitry, from the Jersey docks!"

Dmitry saw his opportunity to join in with the loud gang. He jumped off his stool. "Hey, fellas. What are you guys drinking?" Before they could answer, he called over Svitlana. "Hey babe, a round of Yorsh for all of these guys. Okay?"

She rushed over and said, "sure thing, Dmitry." She smiled and turned red again. She set up five glasses in a row on the bar and reached for the 'Stoly'. Again, she poured a generous shot into each glass followed by the beer. Svitlana passed each glass down a few feet and the gang gave a roar, clinking glasses with their new friend Dmitry. Victor had a huge grin on his face.

Nikita once again turned her head toward the other end of the bar and gazed at Dmitry in the midst of the loud group of mobsters. She took out a clean rag and wiped the bar surface again.

CHAPTER 13

Lieutenant Woods walked out of his office after he hung up the phone. He approached the unit. "Got everything you need from Peggy?"

Del responded, "think so. We'll need the forensics and coroner's reports when they're finished."

"No problem. I'll have Ted and Joey fax them over to the FBI office when they're ready," said Woods. Looking at Corny and Del, "better get going. Gonna take you awhile to get to the Melville office with traffic and all. Besides, the task force is awaiting your arrival." Woods' eyebrows arched. "Those 'special agents 'expect things to get done yesterday."

Corny said, "Copy that, boss. We're out of here."

"Remember, keep me in the loop! A tight loop, Corny," demanded Woods.

Corny added, "Of course Lieu." Turning to Ted and Joey, "you guys do your magic from here. Dig deep. We need to find these bastards. Once you get the DNA, don't forget to check with Interpol."

Ted raised a mug of black coffee to his mouth, "we got this Corny. Take good care. Soon as we learn anything, you'll get it."

It took a solid hour, plus, to get to the Melville FBI office on Pinelawn Rd., just north of Pinelawn Cemetery. After showing their credentials to security on the main floor, they took the elevator up to the second floor. Their contact was Special Agent Samantha Curlee, SAC (Special Agent in Charge) of the task force. She met them at the elevator with a poker face on a head tilt. She offered a stiff-armed handshake, firm and all business.

"Special Agent Curlee, I'm Detective Cornelius Prince and this is my partner, Detective Kristina DelVecchio, NYPD," Corny explained.

"Pleasure, detectives. Let's hit the ground running. We have four youngsters missing and one in your morgue. Parents are frantic and you well know that the longer they're missing, the greater the chance of not getting them back," Curlee explained. "The Suffolk detectives are with my partner, Special Agent Carlos Benitez. Please follow me."

Samantha Curlee, was taller than Del. Maybe 5'8" with shoulder length salt and pepper wavy hair tied in a pony tail. Her sharp gray eyes didn't miss a trick. A strong jawline and high cheek bones defined her as a handsome woman with smooth skin and an aquiline nose. She had more than fifteen years with the FBI and six years in the Dallas police department before that. Curlee wore a fitted navy blue pants suit that revealed her strict workout regimen in the gym.

Agent Curlee brought Corny and Del back into a huge bullpen area with numerous desks in half-wall cubicles. Men and women studied their computers at their workstations. Some walked with documents, coffee cups, or smart phones. Other agents had desks in a large sub-division without half-walls. All of them had state-of-the-art electronics. Many were pecking at the keys in a clickety-click symphony. There were several wide-screen monitors on the walls surrounding the open room. Surveillance photos and pictures of those missing children continuously came into focus on those high definition curved wall screens. Elongated florescent light fixtures hung down from the dark 20-foot ceiling.

"Meet our NYPD partners, Detective Prince and Detective DelVecchio," announced Agent Curlee. "This is SAC John Masters of the Melville FBI office." He nodded and gave a brief smile. He offered a handshake to both of them. "Welcome, detectives, to the task force. You ever work with the Feds before?" Agent Masters asked.

"I have a few times. Del is new at this, but a quick learner," responded Corny.

"My partner of several years, Special Agent Carlos

Benitez," said Agent Curlee. Benitez was a well-built experienced agent of Mexican decent. His generous shock of short black hair was somewhat parted in the center of his head and he sported a slight shadow of facial hair. A boomerang scar was lightly etched in his left cheek.

"Hey there. Welcome aboard. I believe you've met Detectives Morris and Winchester at the Jeffries residence," said Agent Benitez. Morris was sitting on the edge of one of the desks, listening. Winchester stood ramrod straight with a keen stare in her dark brown eyes. They both gave the obligatory nod.

Corny and Del smiled and both turned their heads to the screens. Corny asked, "So how many kids are missing?"

Curlee took the lead. "As of now, four youngsters are missing and, of course, the one you found, Margot Jeffries, is deceased. All from different towns in Suffolk." Benitez worked his computer keyboard and a clear photo of each of the missing four appeared on the screens along with names and addresses. The photos were obtained from the distraught parents subsequent to rather difficult, yet crucial interviews. Del brought the photos of the deceased girl over to Benitez to input into his system so he could post them on the screen as well. Benitez immediately scanned these new photos and posted them along side the other photos.

Everyone stared at the pictures of these missing children and shook their heads. Anger and determination burned within each law enforcement agent. Del felt hot tears welling up.

Agent Curlee said, "Okay, let's get to work. Carlos, post these initial questions on the main screen, will ya?"

Why these kids?
What do they have in common?
Who abducted them?
How did they abduct them?
Where are they now?

"These five questions should be our primary investigative focus? Agreed?" Asked Agent Curlee.

CHAPTER 14

Detective Morris took several steps closer to the surround screen. Saying the names aloud highlighted the horror and pain that these poor kids and their families have been enduring.

"Four girls and one boy abducted. Margot Jeffries, from Bay Shore, allegedly murdered and dumped in Queens. Kimberly Weinstein, Smithtown. Carmen Rodriguez, Brentwood. Brianna Park, Commack. Wesley McArthur, Northport. All from Suffolk County and similar ages."

Del asked, "All of them snatched almost within one week. Organized human trafficking?"

"Latina gang operation or the Russians," guessed Special Agent Benitez.

"Organized, well-planned abductions based on smart intelligence," said Detective Winchester. She used her hands to punctuate certain words as she spoke and remained focused on the screen. "Any camera surveillance of the abduction sites?"

Special Agent Benitez continued, "Margot was taken from her own bed during a home invasion. The mom said there were no security cameras inside or outside the home. Kimberly was grabbed in one of the sprawling parking lots of the Smithhaven Mall. No security footage of the particular aisle she was parked in. And forensics found no relevant fingerprints on her Jeep Grand Cherokee as of yet."

Corny asked, "any film of vans, trucks or cars trolling the parking lots of the mall?"

"Nothing out of the ordinary so far. We'll have our techs check those security films again," said SAC Curlee.

"Carmen was walking home from a friend's house after dark in a residential neighborhood and never made it home," explained Special Agent Benitez.

Corny's thought was that someone's Ring security bell may have caught sight of the perps or their vehicle.

"What about a house Ring..." He was interrupted by Detective Morris, "Our uniforms canvassed each general area of abduction and got nothing. No one saw or heard anything. But, but, but...we got a glimpse of a dark van outside of Commack High School, where Brianna was waiting for her mom to pick her up. One indistinct man, dark clothes, jumped out of the van. He may have injected her with some drug and muscled her into the side door. Then the van drove off. The school's security camera had no angle to see the license plate at all. Just a dark van--either black or dark gray or navy blue or dark green."

Benitez tapped his keyboard and posted the stills of the van and the perp. They all looked closely, willing their eyes to pick something up that could possibly be significant. At this point, they had practically no leads.

"How about the parent interviews? Had we eliminated personal vendettas against family members or conflicts with business partners, business associates?" asked Del.

"No evidence or claims of family troubles, personally or work-related," answered Special Agent Benitez. "But our people will dig deeper."

Corny questioned, "what do all of these kids have in common?"

SAC Curlee jumped in to say, "all high school students except for Wesley, who is a middle schooler. All of them are young and relatively defenseless. All of them live in Suffolk County."

Detective Morris explained, "all of the kids had computers and/or smartphones or iPads."

Del explained, "and what do we know about young people?"

"They are continuously on their devices--either playing, texting, posting. Constant social media interaction," said Curlee. She turned to her left to peer at her task force members. Her arching eyebrows questioned her colleagues.

"The question is: How did these abductors track and monitor these youngsters? Were they randomly chosen or specifically targeted?" posited Detective Morris.

"These kidnappings were targeted. They knew Kimberly was going to the mall and going alone. They knew that Wesley always walks home from school. They knew Carmen was alone at night on the street walking home. They knew Brianna was waiting for her mom," Corny explained.

"So they were probably studied, stalked, and watched for patterned behaviors?" Asked Curlee.

Del said, "there was only one home invasion late at night. And they knew the father was on a business trip. These guys took very few chances."

Benitez asked, "what about the schools? Any relationship between them? Sports, academics, after school activities? Are they interrelated through clubs or organizations?"

"I need each of you to visit each of the schools these kids attended and see what you can find out. Talk with the principals, guidance counselors, deans. Find out how their databases are organized. Ask about sports teams, clubs, groups and their relation to other schools in the county," ordered SAC Curlee.

Benitez gave out the assignments and the members of the task force got their marching orders. Benitez took the last school, Northport Middle School.

"Special Agent Benitez, we came here in one car. We'll take two schools together," said Corny.

"Copy that, detective," responded Benitez.

"Detective Prince, before you leave, have you gotten the forensics or DNA reports yet from your people?" Asked Curlee.

"Not yet, Special Agent Curlee," Corny responded.

Del and Corny followed the Suffolk detectives to the elevator banks. They had a few hours before the schools let out. None of them had much hope they would get any significant lead in the case. The elevator arrived but Corny motioned for Del to take a step back. "You guys go ahead. I have to make a call," said Corny.

"Hey Lieu, it's me. Any info from forensics yet?" He listened to Woods 'response. "Going well. Time to interview school personnel." He listened again for a few moments. "Copy that."

Corny nodded and placed his hand gently in the small of Del's back. Del pressed the down button for the elevator and looked up into Corny's warm brown eyes. "Let's go partner."

CHAPTER 15

Leonid hung up the phone with his boss and leaned way back in his leather desk chair. He opened the top left draw of his desk and plucked out a Cuban cigar, a San Cristobal La Punta. Only one of his bodyguards was in the office with him. Mikhail was busy on his own iPhone at a smaller corner wooden desk. Leonid carefully placed the stem of the cigar between his yellowed teeth. He bit off the tip and spit it out onto the cement floor. He then reached for his Prometheus Magma X Torch Flame Triple Jet lighter, a gift from his wife Irina.

Leonid and Irina have been married for 18 years and have a boy and a girl. Ironically, they are both in high school and are approximately similar ages of the kids he traffics. Of course, to Leonid, 'family is family and business is business' and they remain completely separate.

Leonid and Irina had built a center hall Colonial home in Bayside for over $2 million. Many of their neighbors are also from Russia. Some are mob connected and others own private businesses. They live a charmed social life. Irina gets to buy anything she likes in exchange for never asking Leonid about his business dealings. Leonid comes and goes without answering to Irina which leaves room for him to keep a few women 'on the side'. He secretly owns a well-appointed two bedroom apartment in Douglaston for his trysts. Often he stays over with one of his paramours for a day or two. However, lately, he's been very busy overseeing the abductions and the trafficking for his demanding bosses.

After hanging up with Kuznetsov, he now had a very specific and complicated order, which occupied his full concentration.

"Mikhail, get Alexey and Boris to come here right away. They're probably playing cards or video games in the back. We have a very special order from the higher ups," said Leonid softly.

He puffed on his cigar a few times and sent smoke rings up into the florescent lamp above. Mikhail jumped out of his chair and walked out of the office.

A few minutes later, Alexey and Boris strode into Leonid's smoky office. Mikhail trailed behind and stuffed his large frame back into his chair in the corner. "Take a seat. Both of you," commanded Leonid.

Alexey and Boris sat in the two empty steel chairs across from the desk.

"We have a very specific order and it could be complicated. But I'm very sure that you guys can handle complicated, yeah?" asked Leonid.

Alexey answered, "sure boss. What's the job?"

Leonid explained the basic job without giving the specific details because he did not get the complete file yet. He did feel that they needed at least another two or three good men for the job. They were getting paid a lot of money and couldn't afford to screw up. The buyer was extremely rich with many contacts and connections. They could possibly get more business thrown their way if this job was successful.

"Okay, I understand. I have people...reliable people waiting and ready to work. Just give the word when you get the details," said Alexey.

"The job is in Nassau County. But, it may be in broad daylight. You may have to be very creative so as not to get caught or have any witnesses of the grab. You got me?" asked Leonid.

His bushy black eyebrows bounced up at least an inch. He took another long drag on the Cuban.

"Got it boss. Once we have the details, we'll put together a plan. Once we have a plan, we'll run it by you before we execute," explained Alexey.

"Your people better be professional. No fuck-ups, yeah!

Do I have to say it again?" asked Leonid. Alexey shook his head. Both he and Boris stared at Leonid's beady eyes.

Leonid waved his two men out of his office with the Cuban between his full lips. He picked up his cell phone to call Irina, leaning back in his chair.

CHAPTER 16

The two men walked to the lounge in the back of the dank warehouse. They slumped into the old fabric couch, across from the wide-screen Mitsubishi 55 inch television, and began to brainstorm their next job.

"I've got some guys we could use out of Brooklyn, Alexey. They'd jump at the chance to make some coin," said Boris.

"You mean the guys at *Spasibo?*" asked Alexey.

"Yeah, the club where my sister bartends. I've been there plenty and I know those guys. A few of them work construction. Odd jobs, you know?"

"A daytime grab will be fuckin 'difficult," explained Alexey. "Definitely could use more guys and another vehicle. You know Nassau pretty good?"

"Sure I know the Nassau roads and towns. I drive through all the time and my cousin lives in Westbury," said Boris confidently.

"We don't have the details yet, but a grab during the day usually takes a car switch, more men and of course the magic needle," smiled Alexey. "Who's your guy in Brooklyn?"

"You know Victor Ivanov. He's worked with us a few months ago. He's got a Brooklyn crew and they're good men who are professional. Know how to keep their mouths shut. They get the danger. And they know if they screw up, not only does the money dry up, but they know what the real consequences are. They all saw what happened to Egor," explained Boris.

"Let's set up a meet with Victor and his guys. I need to meet them face-to-face," said Alexey.

"Want me to call him now?" asked Boris.

"Not yet. Once we get the file for this job and we have all

the details, we take a meeting," Alexey reassured him.

Muffled screams and crying came from the cages. Mikhail, the bodyguard, stormed out of the office and marched to the cage area. "What the hell is going on? Why are they screaming?"

Anika, the attendant answered, "I think they saw a few rats running in the cage from the bathroom and these girls panicked." She picked up the 14" hardwood baton from her desk and slammed it into the metal cage. "Shut the hell up!! It's only a rodent! Not going to kill you!"

All of the kids gathered into a tight circle in a far corner of their enclosure. Brianna and Kimberly jumped up onto Brianna's cot. Instantly, they stopped screaming, afraid of Anika scolding and Mikhail's glaring presence. Tears continued to stream down Brianna's face. Wesley sobbed and his whole body trembled. Once they calmed down, Mikhail returned to the office.

Boris looked at Alexey and asked, "when are we shipping these brats out of here?"

"I think as soon as this new job is complete and we have the target. Of course the buyers need to be ready to receive them. They are being very cautious and listening very carefully to the FBI chatter. If the authorities show any movement, we all need to stand down until all is clear to transport them," explained Alexey.

Alexey's phone buzzed. It was Leonid summoning them to the office. Most likely they got the computer file on the new job. "Let's go, Boris. Time to go to work. And remember, no fuck-ups!"

CHAPTER 17

Del and Corny sat in the Hummer and cued the Navi. "Corny, we have Bay Shore and Smithtown. Which one first?"

"Let's hit Bay Shore first. Want to plug in the address?" asked Corny.

"Sure thing big guy," grinned Del.

Corny's cell phone buzzed in the cup holder between them. Corny looked over to Del and pulled over to the curb. He snatched the phone up into his catcher's mitt of a hand and answered. "Hold on Joey. Gonna put you on speaker so Del can hear too."

"Hey. Got some info for you. Forensics found some prints and bits of DNA under the vic's fingernail. No hits on CODIS, but Interpol got back to us. The DNA belongs to an Estonian, Egor Kukk--small time crook, armed robber, involved in B and E's (Breaking and Entering), assaults. He's known to work for whoever is paying him, mostly the Russians."

Del asked, "does he have a passport or did he rabbit across one of our borders?"

"No, he has what seems to be a legitimate Estonian passport. Flew into Toronto three and a half years ago. Probably worked his way across our border," explained Joey.

"Any known address for this guy?" asked Corny.

"Last known address was in Brighton Beach," responded Joey.

"How about you and Ted pay him a visit?" Corny asked.

"Way ahead of you. Ran it by Lieu and we're on our way out the door."

"Keep us posted and tell Lieu we'll catch him up to speed later today. All of us are on our way to interview the school principals and staffs. Trying to connect the dots," said Corny.

"Are the Feds busting balls?" asked Joey.

"Actually for Feds, they aren't too bad," Corny grinned and nodded at Del. "Catch you later."

"Copy that boss."

Corny checked over his shoulder for traffic and swerved back onto the road. He cued the Navi for Bay Shore Senior High School. It was partially sunny and the glare annoyed Corny's eyes even with the shades on. In a little over twenty minutes, he pulled up to the curb outside the main entrance to the school. They didn't feel it was necessary to call ahead to the Principal.

They walked over to the front door and showed their badges to the security guard at the front desk. "NYPD huh? You guys a little out of your normal jurisdiction?" asked the uniformed guard.

Del responded, "Did you hear about the missing student? The story must be all around the school. We need to speak with the Principal now."

"Of course, detectives. Sorry." He picked up his walkie-talkie and spoke with purpose. "Officer James, we need an escort to the Principal's office immediately. We have two NYPD detectives at the front security desk."

"Copy that, William. Be right there," responded Officer James.

"Okay, another officer will be here shortly and escort you. I cannot leave my post."

Corny nodded and smiled. "Thank you, Officer Mackie," he said slowly as he read the name tag that was pinned to the pocket on his uniform shirt.

Officer Mackie switched channels on his walkie-talkie to the Principal's frequency. "Principal Ticher, please pick up ASAP. This is Officer Mackie at the front desk."

Five seconds later, "Go for Ticher," she responded with a strong voice.

"Ma'am I have two NYPD detectives at the front door to

see you ASAP. I called Officer James to escort them to your office."

"No problem. I'm in my office."

Officer James arrived and led the detectives to the Main Office, adjacent to the Principal's office. They needed to sign in first before engaging the Principal. Marjorie Ticher strode out of her doorway and met the detectives at the Main Office counter.

"Hello detectives, I'm Marjorie Ticher. I know why you're here," as she extended a firm hand to each of them.

"This is Detective DelVecchio and I'm Detective Prince, NYPD Homicide Midtown South. We unfortunately need to talk to you about Margot Jeffries."

"Please come into my office."

They both nodded and glanced at each of the secretaries who stared at them as they entered.

CHAPTER 18

The interview with Principal Ticher lasted just short of an hour. From Bay Shore, they headed over to Smithtown High School East in St. James. Again, they needed to register with the front desk security. A teacher who happened to be on patrol near the desk volunteered to bring them to the Principal's office on the first floor. Principal Whitmer was expecting detectives to inquire about his missing student, Kimberly Weinstein. However, he was surprised to be visited by NYPD detectives. They explained the task force and how Kimberly's abduction may have been part of a large human trafficking ring. Just the mention of human trafficking to parents and educators conjured all sorts of dark forces and worst nightmares. Principal Whitmer's face blanched when Corny explained their fears and asked the difficult questions.

Dirty clouds marched across the sky during the afternoon. The Suffolk detectives, Special Agent Benitez and Corny and Del found their way back to the FBI office to post their collective information on the computer screens. They knew they were running out of time when it came to abductions and desperately tried to draw some conclusions in the case.
Once Benitez inputted the results of their interviews, Benitez again posted the questions posed before and the knowledge they had.

Why these kids?
What do they have in common?
Who abducted them?

How did they abduct them?
Where are they now?

Corny jumped in right away, "we got a hit from Interpol on DNA found on the victim, Margot Jeffries, A low level thug from Estonia, an Egor Kukk. With a passport, he flew into Toronto about three and a half years ago and made his way down to the states. In Europe he committed B & E's, assaults, armed robberies. He mainly works for the Russians."

"Russian mob is known for drugs, prostitution, human trafficking," Special Agent Curlee quietly stated. "So we probably have the **Who**, but not specifically who the players are. Now we need to find out **How, Why** and **Where**.

SAC Masters hung up his phone in his office and immediately joined the task force. "I just got a call from the New York office. They've been scoping out the Russian mob for months and have a few agents in deep cover. They are focusing their efforts in the areas of Brooklyn where the Russians are known to live and operate--Coney Island, Brighton Beach, Sheepshead Bay."

Curlee asked, "any chatter by the Russians about grabbing these kids and keeping them under wraps?"

Masters answered, "Not yet. The undercover agents are working on it. One is working on a relationship that may prove to be helpful. The other one keeps an eye on some of the minor players and an ear to the ground."

"We need their handler to press a little harder for info, boss," exclaimed Curlee.

Masters gazed at her over his glasses and continued, "what did we get with the school interviews?"

Morris and Winchester did their interviews together because they came in one car like Corny and Del. They visited Brentwood and Commack.

Morris took the lead, "No issues with either student and their peers. They do not seem to have anything in common. No cross-referencing with respect to extracurriculars, or sports, or clubs. They don't share any common interest but we can check again with the parents."

Curlee asked, "How about the schools 'data bases?"

Benitez asked, "What are you getting at?"

"My point is that nowadays all schools have data bases for their students. IDs, grades, teachers, clubs, psychological evaluations, health information (although HIPAA restrictions pertain to them, I'm sure). There must be anecdotal records from teachers, guidance counselors, etc."

SAC Masters took a few steps forward staring at the screen. "How about the other three schools, people? Data bases for the students? Everything must be on school servers. All the information that used to be on file records must be digitized."

Corny said, "And if they all have computer data bases, that's what they have in common!"

All of the task force members looked at each other. "And if they all have data bases, they all can be **hacked** and **searched**!! The abductions are not random. They are targeting certain types of youngsters," explained Curlee.

"If the Pentagon and other government agencies can be hacked and infiltrated, hacking school data bases is a piece of cake...especially if it's the Russians or other Eastern European countries," said Detective Morris.

"This whole operation could be orchestrated from Russia with operators across the globe. There are probably cells within our country as well as within other countries. All for illicit profit, all for the almighty dollar," said Curlee. "And why... **because they can**."

Del put her two cents in, "What a shit show! We need to find those kids before they wind up...God knows where!"

CHAPTER 19

Even though the autumn night was especially chilly from 20-mph winds, Dmitry's large hands were warm. He wrapped his long arms around Svitlana and felt the contours of her abdomen and her breasts as she fumbled to get the key into the lock on her front door. Svitlana giggled then turned around to press her pink lips against Dmitry's mouth. Her tongue found a slight opening and she flicked and licked. Suddenly, she pulled back, smiling.

"Stop, I can't get the key in the door." She was nearly breathless.

He whispered in her ear, "give me the key, I'll get it in."

"I'm sure you will," Svitlana smirked and relinquished her keyring.

Once the door was opened, they danced inside, twirling and twisting, pushing and pulling. Dmitry kicked the door closed and pressed her body up against the wall. He grabbed her slender arms and forced them over her head against the yellow-painted wall that was marred by cracks and divots. Svitlana uttered tiny groans while he gently kissed her neck on one side, then the other. Her cleavage swelled as he worked his way down to her small, but firm breasts with his tongue. Her lower torso began to grind against Dmitry's erection. She began to pull him out of the galley kitchen.

White wooden cabinets were affixed over the small gas stove and a white porcelain sink. Water droplets and rust stains encircled the drain amidst a few plastic dishes and a small juice glass. A knife and fork rested haphazardly on the porcelain surface. A white refrigerator stood motionless emitting a continuous hum that played a background rhythm for Svitlana's loud groans and high-pitched screams of pleasure from the bedroom.

Their naked bodies performed a ballet of thrust and entanglement. A sheen of sweat coated their chests which heaved and twisted and conjoined. He was not shy to explore Svitlana and she welcomed it. Guttural chirps escaped her lips as she melted into his muscular physique, finally spent. Happily, he released a moment before. Each of them smiled with exhaustion and delight.

The mattress on the double bed was too soft for Dmitry's back, but he did not even think of complaining after his sweet conquest. He looked around the room that had one double window, dressed with cheap dark drapes over plain metal blinds. The walls were a dull gray but decorated with colorful travel posters framed in thin black metal. The small lamp on the wooden nightstand had a 60-watt bulb. It was the only illumination in the room. Svitlana kept the light on while they made love. A tall chest of drawers was the only other piece of furniture in the room. A small stack of paperback books were in the corner atop a plank of wood supported by two bricks on the floor.

Svitlana turned on her side and traced her glossy fingernail up and down Dmitry's hard body. She was still naked and her breasts firmly kept their shape. She discovered a cylindrical welt about six inches above the knee. "What happened to you here?"

"Oh, that. Dock work can cause all kinds of injuries. It never healed properly." He turned his head and kissed her nose and then her lips. "That's why I need to look for work that's not as dangerous."

"Why, you're a strapping guy. I can see you doing physical labor." She ran her soft hand over his strong chest and arm muscles. "Do you work out at the gym as well as work the docks?" asked Svitlana.

Dmitry explained, "Like I said, I'm really looking for less physical work right now. And I go to the gym when I get the chance."

Svitlana flopped on her back next to him and stared at the ceiling. "You know, I could talk to my brother about you. I could see if he has some work for you that doesn't involve working with your hands," she said.

"That would be really helpful, Svitlana. Life is all about connections, huh?"

She responded, "they say, 'it's who you know, not what you know 'I believe."

"And that's how the world goes round." Dmitry combed his lush black hair with his fingers and exhaled slowly. "So what kind of work does Boris do? I'm looking for easier work, but definitely willing to pull my own load."

"Yeah, I get that Dmitry. He does many kinds of work...for very powerful men. Men nobody wants to cross," Svitlana said sternly. She gazed at him with cold blue eyes and no trace of a smile.

"I'm good with that. I know how to follow orders. And keep my mouth shut," said Dmitry.

"Don't worry, I will talk with him. Maybe he needs someone like you." She paused for a few minutes. "But not like the way I need you." She made circles with her pink fingernails around his groin.

Dmitry turned to her and kissed her smooth lips again and nuzzled her neck. More giggles bubbled in her throat. "Are you ready to go again?"

She wrapped her legs around his torso and turned off the lamp. Aside from the thrill of sex with Svitlana, Dmitry thought about all of the skill sets he had acquired in order to be successful. Being persuasive was definitely high on the list.

CHAPTER 20

Teddy and Joey walked up four steps on the narrow stoop. Teddy examined the names on the three bells near the mailboxes. The one on the bottom had the initials of E. K. A thick cloud cover billowed across the sky over Brighton Beach. A few elderly women, wearing colorful head scarves, walked with purpose, clutching heavy plastic bags filled with groceries.

They each stood on either side of the white windowless door. Teddy looked at Joey and chirped," Bingo." Training automatically sent their open palms to the Glocks on their hips. Teddy rang the bottom bell. They both heard the buzzer inside. They waited and watched the door. Teddy rang the bell again. The breeze lapped at the bottom of Teddy's open black raincoat.

"NYPD! Egor Kukk, please open up!" shouted Joey.

A man wearing a checkered flannel shirt was standing on his stoop across the street. He stared at the two detectives, waiting for some action to take place. Most people were compelled to witness any police presence in their neighborhood, similar to rubberneckers on the highway after an accident.

Finally, the front door opened partially and a fifty-ish woman dressed in pressed blue jeans and a red woolen sweater peeked out. "Can I help you?" she asked as she brushed strands of blond hair behind her left ear.

"Detectives Hernandez and Huong," they both held up their badges. "We need to talk to Egor Kukk," explained Teddy.

"Yeah, he lives in the first floor apartment. He doesn't answer the bell because he had an accident and can't move around much."

Joey asked, "do you live with him?"

"No, no, I live on the second floor. I can hear his buzzer

from upstairs."

"Your name, ma'am?" Teddy asked.

"Rina...Rina Sepp." She opened the front door all the way allowing the detectives to enter the foyer. Then she unlocked the inside door and let them into the building. She pointed to the first door on the left. "That's his apartment."

"Thank you, Ms. Sepp. Before you go back up to your apartment, would you mind giving us your contact information?" asked Teddy.

She raised her dark brown eyebrows over her slate gray eyes. "What's this all about?"

"We just have some questions for Mr. Kukk regarding an investigation. We may need to ask you a few questions at some point," said Joey.

Teddy opened his notepad and she spelled her first and last name and gave him her cell number. She explained she had no need for a landline in the apartment. Teddy's gaze wandered up the flight of stairs and Rina took that as a hint to get back up. She nodded and climbed the flight.

Joey knocked hard on the Kukk's door. Teddy's hand hovered near his Glock. Joey shouted, "NYPD. Egor, open up. We need to ask you some questions."

Joey leaned into the edge of the door while Teddy remained on the other side of the door jamb. He heard a slow thumping on wood. He looked at Teddy and placed his hand near his Glock, too.

"Okay, I'm coming," exclaimed a voice from inside.

More slow rhythmic thumping. The sound of locks opening and the door cracked open a hair. "What do you want?" asked a tall, gaunt man in his 30's. He was partially bald and had bags under his eyes.

"Egor Kukk?"

"Who's asking?"

"Detectives Hernandez and Huong. We need to ask you some questions. Can we come in for a few minutes?" asked Teddy.

"Hey man, I'm all screwed up here, man. Had an accident and my leg is killing me. Bad time, man."

"Well Egor, it's either we talk here or we take you down to our station house in Manhattan," explained Teddy.

"I can hardly walk, man. Using these freakin 'crutches, hard to get around."

"Open the door, will you?" asked Joey.

There was a pause of about thirty seconds and Egor took the chain off and opened the door fully. The detectives walked into his small studio apartment. Clothes were strewn around the small sofa and on an unmade mattress on the floor in the corner. A pile of dirty dishes were in the sink. Empty take-out containers littered the tiny two-seat table and countertop. A musty odor of urine and left-over food floated in the dank air. No windows were open at all.

Egor flopped back down on the threadbare sofa and he hung his head to the left. A huge plaster cast encased his knee from his upper thigh to his ankle.

"What happened to you, Egor?" asked Teddy.

"It's a long miserable story, man."

Joey cracked a window near the table and both detectives took a seat at the small kitchen table. After listening to Egor's 'long miserable story' Joey said, "Detective Huong, do you buy this guy's sob story about how he sustained his injury?"

"Well, Detective Hernandez, I can't say that I do. Actually, in view of the fact that we found Egor's DNA at a crime scene, I think there's much more to the story."

Teddy and Joey looked at each other for a few moments in silence and then turned to Egor, who was obviously in some discomfort, wriggling on his disgusting and threadbare sofa.

"Egor Kukk, you are officially under arrest for suspicion of murder. Get up and place your hands behind your back. Detective Huong will read you your rights and we're taking you downtown."

Egor looked utterly shocked. "Hey, you said if I answered your questions here, I wouldn't have to go to the station house.

What gives?"

"Well, we didn't like your answers, Egor. And quite frankly, sometimes we lie."

CHAPTER 21

Leonid slammed both of his meaty fists on the metal desk and spewed curses in Russian through his yellowed teeth. "That fuckin 'Egor! I should have capped him in the head! Somehow the NYPD cops found him and brought him in for questioning. We're fucked now! That stupid prick will spill his guts!"

Pavel, one of Leonid's bodyguards pocketed his iPhone and said quietly, "Boss, he'll never talk to nobody, even the cops. He knows his life will be worth shit if he rats on you and your operation."

Leonid stared at Pavel with fire in his eyes. "That fuckin' Egor is a moron. He's got no loyalty to us. No Russian loyalty. The fuckin 'Estonians are loyal to one thing and one thing only-- money!"

"I'm telling you, we don't have to worry. The kids are shipping out soon anyway, aren't they?" asked Pavel.

Mikhail, the other bodyguard knew enough to stay silent, but he kept a keen eye on his raging boss.

"We have one more snatch up and then we ship 'em all out to the buyers. But that's still a day or two away," explained Leonid. He stared at the doorway in deep thought. He knew if he fucked this up, Kuznetsov will have his balls on a platter. Worse yet, he knows Kuznetsov will go after his wife and kids.

"We need to move these kids out today. Mikhail, is the other site ready to move into just for a few days?" asked Leonid.

Mikhail stood up immediately and put his coffee cup on Leonid's desk. "I'll drive over there right now and make sure, boss."

"Okay, go and get back here right away. I want these kids moved and want this place emptied and scrubbed. I don't want any evidence that these targets were ever here. I heard the FBI has a task force now with the locals. Pavel, you and Anika, get the kids ready to move out within an hour. And get rid of all stuff in their cage. Get one of the cleaning crews to scrub the place down. The lounge, my office, and the cages. Got it?" asked Leonid.

"Got it, boss. I'm on it. Just one question, boss. How do you know about the FBI?" asked Pavel.

"Hey, what do you think we're stupid? We got people everywhere working for us. We got people in the NYPD, FBI, ATF, everywhere. For money you get honey, yeah," said Leonid smiling now and again showing a crooked rack of yellow teeth.

Both bodyguards left the office and Leonid began to box up the few possessions he had in his desk. The smile on Leonid's face quickly morphed into a scowl. Thinking of what Kuznetsov would do to him if he fucked up caused his ample belly to become awash with sour acid.

Chapter 22

Alexey flung the heavy door open. Muffled music filled the entrance to *Spasibo.* He and Boris marched straight to the back room behind the bar. Boris caught a glimpse of a few of the hot chicks on the dance floor as he followed Alexey. Victor and his boys knew they were coming. Alexey was arrogant. He ignored the gold-plated PRIVATE plaque screwed into the upper middle of the varnished walnut panel. They stormed in with one purpose: business.

"Hey, my brothers. How goes it?" asked Victor.

There were four other young Russian guys sitting around a hardwood oblong table. Once Alexey and Boris walked in, they all sat up straight in their club chairs and turned their attention to them. Conversation halted immediately. Two of the guys were smoking cigarettes and they all had shot glasses in front of them. There were three open bottles of vodka and small bowls of caviar with side dishes of Russian rye bread slices and diced onion.

Alexey fixed his eyes on Victor and screwed a slight smile on his face. He needed more men for this job coming up and one of his talents was sizing up guys who could be reliable and loyal to the organization.

"Let's give these guys some vodka and a few chairs, boys," commanded Victor.

Three of the men jumped up and offered their seats to Alexey and Boris. One man remained seated and downed a shot of vodka in one gulp. Dmitry was the new guy and played it cool, showing he had the balls not to grovel. He knew who they were.

"Who the fuck is this guy, Victor?" asked Alexey.

Before Victor could answer, Dmitry turned his head to the two gangsters and responded, "Dmitry Kussov. Who the fuck are you?"

Alexey glanced at Boris, and then at Victor without moving his head.

Without answering him, he addressed Victor. "You checked this guy out? Where did he come from?"

Victor said, "Myshkin, one of the ports on the Volga. Father was a fisherman and Dmitry worked with him when he was younger. Came to America about seven years ago. Waited on tables in a place called *Fellows* in Hoboken, New Jersey for about a year. Then he got a job working the Jersey docks."

Alexey walked over to Dmitry, who stood up to face him. Dmitry was a foot taller than Alexey. "So, Dmitry Kussov, you got some big balls on you," Alexey pointed a finger at his chest with cocky attitude. He twisted his neck to get the kinks out, not taking his eyes off of Dmitry. "So you're done with the hard work at the docks? You want to work for me?"

"Yeah, I could use a job."

"Yeah? You know how to keep your mouth shut?"

"Understood," replied Dmitry.

Alexey's eyes shifted to Victor and lines folded on his forehead. Victor nodded. Alexey said, "I need three guys for this job. You Victor and two more."

74

Dmitry piped up, "What's the job and how much does it pay?"

Alexey stared at him again. "I need a driver and some muscle. That's all you got to know." Boris remained quiet.

"Okay, Dmitry, we'll give you a try. Loyalty is everything. Our boss demands loyalty. And once you're in our organization, you're in for good. Understand?" asked Alexey. He also pointed to Stanislav. "I could use you too, Stan."

Stanislav nodded. Alexey gave Victor a piece of paper with an address on it. Victor opened it and nodded. "Tomorrow morning at 7 am, the three of you meet us there."

"You got it boss," said Victor.

"I asked how much the job pays," said Dmitry.

"As long as you do what you're told and you don't fuck up, 2K," replied Alexey. "And there's more coming for more work."

Dmitry nodded and combed his thick black hair with his fingers.

Alexey and Boris walked out of the back room without saying another word. As they shuffled alongside the bar, Boris winked at his sister, Svitlana and blew a kiss to Nikita. She was replacing a bottle of Stoly back on the shelf. Looking over her shoulder, Nikita smiled and blew one back.

CHAPTER 23

Special Agent Jack Belman was a 26-year veteran FBI special agent who handled all of the undercover agents in the tri-state area. He was still in good shape physically and definitely losing much of his hair, resorting to a modified comb-over. Like many guys, he kept a two-day scruff on his face under a slightly crooked nose which was broken some years ago while playing a schoolyard game of basketball with his boys and some friends. Jack worked out of the Jacob K. Javits Federal Building, 26 Federal Plaza, 23rd. floor and traveled where he needed to share information with his agents for face-to-face meetings. Jack was happily married to his wife Gloria, a real estate agent in Staten Island, where they both lived in a split level home. They raised two intelligent and athletic boys, who were both attending S.U.N.Y. at Binghamton, one a freshman and the other a senior. Jack's financial expenses were such that he needed to continue working for at least another four years. The plan was for him to put his retirement papers in after thirty years with the Bureau.

The two-undercover agents working in Brooklyn were notified via burner phones to meet Jack in a parking lot overlooking the Verrazano Bridge on the Brooklyn side. The meet was called for 1:10 am. Jack arrived first. He parked facing the Lower New York Bay and turned off the engine to his Subaru Forester. He watched the wind whip up the whitecaps and gazed at the street lights that seemed to blink and dot the coast of Staten Island. He liked the salt air filling his nose through the open window.

A dark beat-up 2000 Chevy Silverado drove into the lot and pulled up adjacent to Jack's SUV. There were two undercover agents in the vehicle. Dmitry drove and Nikita was in the passenger seat. Windows rolled down half-way.

Nikita spoke first and dispensed with his official title of Special Agent. "Jack, got some news for you." Her ice-blue eyes reflected the illumination from a nearby streetlamp.

"Good, we need some solid intel. Gotta get those kids back before we lose them forever," explained Jack.

"I heard gang talk about the mob having a warehouse somewhere in Deer Park. I don't know where exactly, but I heard it's in a commercial area of the town. They might have the kids locked up there," said Nikita.

Jack responded, "that's a start, but did they mention a street name or a landmark?"

"One guy muttered something about a place called Tangers I think?"

"Now that helps. Tangers is an outdoor shopping mall. Narrows down the location. Good. We'll get on it ASAP," said Jack.

"And Dmitry, what do you got?"

"Jack, I got a job with the gang. Earlier tonight a few mobsters--Alexey and Boris (no last names) came into *Spasibo* looking for a driver and some muscle for a grab tomorrow morning," said Dmitry, combing his hair with the long fingers on his right hand.

Nikita looked over at Dmitry, "how did you score that gig?"

"Long story short, I had to cozy up to Svitlana, Boris's sister. She put in a good word for me," explained Dmitry.

Nikita smirked and said, "I bet you really laid on the charm, buddy."

Jack interjected, "no time for this petty crap. Stay focused you two. Remember, undercover is life or death."

"Yeah, yeah," said Nikita.

"Where's the job, Dmitry?" asked Jack.

"Don't know yet, but gotta meet Victor and this guy Stanislav at 6am at *Spasibo*. Alexey had the address written on a slip of paper and handed it to Victor. I guess I'm on a 'need-to-know 'status. But there's supposed to be an important grab tomorrow morning. Victor said we'll get the details in the morning," said Dmitry.

Jack said, "I'll have my guys in the office activate and track the microchip we imbedded in your upper thigh. My crew and I will set up surveillance near *Spasibo* early and we'll track you. We'll have a tactical team set up nearby as well. Hopefully, you'll lead us to the warehouse and the kids."

"Any intel for us, Jack?" asked Nikita.

"NYPD picked up one of the Russian goons who got his kneecap blown out. We're hoping with some leverage, we can get some info out of him. Now go home and get some sleep," commanded Jack.

The Forester left the parking lot first. Five minutes later, the Silverado pulled out and slowly drove back to the Sheepshead Bay area.

CHAPTER 24

Corny and Del shared a room at the Courtyard by Marriott near Republic Airport. They each got 4-5 hours of sleep, just enough to function and focus on getting those kids back home safely. They had absolutely no interest in making love, but were still in bed. It was 6:15am and they needed to shower, get dressed and run over to the FBI office. There was an early morning meeting with the parents of the abducted youngsters. None of the detectives nor the Special Agents were looking forward to that kind of discussion.

"Hey babe, how about we shower together? Save some valuable time that way," said Corny with an obvious blink of his eye.

"Umm, I could go for that. Let me make some coffee first. Okay?"

Corny's phone buzzed twice. He reached over Del's exquisite muscular body and purposely brushed her naked breasts. She jabbed him in the ribs as he scooped up the phone, glanced at the name and number and answered.

"Morning Lieu, what's up? Any news?"

Lieutenant Woods got right to the point. "Special Agent Jack Belman and Detective Huong conducted the interview with this low level gangster, Egor Kukk. All they had to do was reveal that his DNA was found on the deceased girl, Margot Jeffries, and he turned all shades of pale. Not smart enough to comprehend that we were able to get info from Interpol. Faced with a life sentence in prison, he didn't wait too long to tell us what he knew with the promise of putting in a good word with the District Attorney for a lighter sentence."

Corny listened and asked, "Did he admit to the murder?

Did you get a location? Names of his bosses and accomplices?"

"He said the girl's death was an accident. She woke up too early from a drug-induced injection and started to scream and grab for the doors on the van. He just tried to calm her down with his 'hands around her neck', so he claims."

"How about a solid lead?"

"Special Agent Jack Belman is handling two deep undercover agents. They heard about a warehouse in Deer Park. Kukk admitted that the kids were being kept in a Deer Park warehouse, too. It's not far from Tangers Shopping Mall. He wasn't too clear on the name of the street. He said it had a name of one of the U.S. presidents a long time ago. He couldn't remember what it was. But, at some point he shut up and asked to call his lawyer. A Russian Mob lawyer, no doubt."

Corny responded, "I'm sure this Special Agent Belman contacted our task force out here with that information.

"Of course. The computer specialists are running down the leases on the warehouses and buildings in the general location of Tangers, especially those located on streets with names of presidents."

"Okay, Lieu. We'll be heading right over to the office. We'll keep in touch," answered Corny.

Del had her coffee in hand as Corny got into the shower. He related to Del all of the information Woods just told him. She placed her coffee cup on the sink and grabbed her cell phone. She began researching the streets named after presidents near Tangers Outlet Mall. Hot water cascaded down Corny's hard 6'2" frame and Del recited some of the street names: "Washington, Grant, Garfield, Madison, Lincoln."

"The Feds must be on it as we speak. They have resources to uncover who owns or leases those buildings," Corny called from the shower. "Make a cup of Joe for me, to go, please."

"I'm on it. Get out of there and leave some hot water for me," Del complained.

Within 15 minutes, they were dressed and out the door.

"We need to find those kids, Del, and fast."

CHAPTER 25

Victor, Stanislav and Dmitry stopped off at a Dunkin 'in Merrick, Long Island, for coffee and muffins at 6:35am. They took their breakfast with them to eat in the car. The sun was flirting with the eastern horizon and the skies were clear. Only a few truckers and some early workers were on the local roads. Very light pedestrian traffic added to the serene suburban milieu.

"Let's finish up guys. Alexey does not like to be kept waiting," explained Victor.

"Where is the meet?" asked Dmitry.

"Don't worry about it. I got the address," answered Victor. "We're only about 10 minutes away. Wanna throw away this crap so we can get going," asked Victor.

Stan said, "I got it. Give me the wrappers and cups." He jumped out of the back seat and tossed the garbage into the trash bin outside of the store.

The blue van pulled into a small strip mall with seven or eight local stores in North Belmore. There was a bagel shop, a barber, a small grocery store, a dry cleaners, a small liquor store, a CVS pharmacy and a pizzeria. Victor craned his neck looking for the gray Ford Transit Connect that Alexey and Boris were driving. It was good that the Brooklyn guys got to the meeting point first.

Five minutes later, the Transit pulled alongside the blue van. The passenger door opened and Alexey hopped out and swiveled his head checking for police. He opened the rear van door and got in next to Stanislav. "You guys ready?" Alexey asked.

The three of them nodded. Alexey explained the plan for the grab which included two targets--two 17 year-olds. He repeated the plan again and asked if anyone had any questions. Victor looked at Dmitry and Stan and raised his eyebrows. They all understood their roles.

" Okay, let's hit it. Remember, no fuck-ups!" demanded Alexey.

Both vehicles slowly drove out of the strip mall parking lot and headed to the street with the target house. The Ford Transit lead the way. In less than ten minutes, they arrived at their destination and pulled up to the curb on the south side of the street. They all watched the target house and waited. Fifteen to twenty minutes later, a detailed black town car drove down the block and pulled into the driveway of the target house. The driver, who wore a black suit, white shirt and gray tie turned off the engine and got out. He was a beefy guy, in his 50's, about 6' tall, and sported a salt and pepper crew cut. He rang the front door bell.

The inner door opened and one of the targets, a 17 year old bronze-skinned girl answered. There was a brief dialogue and the driver nodded. He waited on the top step while the girl went back inside. After a few minutes, both targets exited the front door wearing opened bomber jackets. Each girl clutched the handle of her own pale yellow suitcase on four wheels. The driver picked up both cases by the handles and carried them down to the trunk of his town car. An older woman, their mother apparently, also excitedly emerged through the front door and skipped down the steps. She hugged both girls and kissed them both on the cheeks. The girls got into the town car, rolled down the windows and waved goodbye to their mother.

"Call me when you get to the airport. Okay?" asked the mom.

Both girls in unison agreed to comply. They both shouted back to their mom, "we love you. We'll call you each day from the road." Twins often had similar thoughts and made similar statements. They also discovered that finishing each other's sentences was cute and cool.

The driver backed out of the driveway. More waves back to their mom. She had a few tears in her eyes. This was the first time the girls would be away for an extended period of time.

Boris and Victor started their engines up the street. The town car rolled down the block and around the corner. It was headed to Kennedy Airport. The trip should probably take about a half hour. The gray Transit and the blue van followed, but not too close. After a few blocks, the Transit and the van took different routes to intercept the town car.

A few minutes later, on Jerusalem Ave., just east of Newbridge Rd., the van cut in front of the town car. This maneuver forced the chauffeur to screech to a halt. The Transit stopped abruptly right behind the car. The driver of the van, Victor, jumped out of his vehicle and began shouting at the chauffeur, who was angry that the van had cut him off. He opened his door tentatively and simultaneously checked on the safety of the two girls in the back seat. Both girls stopped texting on their phones and looked up in surprise.

Victor strode over to the town car and said loudly, "You cut me off, man. What's wrong with you?"

The chauffeur tentatively got out of his car and answered back.

"I had the right of way, pal. You were wrong, not me."

Taking a few breaths and forcing himself into a calm zen, especially since he needed to get these girls to the airport, the chauffeur said, "look, there was no accident here. No damage. I'm sorry. Let's just be on our ways."

Before he was able to get back into the car, a muscled arm snaked around his neck and applied a tight choke-hold. Dmitry made sure the driver was unconscious and lowered him to the asphalt. Watching the drama unfold outside the car, the girls began to scream. Alexey and Boris jumped out of the Transit and opened both back doors to the town car. They each had a switchblade and menaced both girls to keep quiet. The hoodlums grabbed both phones and pulled on the girls 'arms to get out of the car.

Emma cried, "what are you doing? We have to get to the airport."

Alexey smacked her across the face with the back of his hand and pressed the knife into the skin of her neck without drawing blood. "Shut up and move it. No fucking screaming or we kill your sister. Understood?"

Emma nodded quickly and her eyes bulged in fright. She stopped breathing.

"Just do what they want, Emma," exclaimed Jordan.

They were both ushered into the back of the Transit. Alexey injected both girls with a ketamine cocktail to put them out. It happened so quickly, they barely had time to put up a fight. Boris got back behind the wheel and Alexey got into the passenger seat. He menaced the girls with his knife, swinging it back and forth in front of them. "Quiet!" The Transit slowly moved along Jerusalem and made a right turn onto Newbridge Rd. The entrance to the Southern State was just ahead about a half mile.

Dmitry and Stan picked up the chauffeur and placed him in the back of the town car. Stan injected him, too, with a ketamine cocktail that would keep him out for at least an hour. Victor got behind the wheel of the town car and Stan sat in the passenger seat watching the driver who was out cold. Victor purposely drove slowly down Jerusalem, not wanting to be noticed.

Dmitry got behind the wheel of the van and drove down the avenue. He also headed toward the west entrance to the Southern State. His job was to return the blue van to *Spasibo*. Both vehicles were going back to Brooklyn. The grab was so fast and efficient that no one on the street seemed to notice the abduction. Not too many people were out and about at 7:30am on a Saturday morning anyway.

Five minutes later, Special Agent Jack Belman and two

younger agents arrived at the scene of the grab in the command car. The tactical team pulled alongside the curb nearby. On his laptop, Belman was able to hone in on the gang's location utilizing the signal that had been emitted from the microchip embedded under Dmitry's skin. It was crucial not to make contact now, hoping that the criminals would lead them to the location where all of the other kidnapped kids were being kept.

Starring at his laptop, Belman exclaimed, "Shit, that was a mighty fast grab. Gone already. I wanted to follow them to Suffolk. Our man's signal shows he's going west on the Southern State, probably back to Brooklyn or maybe Queens."

"No clear evidence that anything happened here," said Agent Myers.

"But the intel is that the Russians have the kids somewhere in Deer Park," said Agent Myers.

"I was hoping that they'd have Dmitry drive out to Suffolk. We'd then have a location of the abducted kids," said Belman.

"Sly Russians. Maybe they're transporting the targets to another Brooklyn or Queens location. Or maybe they don't fully trust him yet. After all, he just got the job. They're keeping him close to their Brooklyn headquarters," said Agent Myers.

"That's a lot of 'maybes'. I fucking hope they didn't make him for a Fed," said Belman.

"If they did, he'd be dead by now," answered Myers.

"For everyone's sake I hope he's alive and well," scowled Belman.

Belman called the commander of the tactical team in the vehicle behind them. He explained how the signal tracked back west, probably back to Brooklyn. He was pissed that they had lost the Suffolk County connection.

"Okay, we follow the only signal I have," said Belman.

"Copy that," responded the commander.

Both vehicles pulled out and headed to the Southern State entrance west.

CHAPTER 26

When Del and Corny arrived at the FBI office, they were directed to the large conference room. SAC Masters, Special Agents Curlee & Benitez, and Detectives Morris & Winchester were standing at the front of the room chatting softly. Most of the parents were seated already and a few had filled up coffee cups from the credenza near the windows. Mr. and Mrs. Weinstein, each dressed impeccably in office attire, were at the far end of the huge oval cherrywood table. Mrs. Weinstein dabbed at her flowing tears with balled-up Kleenex underneath carefully applied eye make-up. Mr. McArthur, who lost his wife to cancer a few years ago was present with his girlfriend Sally Barnes. She was trying to console her boyfriend, Frank, who kept looking at the ceiling. They sat to the Weinsteins 'left, near the windows. Mr. and Mrs. Rodriguez, dressed casually neat, beneath dour facial expressions, sat to the Weinstein's right. Mrs. Rodriguez was forcing herself to hold back the sobs. Mrs. Park, a single mom, had not arrived as of yet.

SAC Masters poked his head out the door to the conference room and said to his secretary, "Please call Mrs. Park again. Find out if she's on her way, please."

"Yes sir."

SAC Masters addressed the group of parents. "We are just waiting a few more minutes for Mrs. Park to join us. Please be patient folks."

Mr. Rodriguez shouted out, "Look, we need to know the latest news now, Special Agent! Please! We're all waiting patiently, but our kids are out there. Only God knows where." He leapt out of his office chair.

"Tell us what you know. We're all jumping out of our

skins," pleaded Mrs. Weinstein.

SAC glanced through the glass window of the door. His secretary shook her head from side to side. "Alright. Seems as though Mrs. Park couldn't make it."

All four detectives stood by the windows and SAC Masters, as well as Special Agents Curlee & Benitez took control of the meeting by standing in front. Masters began.

"Thank you for coming in. We could only imagine how traumatic this is for you. We could only imagine how you can become frantic and lose perspective. However, we need you to try to think clearly and do what we instruct you to do." Masters paused and looked around the table.

" I'm going to get right to the crucial points. First of all, please, under no circumstances are you to talk to the press! Safety of your children depends upon you keeping whatever information you hear this morning to yourselves. The members of the media will hound you for information. DO NOT ALLOW YOURSELF TO GIVE COMMENTS! It is crucial that our investigation is kept confidential in order for us to rescue your youngsters. The perpetrators of these kidnappings must not be privy to our advancements in the case. Is that clear?"

He made sure to make eye contact with each parent. They all either nodded their heads or said that they fully understood.

"Special Agent Curlee will disclose certain information and exclude other facts that could jeopardize our investigation. Are we clear?"

Again, they all agreed.

"Good morning. We have four detectives, (two Suffolk County and two Manhattan) and two Special Agents directly working this case."

She reintroduced the detectives and the two FBI Agents on the task force, herself included.

"We also have all of the resources and personnel of the entire FBI and local police agencies working to find your children. We will take questions after the presentation."

She began a brief powerpoint presentation on the large

Smart Board in the front of the room by operating a small remote control in her left hand. She read aloud as she produced each item.

This is what we know

1. Each child was specifically targeted for abduction
2. Details of your child's actions and habits were somehow made known to the criminals
3. Each child attends either high school or junior high school
4. There is no connection or relationship between your child and the other children abducted
5. Most, if not all, of your youngsters are being held somewhere in a warehouse in Deer Park

This is what we infer currently

1. All of your children are victims of human trafficking
2. The perpetrators are probably members of a Russian criminal cell
3. All of the school data bases were hacked to get information about your child based upon specific orders placed by potential buyers
4. Hopefully your children have NOT been delivered as of yet and have not been harmed
5. After interviewing all of you, we are in possession of and currently analyzing your children's smart phones, computers and/or tablets
6. MUCH OF THEIR DAILY LIVES ARE CONTINUALLY PLACED ON THE INTERNET to conduct daily communication with friends, relatives, etc. all for evil doers to easily harvest.

Some of our work to rescue them

1. Arrested one of the lower level gang members who gave us some important information
2. Known location of some of the gang members

3. *FBI in deep undercover gaining information*
4. *World class computer analysts working to uncover from where and when the hacking takes place*
5. *Other intelligence analysts searching for possible location of criminal-controlled warehouse and other properties.*
6. *Surveillance cameras give us additional information.*

As soon as Agent Curlee mentioned the two terms: human trafficking and Russian criminal cell, there were several audible gasps. Tears began rolling down distraught faces again. Most of the parents were in shock. Some placed their hands on their heads and some of their shoulders visibly stooped in defeat.

"Now we can take questions you may have," explained Curlee.

Corny's cell phone buzzed in his pants pocket several times. He looked at Del and walked toward the door to take the call. He stepped out of the conference room and placed his phone to his ear in the hallway.

"Prince."

There was crying and muffled sobbing. He pressed the phone closer in an effort to hear.

"Who is this? I cannot hear..."

"Corny, Corny!" his sister yelled.

"What? What's wrong?"

She was sobbing again. "The girls never made the plane." She cried and struggled to compose herself. "The girls are missing."

"How do you know?" asked Corny.

"The chaperone from the travel tour called the house. All of the kids were accounted for except for Emma and Jordan," she cried again.

All of the color drained from his face and heat began to rise in his neck. "Did you call 911?"

"No Corny. I knew you'd know what to do."

"Is Doug home with you?" Corny asked.

"He's on his way.   Left his shift early," Cara's voice trembled.

"Don't move. I'll be there in a half hour! I'm coming! And when you hang up, call 911!

"Yeah, okay. I will."

Del starred through the door window pane and saw that something was very wrong. She ran to the door and breezed through to see who called him. "What? What?"

"We gotta go, now. The girls are missing!"

"What? Weren't they taking a flight to California today?"

"Never made it to the airport!" Tears stained Corny's eyes.

Benitez exited the conference room seeing Corny and Del in turmoil.

Corny pleaded, "My nieces are missing. Never made it to the airport. I need to be with my sister and find out what's going on."

Benitez 'eyes grew large. He exclaimed, "you guys go. Keep us in the loop."

CHAPTER 27

A navy blue unmarked Ford sedan was parked in front of Cara and Doug's house. Del drove the Hummer from the FBI office, knowing full well that Corny's anxiety was spinning out of control. On the trip back to Nassau County, she tried to keep his mind occupied with light conversation about their case with the task force. Corny stared out the window, pensive and quiet. Del could make out a reflection of his stoic face with muscles clenched and moist eyes. He white-knuckled the leather handle above the window.

Corny jumped out of the vehicle before Del came to a full stop in the driveway. He took the steps two at a time and stormed through the opened door. Del was on his heels. She got a whiff of whatever Cara had been baking in the kitchen before she got 'the call 'about the girls.

Doug and two men with sport coats were standing in front of the mauve-colored leather sofa in the living room. Cara was sitting on the very edge, dabbing her eyes with a few tissues. Doug's hands were dug deep into the pockets of his jeans and was the first to notice Corny and Del enter the house. Cara shot up off the sofa and Corny gave her a tight bear hug. Cara cried uncontrollably on his broad left shoulder, wetting his grey suit jacket. Del and Doug hugged briefly.

"Corny, they're just gone. Never got to Kennedy," Cara's voice traveled off into the air.

The two Nassau detectives introduced themselves. "This is Detective Parlefsky and I'm Detective Kurz. We normally don't investigate missing persons before a 24-hour period, but when we were told you were on 'The Job 'and we are well-aware of the task force involving the FBI, our captain thought we should come out ASAP."

"Thank you for that. This is my partner, Detective DelVecchio, and I'm Detective Prince, Midtown Precinct South Manhattan. FYI, we are both working in that task force case." Corny gently guided his sister back to the sofa and stroked her back with his left hand.

"Got it," said Detective Kurz who glanced over at Parlefsky. Kurz was tall, broad and wore a receding gray crew cut, reminiscent of his days in the Marines. He had an etched two-inch scar just below his high cheek bone on the right side of his chiseled face. Parlefsky's solid frame was shorter and barrel-chested. He had a full head of straight sandy hair combed from front to back. His bushy mustache wriggled as he continually repositioned a wooden toothpick between his teeth.

"What the hell happened?" asked Corny.

Cara composed herself somewhat and began to explain. "As I was telling these detectives, Doug had to work a shift this Saturday, so he could not take Emma and Jordan to the airport. I mentioned to Mom and Dad that I was going to drive them. Instead they volunteered to pay for a car service to drive the girls 'in style', as they put it, since it was their special graduation trip. So I said okay."

Del and Corny, simultaneously, looked at the Nassau detectives for additional information. Detective Kurz instinctively responded, "Platinum Limousine Service, based in Plainview. We called already. The owner, a Freddie Militokis told us that both the town car and the driver, Peter Volk, a 54 year old Caucasian, are missing. Peter never called in and the dispatcher couldn't reach him on his cell after trying several times. He's been driving full and part time over an eight year period for them. Never had a problem with him."

Corny asked, "He could be involved. We don't know. You put out a BOLO (Be On the LookOut) on the car?"

Detective Parlefsky responded, "Called the BOLO in immediately. No results yet. We also alerted NYPD, as well as Suffolk."

"We may want the entire tri-state area. They could be anywhere." said Corny.

Detective Kurz added, "We're looking at all of the surveillance cameras at all of the bridges, tunnels, tollbooths, ferries, etc. in the tri-state area."

Corny nodded, "good. Please keep us in the tight loop." He handed Detective Parlefsky a card with his contact information.

Del pulled out her iPhone and interrupted, "Gonna inform Woods. I want him informed. He'll make sure the all of the city's precincts are on full alert."

Detective Kurz asked Corny in a low voice, "You think this is part of your case?" He glanced over at Cara.

"What case Corny? Involved in what? What are my girls involved in?" Cara began to panic and stood up. Her whole body became rigid.

None of the detectives said anything for a few moments, but everyone looked at Corny.

"Look, Cara, we have very little information right now. But it's possible that they may have been abducted," he said very slowly.

"By who? Who would want two girls taking a trip to California?"

Del rushed over to Cara, put an arm around her and shot a look at Doug.

"Cara, we are investigating human trafficking with the FBI. A few other youngsters have been abducted recently from Suffolk County."

"But this is Nassau. I don't understand," Cara pleaded.

Corny said, "We think it's a Russian Mafia cell that's grabbing these kids. We feel that there are some sick, rich people, probably on the dark web, who are paying a lot of cash for these young adults. Mainly high school kids."

"What? How do they find these kids?" asked Doug, getting closer to Corny and Del.

"There are databases that these bastards hack into to find personal information. We also feel that once they find the kids they want, they track them on social media. Instagram, Twitter, Snapchat, Facebook, TikTok, etc." explained Del.

Detective Kurz directed his comments to Cara and Doug. "I'm sure your daughters have cell phones, iPads and/or laptops. I'm also pretty sure they communicate with their friends quite a bit about their lives."

Doug responded, "Well, sure. Just like every other kid their age. All of the kids, as well as adults, are constantly posting photos, events, things they are involved with. Always texting."

"Shit! Shit! Emma's and Jordan's lives are open books on the internet. These bastards can find out all about their intimate information. Where they go, when they go, what they do..." Cara got up and Doug wrapped his strong arms around her. They searched each others 'eyes, wet with tears.

Corny said, "We will find them, Cara. We are beginning to get information about this criminal cell. I promise, we will bring them back home. I promise."

Del reiterated, "we will not rest until we bring Emma and Jordan home."

Detective Kurz and Parlefsky left their contact information with Doug and Corny. Del gave the detectives her cell number, too. They all agreed to keep in touch if anything new came to light. The two detectives let themselves out of the house. There was a soft clack as the screen door closed shut behind the Nassau detectives. Corny and Del sat with Cara on the sofa for a short while, trying to console her.

CHAPTER 28

The gray Ford Transit pulled around the warehouse to the back loading area. The van's windows were heavily tinted to prevent police from looking inside. No one else was around and no other building faced the loading dock. Only a half an acre of trees and bushes served as the rear perimeter. Another reason why this warehouse was chosen. A mixture of clouds and sun bathed the mid Saturday morning while the men carried their targets, still unconscious, into the warehouse. Once Leonid gave the word, they'd begin to move out to their other location further east.

Alexey stepped into the office. "Okay, boss. We got our targets. Smooth as silk."

Leonid lit up another Cuban cigar and leaned back on his office chair. "Smooth as silk, yeah. Any witnesses on the street? In a store?"

"Not many people around on a Saturday morning. No witnesses. Went off without a hitch. "Victor take care of the driver and the car?" Asked Alexey.

"That's what he tells me. Torched the car and left it by a beach on the south shore. But now that we have all of our targets safe and sound, we have to move out east. Then we need to clean this place up fast. I don't trust that Egor. He's gonna spill the beans, as the Americans say," sneered Leonid.

He took a long drag and shot smoke rings into the lights above.

"Won't be long before the FBI finds this place. But I'm thinking they need a diversion to keep them occupied," Leonid took another puff. He stared at the ceiling.

Alexey asked, "what do you have in mind, boss?"

"Egor's lawyer shut him up as soon as he got to the precinct. But he also met the two cops who questioned him. One FBI and one NYPD detective. I'm thinking we need to make their lives a little more difficult, if you know what I mean," smiled Leonid. "Make them think twice about coming after us."

Leonid sat up and glared at Mikhail and Pavel. "Let's get going, yeah! You guys know what to do. Get the kids ready to move out."

Leonid picked up the phone and made two calls. One to Kuznetsov, his boss, to keep him informed of their progress. The other call was to Sophia, the computer hacker in St. Petersburg. He needed inside information on Jack Belman and Teddy Huong and fast.

CHAPTER 29

"Corny, we got to get back to the task force office. We need to coordinate with Agent Curlee and pool our information," Del whispered. She knew he didn't want to leave his sister, but knew full well that they would not get anything done sitting with Cara. She stood up and hugged Doug again. "We'll keep you informed. I promise."

Corny nodded and kissed Cara on her forehead and stood as well. "I'll call you if we learn anything. Okay?"

Cara forced a strained smile.

As they opened the doors of the Hummer, Del's phone buzzed. She removed it from her suit pocket and jumped up into the driver's seat.

"DelVecchio," she answered and pressed the button for the navigation system so that with Bluetooth, they can both hear the conversation. She started the car and drove down the block and around the corner toward the highway.

"Del, this is Detective Winchester. We think we found the town car that picked up Detective Prince's nieces."

"Are my girls with the car, Winchester?" Corny spit those words in rapid fire.

"No, no. No evidence of the girls bodies at all. We do have one body in the rear seat. The car was flamed and left in a remote parking area of Captree State Park. Difficult to identify the deceased, but looks like a large male matching the description of the driver. Matching luggage was found in the trunk. Whatever items in the bags that we can salvage, we'll bring back for analysis."

"Thank God they weren't in the car. They were abducted like the others. Del, we gotta find them and fast," exclaimed

Corny. "Thanks, Detective. Meet you back at the office."

It took another half hour to get back to Melville. Corny was hesitant to call Cara to explain where and in what condition the limo was found. He decided to wait for more information before he called her.

Benitez met them at the elevator. "How's your sister and brother-in-law holding up?"

"As well as can be expected. Did you hear that Winchester found the town car at Captree? They killed the driver so he couldn't finger the abductors."

"Yes, we got word. The forensics team will flatbed and process the charred limo back here in our garage downstairs. Doubt we'll get anything, but you never know. Fingerprints, DNA, something that could identify these guys," explained Benitez.

They all walked back into the bullpen and looked up at the computer screens. "Our researchers think they may have found the Deer Park warehouse. A building on Cleveland Ave. used to be owned by Ford Motors. Now a nondescript holding company with ties to an overseas corporation seems to hold the deed. Remember the Estonian that your guys picked up in Brooklyn said the warehouse was on a street with a president's name on it?" asked Benitez.

"Do you have a tactical team ready to go with a warrant?" asked Del.

"Special Agent Curlee is in the process of securing that warrant from a Suffolk County judge as we speak."

"Okay, we're ready when you are," said Corny. He noticed that Detective Morris was pouring a cup of coffee and heading over to them.

A hulk of a man, an incessant twitch over his right eye plagued him on a daily basis. He was definitely looking forward to his well-deserved retirement at the end of this year.

"Morning detectives. Hopefully, we can find these kids in Deer Park and bring them home to their families. Curlee is getting the warrant. Glad I sent Winchester to Captree. I want to be there when we breach."

Curlee walked out of Masters 'office. "Alright, it's a go. The tactical team will meet us downstairs. Got the warrant. Let's move."

They all hustled down the stairs, not waiting for the elevator.

CHAPTER 30

A small, yellow Penske box truck rolled up to the front of a five-story red brick apartment house in Jamaica. Two men, wearing dark windbreakers and brown construction boots fitted black latex gloves on their hands and navy blue baseball caps on their heads. In unison, they jumped out of the front cab and walked to the rear of the truck. The taller one stepped up onto the rear bumper and inserted a key in the lock. The shorter deliveryman kept his head on a swivel while the taller one pulled the accordion door up into the roof of the cavity. A musty smell escaped and the delivery man grimaced. There were several cardboard boxes within the storage area and a green-handled hand truck laying down, wheels up.

He selected a large cardboard box marked Whirlpool Dryer and fitted the hand truck underneath. He placed two moving straps around the box and the hand truck, affixing the box securely. He placed his left boot on the back rung of the truck for leverage and pulled back. The box tilted back nicely and he wheeled it over to the doorway. The smaller man, who was built like a tank, reached up and grabbed the bottom of the hand truck. They slowly guided the box to the ground. Then the taller one closed the squeaky accordion door with a rattle and locked it. He jumped down to the asphalt.

The small delivery man took the hand truck and walked it over to the three-step entranceway to the front door. He turned around and quickly pulled the truck up the three concrete steps. The tall man opened the front door and both entered the vestibule. The inner door was locked and there was no doorman. These men already knew that no doorman or concierge serviced this building. That made their job easier.

There was a bank of buttons underneath numerous names encased in a large silver metal frame. The tall man began to ring random bells and waited for a response. A woman's voice became audible from the slotted speaker.

"Who is it?"

The tall man said, "Delivery ma'am" with his hand partially covering his mouth.

"What? Did you say 'delivery'? I'm not expecting anything." Her voice trailed off into a raspy whisper.

The tall man rang the bell again and again. After several seconds the inner door electronically clicked open. Bingo, they were in. There was a sign for the elevator. They needed to find apartment 412. Once on the fourth floor they wheeled the box to the correct door. The tall man rang the red button bell that was imbedded in a gold rectangular frame in the center of the metal door.

After several seconds a man responded, "Who's there?"

The small delivery man said, "Superior Appliances. Delivery."

"We no get delivery. Wrong door. Not us." The man's response had a strong Asian accent.

"Sir, your son-in-law, Teddy Huong, bought you a new dryer. Please, we need you to accept the dryer and we have to install it. We have other stops to make."

There was muffled murmuring behind the door. Evidently a husband and wife discussing a surprise delivery. The door opened slowly.

"Hey, we have your new dryer. Teddy Huong ordered it and set up delivery." The old man opened the door wider. The small man entered the apartment pushing the hand truck over the oak door saddle with the tall man on his heels. "Where's your old dryer?"

The tall man closed the door behind him and reached into his pocket for an object. The old man and his wife stepped back, still a little puzzled, but smiling at the generosity of their son-in-law. A nine-month old baby boy was swatting at small stuffed animals hanging from a hard plastic blue arm above his baby swing. The swing was situated next to the plain upholstered sofa in the living room.

The old man pointed to the small laundry room off the kitchen. As he turned to point, the tall man hefted a hard-rubber mallet and clubbed the old man in the back of his head. The old man crumbled to the hardwood floor.

The old woman ran to protect the baby and stood in front of the swing. "What you do? Why you hit my husband? Get out of here. I call 911," she screeched and the baby boy started to wail.

The tall man took three strides to her and clubbed her at the base of her neck. She fell over but was still conscious. He viciously clubbed her again on the head. The small man took a roll of gray duct tape from his pocket and tied each of them up securely. The tall man took a knife from his other pocket and poked holes on the top and sides of the Whirlpool box. He opened the lid flaps. The box was a quarter filled with bricks. On top of the bricks were two soft moving blankets.

The small man scooted over to the swing and snatched the baby boy gently. The baby studied the man's face and his mouth began to quiver. He was about to cry again. The man took a small bottle with amber liquid filled half-way. He unscrewed the cap, poured a little liquid on his fingers and placed them in the baby's mouth. He figured some diluted bourbon would calm him down. The small guy then placed the baby on top of the blankets in the box and wrapped the top one around his little wriggling body. This man knew how to swaddle since he and his wife raised two little guys himself. He closed the lid flaps, duct-taped them shut and was ready to go.

The tall guy removed a typed sign from his inner jacket pocket and taped it to the old man. It read, "Back off Teddy. If you want to see your little boy again, back your people the fuck off. We'll be in touch."

CHAPTER 31

Three black SUVs silently converged on the front entrance of the gray warehouse on Cleveland Avenue. All doors swung open and several SWAT officers piled out of two of them with full tactical gear. Some carried H&K 416 assault rifles and some used MP5/10 submachine guns. The third vehicle contained the FBI special agents and the detectives. They had donned their Kevlar vests in the car and drew their Glock sidearms. One black SUV sped around to the rear loading dock. More SWAT officers immediately emerged, ready to breach.

Special Agent Curlee was SAC in this operation and spoke into her communication mike to coordinate with the tactical teams and the other agents who wore earbuds. "All teams check in and wait for my 'GO' signal."

The tactical team leader whispered, "Copy that."

Each detective responded the same.

"Before we breach, we need eyes inside. Insert camera snakes into the front, side and rear windows."

The tactical team leader responded again, "Hope this is the place. Only two vehicles parked near loading dock. How many in front?"

"Two sedans and one van parked in front," responded Curlee. "As soon as your cameras are in, please report."

"Copy that Special Agent Curlee.

Within minutes the team leader responded. "We do not have eyes on the entire interior. The areas that we can see have empty cages and what appears to be a cleaning crew."

"Any combatants with weapons visible?"

"None that we can see."

Special Agent Curlee shut her mike for a moment. She

conferred with Special Agent Benitez and the three detectives. "Don't know if the kids are here anymore. Only one way to find out."

She turned the mike on again. "Get ready to breach. Front and rear doors. Place your charges and have the flash bangs at the ready. If there are combatants, DO NOT SHOOT TO KILL unless absolutely necessary. I repeat, DO NOT SHOOT TO KILL. Priority is to find those kids and keep them safe."

Both front and rear team leaders responded, "Setting charges and we copy Special Agent."

Three minutes later each leader responded that they were ready to breach.

Special Agent Curlee nodded to the detectives and Benitez. "All teams go, go, go!"

The explosive charges blew each door off their hinges causing loud booms. All of the breachers had wedged earplugs prior to the explosions to save their eardrums. SWAT teams cautiously entered the warehouse, weapons at the ready. The agents and detectives followed on their heels. Flash bangs were not warranted during the breach since it appeared that only a cleaning crew was at work.

Upon seeing the SWAT officers aiming their weapons, the four cleaning people (two young women and two young men) dropped their mops, brooms, and other cleaning utensils to the ground and shot their hands in the air.

"Get down on the ground. On your knees. On your knees!" commanded one of the SWAT officers. They all complied. Fear gripped each one of them. One of the women began to cry. They began yelling in Spanish that they were only hired to clean the warehouse. They swore they had no weapons. Two other officers surrounded them and placed zip ties around their wrists and brought them to one corner of the caged-in area that they were currently working in. They were told to sit on the floor.

All of a sudden the nearly empty warehouse was filled with loud gunfire. Two SWAT officers remained with the cleaning crew while the rest followed the cacophony of machine gun and rifle fire to the rear of the warehouse. By the time they got to the area of action near the loading dock, what appeared to be three plain--clothes combatants were contorted on the floor. All three had crimson holes in their torsos. One officer knelt beside one of the gunman, checking for a pulse. The rear tactical team had possession of their submachine guns.

Special Agent Curlee's head was figuratively about to explode. "What the hell? What part of DO NOT SHOOT TO KILL didn't you officers understand? Sergeant Barnes, what the fu..?"

Barnes looked up at the agents and detectives. "This one is alive. Call for an ambo! Call for an ambo!"

"Sergeant, what the hell happened?"

"Agent Curlee, I know what you said, but in this situation it was necessary to use deadly force. These gunman were pros. They refused to drop their weapons. Two of my team took bullets--one in the thigh and one in the shoulder."

"They moved these kids. They must have known we were coming. Shit. Do we have a leak in our office? A mole? Special Agent Benitez, call in a forensic team to process the entire warehouse. Let's hope we can get some clues to figure out where they stashed these kids," said Special Agent Curlee.

"Jesus," said Corny. "What now?"

"Get Agent Belman on the line. Hopefully his undercover agent has some news."

Del whispered in Corny's ear. "You gonna call Cara and Doug?"

"I promised, but not happy to tell her we struck out. Shit," said Corny.

"Check the caged areas for something, anything that might give us a lead," said Del.

"Sounds like a short-term plan. Come on," responded Detective Morris. The twitching over his eye was driving him nuts. He wondered if it would disappear when he retired.

The three detectives walked back to the cage area fitting black latex gloved over their hands. Corny fished his iPhone out of this pocket and reluctantly speed dialed his sister.

CHAPTER 32

She usually worked until 5:30, but today she needed to finish up a project for her boss. After all, it was the beginning of tax season. Maggie Huong was a CPA in a small Manhattan firm. Maggie believed in the old adage that if she 'dressed for success 'and worked hard, she'd soon be able to score a position in one of the larger accounting firms in New York City. She thought that the larger the firm, the bigger the clients--thus the more lucrative the rewards. Both she and her husband, Teddy, were hungry to earn more money to afford a house for their growing family in the suburbs someday. Luckily, her parents were willing to babysit Micah on a regular basis while he was a toddler. At some point they'd look into a good pre-school program for him since her parents were certainly getting on in years.

Maggie edged her way down the subway steps at about 6:40pm. Her high heels clacked on the gritty platform floor. Even though the platform was still crowded, she positioned herself at a spot where the train doors would open. Maggie had a curvy figure and jet black straight hair at shoulder length. Lightly applied makeup and pink lipstick accentuated her very pretty face. Alert dark brown eyes darted from person to person since her husband, a New York City detective, always warned her to keep vigilance in the subways system at all times.

She emerged above ground in Jamaica and had to walk 5-6 blocks to her parents 'apartment. There was no need to call to tell them that she would be a bit late because they loved indulging in Micah and spending time with their only grandson. She used her own key to open the vestibule door. Two elderly women were walking toward her from the elevator and they smiled at Maggie, indicating familiarity. Most evenings, Maggie was the one picking up Micah. Teddy's hours were irregular and longer than hers.

Once at their door, Maggie inserted her keys into the two locks. She was a little surprised that there was no laughter or playful sounds coming from the apartment. Maggie also thought it strange not to detect any cooking aromas, since her mom should have been preparing for the evening meal. Normally she was greeted by her father when she came in. This evening she opened the door and called out.

"Mom! Dad! Micah, it's mommy. Hello!"

Maggie closed the door behind her and looked into the living room. She immediately spied her mother's feet on the floor. "Mom, mom!"

She ran over and found her mother and father lying on the rug, tied up with duct tape. There was blood under their heads and they seemed unconscious. She sunk to her knees and frantically ripped at the tape around their mouths. She spun her head around searching for Micah.

"Micah, Micah honey. Where are you?"

Panic gripped her throat. Her hands trembled while she tugged at the duct tape. Her father started to wake. His eyelids shot open. Tears spilled down his cheek. The blood was all over the rug and under his nearly bald head. Maggie tore at the tape around her mother's mouth.

"Mom, mom! What happened?" She tried to wake her up. She gently shook her mother's arms.

Her father croaked out a few words. "Maggie, sorry, sorry. They took Micah. They took Micah." His throat was parched.

She got to her feet and checked the bedroom and the bathroom. No Micah. The swing was empty. She checked the lower cabinets. No Micah.

She went to one of the kitchen drawers and grabbed the red-handled scissors. She ran back to her mom and dad and cut through all of the tape. Her mother started to stir. She also had some blood encrusted in several strands of gray hair. Blood pooled on the rug under her too.

Then she noticed the note pinned to her father. She read: "Back off Teddy. If you want to see your little boy again, back your people the fuck off. We'll be in touch." Tears welled up in her almond eyes.

She opened her bag and scooped her cell phone out. She immediately called 911 for an ambulance. Then she speed-dialed Teddy with trembling fingers. His phone rang three times and then he picked up.

"Teddy, Teddy, it's me." She sobbed uncontrollably.

"Maggie, what's wrong? Maggie. Maggie, talk to me."

"Teddy...they took Micah. My parents were attacked in their apartment. They took our little Micah. Teddy--they left a note."

"Oh my God. I'll be there in a half hour. Leaving right now. Call 911 now and try not to touch anything else."

"I did. Thank God my mom and dad are alive. Come quick, Teddy."

Teddy hung up and took his Glock out of the desk drawer and grabbed his sport coat. He ran to Lieutenant Woods' office and shouted, "Lieu, they took Micah. I gotta go."

Woods looked up and shot out of his chair. "What the hell happened Teddy?"

Maggie just called. "My in-laws were attacked in their apartment and Micah is gone, Lieu!"

"Jesus! You think this is related to the Russian mob case?"

"They left a note with my name on it!"

"These guys stop at nothing. They're brutal. Get going and take Joey with you. I'm gonna get the FBI involved. It's a freaking kidnapping for Christ sake!"

"Thanks Lieu."

"Take care of your family and keep me posted."

"Copy that." In two seconds Teddy was out the door with Joey on his tail.

CHAPTER 33

Tuesday was a slow night in *Spasibo*. At 6:30 PM, half the restaurant tables were filled with weekday patrons. A handful of millennials and members of the 'Gen Z 'were standing up at the bar in groups of twos and threes. A Bruno Mars tune was pumping through the speakers in a moderate volume. The mobster wannabees were drinking and bragging about their conquests in the back room. Nikita volunteered to serve them, hoping to hear some bits of information to pass on to her handler. Every night she worked the bar, she dressed in a short, tight skirt and a low scooped satin blouse, revealing a generous portion of her cleavage. She readily flirted with the guys and allowed an occasional ass pat or a lascivious hug or grope, encouraging them to let their guard down. Part of the undercover job. On her way back to the main room, her phone buzzed in her ass pocket.

"Vlad, going outside for a smoke. The boys in the back room are good for now. Be back in five," Nikita assured him. She spoke loud enough for Dmitry to hear at the other end of the bar.

"Okay, babe. If I need you, I'll call you in," said Vladimir. As he wiped down the bar his eyes followed her cute little ass as she sashayed to the rear door. He had a 'thing 'for her, but hadn't made a move yet. He was still watching her closely since she'd only been working for 7 or 8 weeks in *Spasibo*. She had to prove her loyalty before they trusted her 100%.

Dmitry was at the other end of the bar and had been flirting with Svitlana while nursing a beer. She broke away to serve two twenty-year olds who walked in. Dmitry glanced at Nikita and their eyes met for an instant. He had gotten the call too. He took it outside in front a few minutes ago.

Unfortunately, he had nothing to report.

Nikita closed the heavy metal rear door gently behind her and removed a Marlboro from her pack as she walked to the other side of the dented green Dumpster. She placed the cigarette between her lush red lips and lit it with a plastic Bic lighter. She took a well-deserved full drag and raised her head to blow out the smoke. The cool air swirled around her body and it felt good. She took another drag and inhaled deeply. She needed the nicotine to calm her nerves. Undercover was no picnic, especially with these guys. Nikita removed the phone from her rear pocket to check the caller ID. She checked the door, which was still slightly ajar and then speed dialed her handler. After two rings, he picked up.

"What do ya got for me?" Agent Belman asked.

Nikita gazed at the door again. "Not too much. Bits and pieces. Talking about Deer Park and how they left with the goods."

"And took them where?"

"One guy mentioned the 'farm'. Somewhere out east. North Fork I think. I heard something about wine. Probably the Long Island wineries. They've been there before," she whispered.

She turned her head and took a third drag on the Marlboro, facing the brick wall.

Vladimir opened the rear door with a garbage bag in his hand. He glanced at Nikita with a raised eyebrow while tossing the bag into the Dumpster.

"Hey babe, who you talking to?" he asked suspiciously.

Nikita ended the call abruptly and sucked on the cigarette one last time before she tossed the butt on the ground and crushed it with her heel. Her ears flared with a red hue.

"Just a friend. Trying to make some plans on my day off," she replied casually.

"Oh yeah? Anyone I know?"

"No. Just a good friend."

"A boyfriend Nikita? Friend with benefits?"

She let out a throaty chuckle and looked him straight in the eye. "Why so curious Vlad? Huh?"

He got closer to her and tried to back her up against the brick wall. He leered at her and gave her a lustful smile. Vlad figured this was the time to put the moves on her, yet he suspected she wasn't making plans with a friend. He knew full well that the mob had a few properties on the North Fork. She placed a solid hand on his chest to hold him back.

"Hey, if you're interested in me, put the brakes on. I don't date where I work."

She continued to stare into his cold dark brown eyes and wondered if he heard her conversation. The diversion of the flirting actually gave her comfort.

"Speaking of work, time to get back to it. I gotta get inside," she said.

Nikita slowly circled around him and opened the metal door. As she reentered the bar, Vladimir took his phone out to make a call.

CHAPTER 34

Corny, Del, and Special Agent Benitez waited in the Deer Park warehouse for the forensics team to analyze the crime scene. Special Agent Curlee and Detective Morris drove back to the FBI office and the SWAT unit followed. Curlee needed to see if her research team and surveillance experts had uncovered any more information.

Suddenly, Corny's phone vibrated in his pocket. He scooped it out without looking and placed it to his left ear. "Detective Prince."

"We've got another huge problem Corny," explained Lieutenant Woods. "We have another abduction, but this one is close to home."

"What? Who?"

"Teddy's little boy was snatched from his in-laws. They were assaulted and little Micah is gone. They left a note. Definitely the Russians! Told Teddy to back off," said Woods.

"Shit! Those fuckers stop at nothing," exclaimed Corny.

Del raised her head and mouthed a 'what', staring into Corny's eyes.

Corny nodded and raised his forefinger.

"Where's Teddy now?"

"He and Joey are rushing over to his in-laws 'apartment. Maggie found her mom and dad unconscious and tied up with duct tape. Called 911. Her mom and dad were taken to Jamaica hospital. Maggie's waiting for Teddy to arrive."

"Del and I will meet them there. This is all related. Did we get any other leads on these guys at all? Something's got to pop," said Corny.

Woods responded, "actually we got a hit on one of Egor

Kukk's associates: a Boris Petrov. He's got a girlfriend on the Queens/Nassau border. Glen Oaks. I'll text you her address. You may want to contact the two detectives you met at Cara's house. Get them to meet you there instead of the hospital. You said they'd share info. I'll get a judge to give me an emergency warrant due to exigent circumstances."

"Copy that Lieu. We're on our way. Send Del the address."

Lieutenant Woods hung up.

Del grabbed Corny's arm. "What happened?"

"The Russians abducted Teddy's son. His 9-month old son, Micah."

"Bastards. Where do we start? Where's Teddy now?" asked Del.

"Lieu gave us a lead to track down. He's gonna text you the address. I'll drive. Once you get the address, call Detective Kurz and see if he can meet us there."

"What's the lead?"

"An associate of Egor Kukk's. His name is Boris Petrov and he has a girlfriend in Glen Oaks. Woods is getting us a search warrant."

"Copy that. Let's go." Del was out the door already when she got the text. "Got it." She fished for Detective Kurz's card in her back pocket.

Del flipped the keys to her Hummer to Corny and got in the passenger side. Should take about a half hour.

"I hope to God Micah is still alive. Gonna call Teddy. He'll definitely want to drive Maggie to the hospital so she can be with her mom and dad. I'm sure he'll meet us at the Glen Oaks address afterwards."

"Of course," said Corny.

Corny sped out of the Deer Park warehouse parking lot and headed for the highway.

"Del, the Russians have got us coming and going. We really need a break here. We've got several teenagers missing and now a toddler. Telling you now, I'm not gonna play nice anymore."

Del knew what that meant. Her eyes widened and her eyebrows arched. She tenderly stroked his thigh with her strong left hand.

All the muscles in Corny's face hardened as he stared straight ahead. "I'm tired of being jerked around. These guys play hardball. And now, so am I!!"

CHAPTER 35

It was closing time at *Spasibo*. Nikita twirled her light blue jeans jacket around her muscular shoulders and slid her arms into the sleeves. Before she exited the door, she placed a cigarette between her lips and dug out her lighter.

"Good night guys. Tomorrow..."

The autumn wind whipped through the trees ripping dried leaves off slender branches. Nikita welcomed the fresh air and wondered how much longer she'd need to spend in the lion's den. Of course the end game was rescuing those kids from these cruel and greedy mobsters. She was proud of the undercover work that she and Dmitry volunteered to do as FBI agents. She was also proud to be a member of her Russian community of loyal and hardworking American citizens. Nikita knew very well that only a very small percentage of Russian emigres come to this country to run criminal operations with reckless abandon. Her cover was solid, but she'd hope Vladimir wasn't getting suspicious of her. The afternoon communication with Belman was a close call. She took a long drag on her Marlboro and a giggle escaped with a plume of smoke from her throat as she thought of the play on words: 'the call was a close call'.

Nikita turned left at the corner and swiveled her head left and right to see if she was being followed. No one was walking the dark streets at this time. Her seven year old Volkswagen Beetle Hatchback was parked up the block and around the second corner. She was short but her stride was powerful from many years of running to build up her leg muscles. Besides, before she got home, she had another meeting with Dmitry and Belman at the same spot as the last meet. As she power-walked up the street, she turned up her collar to cover her neck somewhat. Only a few homes had lights on the outside of their doors. The rest were darkened as were some of the street lamps. She wondered what the hell the city did with their tax money. Keys in hand, Nikita approached her powder blue ride. Another head twist around, but she heard a noise. It sounded like crushed glass on cement. She still could not see anyone approaching.

She placed the key in the lock and began to unlock it. Then she heard footsteps, light and quick. In an instant she thought--rubber soles. And then felt an iron grip around her neck from behind and her legs gave way.

"What the fu..?" she gasped.

Her half-smoked cigarette fell to the sidewalk and a few sparking embers shot from the tip. She had no weapon because she was afraid someone in the bar would discover it. Her training kicked in, in a fraction of a second. She grabbed the arm around her throat and dug into his wrist with her fingernails. Her right elbow weaponized, shot back and caught him in the solar plexus. The 6-foot attacker grunted and loosened his grip on her throat. Nikita took the advantage and crushed the instep of his right foot with the heel of her shoe. She then spun around and kicked him hard in the knee cap. When she looked up, she recognized him from the back room of the bar. Stanislav! One of the slime-ball mobsters.

Nikita was breathing hard from the rush of adrenaline. And then, Stanislav squeezed her throat with his large beefy hands and shoved her against the Volkswagen. She was about to fight back again when another set of strong arms wrapped around her struggling torso, raised her off the ground and threw her to the concrete. Her head bounced off the concrete, leaving a small pool of blood near the rear wheel of her car. She remained motionless. The second attacker, Victor, checked for her pulse. She was still alive. But he had his instructions.

Victor took an 12-inch hard wood club from his jacket pocket. He viciously swung it at her head three or four times splitting her skull open.

Her red mouth formed a limp oval and her ice-blue eyes starred up at the cloud-covered indifferent moon.

"Fucking undercover cop. She got what was coming to her! Bitch!"

Victor stood up and looked all around. Nobody was on the street.   "Stan, open the door to the Volkswagen. You take the legs, I've got her shoulders. Lay her down on the floor in the back seat. We'll drive it into fucking Sheepshead Bay. Take her bag and search it. Probably no real ID. When the job is done, I'll make the call to the boss," explained Victor.

CHAPER 36

Dmitry's Silverado pulled up to Special Agent Belman's SUV more than a half hour late. Dmitry got out of the car and lit a cigarette and shook his head back and forth as he took a puff. He looked around for pedestrians or cars with young lovers parking in the small lot. Spotting no one, Dmitry approached Belman's driver's side window and threw his cigarette on the ground.

"Big problem. She's nowhere to be found. She's not at the club, not at home, not on the street." He coughed up some phlegm, turned his head, and spit a small wad on the asphalt.

"They must have made her. Fuckers!" exclaimed Special Agent Belman. "Somebody must have overheard our conversation this afternoon."

"It's been more than 45 minutes and she's never been late before," said Dmitry.

"What's going down? What do you hear?"

"Going out to the North Fork of Long Island tomorrow. I assume that's where the kids were moved to until they ship them out to the buyers."

"Okay, we'll track you tomorrow and make sure SWAT teams are ready. We got another problem, too. The NYPD detective, who worked with me on the interview of Egor Kukk, discovered that his toddler son, Micah, was kidnapped from his in-laws in Queens. Members of his squad are tracking down a few leads," explained Belman.

"We must be getting close since those Russians felt the need to split us in different directions," said Dmitry. "Meanwhile, let's try to find Nikita." He glanced at the laptop next to Belman.

"Just about to do that."

Agent Belman opened his computer and placed it on the custom-made slide-out tray from the dashboard. He typed in some commands and the program that coordinates with the microchip implant appeared. The GPS tracking signal was weak, but visible. They both gazed at the screen.

"Looks like she's standing in place near the mouth of Sheepshead Bay," said Dmitry.

"Get in your Silverado and follow me. Let's see what they did to her. God, hope she's still alive," whispered Belman.

It took the two vehicles ten minutes to get to the bay. They both parked their cars away from each other and got out 5 minutes apart. They searched the area in all directions casually. They could not spot either Nikita nor her Beetle. The inevitable slowly became a miserable reality to both men. Belman returned to his car and checked the computer screen again. Dmitry approached with a sour look in his face and looked at the screen from the passenger side. The signal continued to pulsate from the same spot--the beginning of Emmons Ave., near Plumb Beach. They looked at each other and came to the same conclusion. She was underwater.

"Gotta call the dive team. You better get home and get some rest. Don't want any of your buddies seeing you out with us Feds," explained Belman.

"Copy that. Keep me in your sights tomorrow," said Dmitry.

"Don't worry. We'll be dogging your trail."

"It's all about those kids. We gotta get them back!"

"Yeah. Watch your six."

Dmitry began to walk toward his Silverado.

"Hey, sorry about Nikita. Know you guys were tight," called Belman. "One last thought."

Dmitry raised his eyebrows and stopped in his tracks.

"Only one positive, Dmitry. If they made Nikita, most likely they won't be looking for another mole in their organization."

"This fucking job." Dmitry shook his head again and then nodded. "But somebody's gotta stand up to the bad guys." He waved his arm and got in the driver's seat.

CHAPTER 37

Corny's phone rang through the Bluetooth in the Hummer. After the first ring, Corny immediately pressed the green button.

"Go for Prince and DelVecchio," Corny answered.

Special Agent Curlee asked, "What's your status detectives? Where are you?"

Dispensing with formalities, Corny responded. "Curlee, Woods called with more bad news. The Russians abducted the son of one of our detectives on the squad. Teddy Huong partnered with Belman on the Egor Kukk interview. They snatched Teddy's 9-month old son and beat up Teddy's in-laws. Left a message for Teddy to 'back off'."

"Oh shit. They are going for the jugular. Making it personal," said Curlee.

"They are definitely playing hardball. Time to take the kid gloves off, Curlee. First they took my nieces and now a little boy. You got anything else. Any more leads?"

"Okay, first, our agents got a chance to talk with the guy who was shot in the warehouse. He finally came out of surgery and gave up his boss's name with a little encouragement. He was ready to make a deal to reduce his prison time for kidnapping, extortion, gun possession, and God knows what else," explained Curlee.

"What's the name of the boss?" asked Corny.

"Leonid Vasiliev. Some years back we arrested him on drug tracking and gun-running. Unfortunately, his high-priced lawyers were able to get him off on some technicalities," said Curlee.

"We have any other info on him or his associates?" asked

Del.

Curlee continued, "Got a wife and two teenage kids living in a huge house in Bayside. We think he also has a second house somewhere in Sag Harbor."

"Really. Good place to start, don't you think?" asked Corny.

"I've got more, detectives. We think one of our undercover agents was made and killed last night in Brooklyn."

"Shit. God damn it. Our ace in the hole," said Del.

"Well, yes and no. We have another undercover agent in Brooklyn and his assignment tomorrow is to drive out to the North Fork. We think they are getting ready to move the kids to their respective buyers. Another ace in the hole, as you put it, is that our agent has an implanted microchip under his skin. We'll be tracking is every movement. Hopefully, he and his mob friends will lead us to the abducted teenagers," explained Curlee.

Del jumped back into the conversation. "How are we going to know where the kids are going, assuming they all have different buyers?"

"Our computer researchers are working on it. They are going through internet back channels from the hacks of the schools the kids attend. What we do know is that the computer hackers are working from Russia, specifically St. Petersburg. Most likely one of the uber-wealthy oligarchs is running the whole criminal organization, with tentacles in the U.S., Germany, Great Britain, Scandinavia, France, Italy, etc." said Curlee.

Corny asked, "Can we work the angle of Vasiliev's family? You, know, apply some pressure..."

"Detective, I know what you're thinking, BUT NO. The FBI doesn't work that way. We must work within the confines of the law. Besides, if we want convictions, we must go by the book. Is that understood?"

"Okay, okay. Just saying we have options to GET THOSE KIDS BACK!" Corny demanded. He was so enraged that his ears became beet red.

Del cut in again. "Agent Curlee, our Lieutenant gave us a solid lead to follow. Looking to get Teddy's boy back safe and sound. They discovered that a known associate of Kukk is Boris Petrov. Didn't have an address for him, but our people found his girl friend. She's got an apartment in Glen Oaks. On our way there now and we've asked the two Nassau detectives we met at Corny's sister's house to meet us there. Okay with you?"

"Sure, go. We'll work the North Fork, but keep me informed. That little boy needs to be returned to his mom and dad. Go."

Del responded, "Copy that."

In 5 minutes, Corny pulled around the corner of 82nd Ave. and 257th St., looking for the texted address. He spotted the house and drove past it and parked at the far corner of the block.

"The fifth brick house with a white front door and black awning above," said Corny.

"What's the name of the girlfriend? asked Del.

"Marta Stepanova."

"Have you spotted the Nassau detectives yet?"

Corny replied, "They rounded the corner a second ago. Dark green sedan."

"Did you get the warrant?"

Corny nodded. "But we wait for Teddy and Joey. And then we breach."

Del and Corny drew their Glocks, each making sure a round is chambered.

CHAPTER 38

Five or six grimy and stained mattresses were spread haphazardly on the dank concrete floor. An acrid odor of mold filled the stale air that surrounded a dozen large, empty oak barrels. The windowless subterranean room was approximately 30 feet by 45 feet. Four single low-watt bulbs hung from thick black wires attached to circular metal fixtures spread evenly from the low wooden ceiling. No sound could get out; no sound could get in. At one end of the room was an old mahogany door made of vertical panels and one diagonal bar. Black metal hinges and a thick black metal doorknob secured the door locked. There were two buckets, a roll of toilet paper and hand wipes in the far left corner of the room where it was dark. Suddenly the heavy door opened and one of the guards walked in with a large paper bag and a small case of bottled water. He placed them on the floor and exited, locking the door from the other side.

"Our gourmet meals have arrived guys. I guess it's bologna or bologna," Carmen sarcastically explained.

The others were sitting on the filthy mattresses, some cross-legged, some with outstretched legs. Wesley got up and headed for the bag with sandwiches. He looked inside and shook his head.

"You're not gonna believe it ladies. It's not bologna. No, no, no. We hit the jackpot!" exclaimed Wesley.

Jordon responded, "the suspense is killing me, Wes. What gives?"

She stood up and walked over to Wesley and snatched the bag from his hand and rummaged inside. "Okay, girls. Who wants cheese on a roll? And who wants a ham & cheese wrap? We got what looks like chicken salad on a seeded bagel. And tuna on another roll. And a few more delicious sandwiches."

Brianna got up and distributed the meals to the others along with bags of potato chips and chocolate bars. Wesley handed out bottles of water. They were weary, scared and anxious, but now they focused on getting their hunger and thirst quenched.

In between bites, Emma posed a question. "So why do you think all of a sudden they give us better food?"

Kimberly asked, "the better question is, where the hell are we and what's the next step?"

"I want to know why it's taking the police so long to find us?" asked Carmen. "It's been three to four days already. They must be ready to farm us out to some rich sultan or wealthy sleaze bag from China or something."

"Well it took over an hour to drive to this place. And it looks like an old winery or whiskey..." Wesley hesitated.

"Distillery. Is that the word you were looking for Wes?" asked Jordon.

"Yeah, dddistillery. It smells like mmmold in here. No windows, no air," he said.

Emma said, "look up at the ceiling. There are vents up there and I do feel a little bit of air flow."

"Look, I know you guys are gonna laugh, but my uncle is a NYPD detective and I know right now he's out looking for us. He and his partner Del are probably working with the local police searching and investigating. He's gonna find us. Let's not lose hope, okay?" said Emma.

Jordon nodded with confidence and the rest of the teenagers seemed to relax a little. They all hungrily finished their sandwiches and chips. Some of them saved the chocolate bars for later. They stuffed the wrappers back into the paper bag and looked around for the toilet.

"So the toilet and sink is...where?" asked Carmen.

"We looked around before. Did you see the buckets in the corner?" asked Jordon.

"No, no...no. I'm not...no. Not in front of our boy Wesley."

Carmen complained.

"Oh don't worry about me. I'll walk over to the door and face the wall. I won't peek. Promise." said Wesley. A small smile crept only his lips and his eyebrows did a dance.

"Oh shit. Wesley McArthur I will kick your ass if you look. I swear." Carmen blurted out as she walked over to the bucket corner.

The other girls giggled and polished off their lukewarm water bottles. They heard low groans coming from Carmen in the corner of the room. After cleaning up she announced, "Who's next?"

The rest of the girls just stared at each other. And then the door opened again on squeaky hinges.

CHAPTER 39

Joey and Teddy showed up ten minutes later and parked near the first corner of the street. They both jumped out, eyeballing the address they'd been given. Teddy rushed across the street, laser-focused on the front door. Joey spotted the Hummer on the far corner and waved at Corny and Del. Detectives Kurz and Parlefsky hopped out of their unmarked sedan. All six had their handguns at the ready, adjacent to their legs. All approached the house quietly and quickly.

Corny placed a firm hand on Teddy's shoulder and made eye contact with him. He said quietly, "you've got to slow it down Ted. I know you're hurting, but we're not going in with guns blazing. You have to think of Micah's safety. Follow my lead."

Teddy nodded and took a short step back. He was fuming and he glanced at the sky with a few tears in his eyes. "I know boss. But I gotta get my little boy back. Those bas..."

"Yeah, yeah. We'll get him back. My way. We're not going in half-cocked. Get your head in the game or you're gonna sit in the squad car. Understand?" asked Corny.

Del knew Corny was 100% correct. If Ted ran in with fury, he could screw up the entire breach which needed to be done as per their training.

Teddy stared at Corny. His jaw muscles were flexing and he was twisting his head in semi-circles.

"You good? Teddy, you good?" asked Corny.

"Yeah, I'm good," nodded Teddy.

Detective Kurz stepped up to Corny. "You got a warrant, detective?"

"Exigent circumstances! Teddy's little boy was

kidnapped, Kurz."

Detective Kurz arched his eyebrows, gazed at Parlefsky and said, "well, what are we waiting for. Let's go."

Teddy knocked on the front door with several powerful raps. No answer. He knocked again, harder. And he listened for foot steps or any sign that someone was home. Finally a woman answered from inside.

"Who is it? Why you knocking on my door?"

"NYPD. Looking for Marta Stepanova. Open the door," demanded Teddy.

"Why you looking for her?"

"Open this fucking door NOW!" Teddy demanded a second time, and getting more agitated.

All of a sudden, Del heard two metal clicks and the door swung open two or three inches. There was a safety chain between the door and the door frame.

"Why are you here? What do you want?" asked Marta.

Corny took charge. "Are you Marta Stepanova?"

Before she could answer, Corny blurted out, "either you open this door all the way, or we'll break it down. Your choice."

Marta hesitated, then closed the door momentarily to unhook the chain and opened the door fully. All of the detectives entered her doorway, guns drawn and spread out looking for Micah immediately. They called out for anyone else who might be in her house with her. They cleared each room methodically and found no one else.

Teddy grabbed Marta firmly by the left arm and snarled inches from her face. "Where is the boy? My little boy. Where is he?"

Marta, a pretty dark-haired woman in her early thirties, had an hourglass figure. She wore a jade green cotton sweater, tight blue jeans and black patent leather high heels. Black eye liner framed her green-blue eyes and she wore pastel pink matte lipstick. She leaned her head back away from Teddy's fury and the color drained from her face. Her mouth made an oval gasp.

"I don't know what you talking about. Leave me alone!

You're hurting me! Let me go!" exclaimed Marta.

Del rushed over and pulled Marta down into one of the wooden kitchen chairs. "Look, Marta. We know your boyfriend, Boris Petrov, runs with the Russian mob. We also figure he brought a 9-month old little boy here after they kidnapped him. So where the hell is this boy? This detective is his father! If you don't talk, he's gonna teach you a serious lesson you'll never forget," yelled Del.

The veins in Marta's neck bulged and visibly throbbed. She knew she was in serious trouble.

"Now cut the shit about how you don't know anything and give us a clue. You're facing 20 years for aiding and abetting a kidnapping. You're young and beautiful now. You want to spend your best years in prison, Marta?" asked Del.

Marta began to tremble and breathe erratically. "I can't tell you. They kill me if I talk." Tears welled up in her eyes.

"Marta, we can protect you. We can arrange for the witness protection program. Set you up with a new life," explained Corny.

Teddy grabbed her straight black hair and yanked her head back. He almost tilted her chair back so she'd land on the floor.

"Where is my BOY?"

Joey stepped in and pushed Teddy back a few steps. "Teddy, we need you to focus. Back off, man."

Del asked Marta again. "Where is the boy, Marta?"

Tears rolled down Marta's smooth face and blood rushed back. Her mascara mixed with watery rivulets down her cheeks. Del filled up a glass with water from the kitchen tap and handed it to Marta. She managed to take a few gulps slowly.

She whispered with a hoarse voice, "my cousin. My cousin is looking after him. He's not hurt. He's fine. But you gotta protect me. They're gonna cut my tongue out. Please!" Marta pleaded, obviously terrified.

"What's the address? What's her name? Who else is there?" shot Corny.

She gave the detectives the name and address of her cousin in Great Neck. She also said that the two thugs who kidnapped Micah were guarding him there as well. Marta swore that was all she knew.

"Joey, you stay here with Marta and call for a few uniforms to take over. We need to keep her safe and make sure she makes no phone calls," said Corny.

"Copy that boss."

"Okay, let's go. This is the borderline of our turf now. Parlefsky, call it into the squad. We're gonna need a SWAT team to meet us there. We need to get this little boy back to his dad, safe and sound. Don't worry Teddy. We got your six," said Kurz.

The five detectives rushed out of the house and climbed back into their sedans and headed for Great Neck.

CHAPTER 40

Two thugs stepped into the cavernous room. They were Leonid's bodyguards. All six teenagers sat up erect, wondering what was going to happen next. They stared at the two men who were obviously on a mission for their boss. Emma and Jordan clutched each others 'hands. Kimberly wrapped one long arm around Wesley's torso and pulled him close to her. Carmen defiantly made eye contact with one of the smug mobsters. Brianna's eyes began to water. The smell of fear and anxiety permeated the cool dank air.

Mikhail spoke. "Who's Brianna?" He searched faces of the frightened kids. No one answered. "I said, who is Brianna? We need you to come with us."

A small wet blotch spread in the center of Brianna's blue jeans. Hot tears welled in her eyes. She reluctantly raised her slender arm. The others felt for her. Wanted to protect her. But, they knew they were powerless. Brianna stood up on shaky legs.

"Don't worry and don't be scared. It's your turn to take shower and get nice clean clothes. You'll be back soon. Come on." Mikhail gestured with his muscular forearm.

Brianna walked slowly toward the two guards. She knew that she could not resist their 'request 'and she desperately needed to get cleaned up. Right before she walked through the doorway, she turned back to her new found friends, longing for their support. And then the heavy wooden door hinges squeaked and groaned, followed by a loud thud that echoed in the old wine cellar.

The two men escorted her out of the abandoned winery and into a navy blue SUV.

"Where are you taking me? I thought you said I was to

take a shower and get clean clothes," she protested.

"Don't worry. You will. No shower here in this building. We drive to the farmhouse and you'll get cleaned up," explained Pavel.

It took approximately 15 minutes to drive to the farm off of Anchor Way in Southhold. It was definitely off the beaten path and rather secluded, which was perfect for Leonid's purposes. Once on Anchor Way, they took a few left turns and up a long and curvy pebble & shell driveway led to the battleship gray house in desperate need of a paint job.

The two-story clapboard building had a wrap-around porch with a few old white rocking chairs sitting idle under large white-framed windows. Inside there were several bedrooms upstairs and at least three full bathrooms. A sizable foyer opened up to a dining room on the right and a large living/ sitting room on the left. The huge kitchen took the rear expanse of the house.

A huge wooden barn sagged its shoulders about 30 feet behind and to the right of the place. There were five acres surrounding the farm. Most of the land was barren. But a small tract of land had short pine trees growing for the Christmas season. Three dark SUV's were haphazardly parked in front of the old building. Several pitch pine and Eastern red cedar trees supplied much shade and privacy for this old hidden gem.

"Okay little girl. Let's get out and into the house. Anika will take you to get cleaned up. Come on girl," said Mikhail.

Brianna saw she had no other options. She hesitated getting out of the car. She used the back of her hand to wipe her nose and eyes and jumped out of the SUV. She slowly walked up the creaky porch steps while she looked around at the house and the front yard. She noticed the tiny pine trees in the field beyond the shade trees. Anika greeted Brianna as she stepped into the foyer. She had fresh towels hanging from her arm.

"Come. We go upstairs to the shower. Come."

Brianna began to tremble. "What's gonna happen to me?"

"Come child. We get you clean first. Don't be scared.

There's nobody upstairs," explained Anika. "The men are in the kitchen eating lunch."

Brianna heard hushed conversation and some dishes clattering coming from the kitchen. She slowly walked up the steps behind Anika, wondering if she would see her mother ever again.

CHAPTER 41

"Agent Belman, what is your progress?" asked Curlee.

"Agent Curlee, we should be near your office in about 20 minutes. We're tracking undercover Agent Dmitry Kussov as he heads east. He's currently on the L.I.E. with other cell members. The organization needs drivers to deliver the abducted youngsters, wherever that may be. Are the tech people having any luck uncovering that information?"

Curlee responded, "they're working on it. A few weeks ago we were able to snag a couple of young hotshot hackers who know their way around the dark web."

"Is SWAT ready to roll?"

"Locked and loaded, Belman. SAC John Masters is always on top of his people."

"Okay, see you in a few. We'll coordinate with you and your agents in the parking lot. Having a bead on our undercover guy makes life a lot easier."

"How much longer Victor? My legs are getting cramped. Where are we meeting the others?" asked Dmitry.

"Hey, what are you worried about? Stan knows the way. We'll be there soon. Time to transport the goods," chuckled Victor. "This is what you're making the big money for my friend."

"How about stopping at a place where I can take a leak and get a cup of coffee, huh? Ten minutes tops," said Dmitry.

"Fuckin 'pussy Dmitry. I thought you were this tough guy from the docks. What do you say, Stan? You need to take a leak too?" asked Victor.

"A ten minute stop'll do us all some good. I could go for a

sandwich or something," said Stan.

Victor gave in. "Okay, okay. Pull off at the next place for a quick stop." Under his breath he murmured, "two fuckin' pussies in the front seat." He scowled and stared out the window as Stan veered into the right lane.

In about 5 minutes, Stan signaled for the rest stop in Dix Hills, right off the expressway. It seemed like a fairly new welcome center with a lot of food choices. He pulled into a spot and the three of them got out.

Stan and Dmitry headed straight for the Men's Room and Victor strolled around the center, eyeballing the food counters. Suddenly, his phone buzzed in his jeans pocket. Victor took his iPhone out and checked the number. It was Leonid.

"Yeah, what's up boss?" Victor walked outside for some privacy.

"Where are you now?" asked Leonid.

"A rest stop on the L.I.E. Dix Hills I think," answered Victor.

"Are you alone?"

"Yeah. The other two are taking a leak."

"We got more trouble Victor."

"Listening boss."

"Got a call from Sophia. That story about Kussov's father. Fisherman from Myshkin on the Volga. Bullshit! Sophia dug deeper. The father was from Moscow and he taught languages in the English School of Science and Technology. Your boy's got to be a fuckin 'undercover cop too! Just like that bar bitch Nikita."

Victor looked at the front door of the welcome center. His men were headed outside. Dmitry was carrying a cup of coffee and a banana. Stan had a wrapped hero sandwich and a bottle of Snapple. Victor turned and walked a little further into the parking lot.

"Boss, what do you want me to do?"

"Take care of him. Under no circumstances should you bring him here. The cops and the FBI are probably on your tail. Keep your eyes open. You know what to do. Make it hard for them to find that prick."

"Got it boss." Victor hung up.

"Hey Victor, did you get something to eat?" asked Stan.

Victor stared at him and shook his head. "Not hungry like you pussies."

Dmitry asked him, "don't you need to take a piss? What are you, a fuckin 'camel?"

Victor smiled and walked back to the car, thinking of how he was gonna kill Dmitry and hide the body.

CHAPTER 42

The house was nestled on Deepdale Drive in Great Neck Estates. It was a sprawling all brick and stone Tudor mansion that had to go for over $3,000,000. A pre-war (WW II) design and solid construction, the home had to have at least 5 bedrooms and a minimum of 5,000 square feet. Eyeballing the property, it looked to be on approximately one third of an acre. There were houses on both sides, so the breach had to be carefully planned and executed.

All three detectives 'vehicles did a drive-by 5 minutes apart and they parked around the corner on Glenwood. Detective Parlefsky reached out to the Great Neck Estates Police Department, explaining the lead they got regarding a possible kidnapping of the son of NYPD Ted Huong. They believed the boy was being held in a residence on Deepdale Drive. The Chief of Police responded with a promise of support from their detective unit. Two detectives, Matt Johnson, a young 6-foot, 3-inch ramrod-straight beanpole and Sheila Manes, an older curley-haired blond female who was wiry and solid, were leaning up against their unmarked SUV when the others arrived.

All eight detectives exchanged pleasantries and sized each other up. Detective Manes took the initiative to orchestrate the plan since the home was in her jurisdiction.

"Okay, this house, although it's on a third of an acre, is dangerously close to neighbors. We called in the uniforms to warn the occupants of several homes surrounding the address in question to stay away from windows and to quarantine in their basements during our approach. If we evacuated those folks, the element of surprise when we breach will be gone. The house has 5,500 square footage with 5 bedrooms upstairs and a large backyard. We are currently in the process of accessing the building plans so we can plan our entry and get a look at each floor plan. Any questions so far?"

"Do you know who owns the house or who lives there? Do we have an idea how many are inside?" asked Kurz.

Before Manes could respond, Teddy spit out, "do you know if my boy is inside? Have you seen any trace of Micah?"

Joey put a hand on Teddy's shoulder and stood close by. Del walked over to Ted and joined Joey to show support. She pursed her lips and listened closely as well.

Manes continued, "actually we were able to snag a truck with a thermo infrared imaging scanner from your Nassau Country Great Neck department. They arrived a few minutes before you guys got here. They're parked on the street and should be sending us a report momentarily."

Johnson said, "The house is owned by an LLC with ties to an overseas conglomerate within Eastern Europe."

Corny suggested, "Well that's sounds like they're connected to the Russian mob cell. Why don't we begin planning for a breach and make adjustments once we get the floor plan and the imaging report."

Manes's phone buzzed. "Hold up. Could be the housing department."

She opened her email and found the note. Instead of opening the email on her phone, she ducked into the SUV for the laptop. Since it was powered up already, she hit several keys and opened the email in the computer. Now she had the floor plan for the home and placed the laptop on the hood so each detective could get an idea of the layout.

"Now all we need is the imaging report of how many in that residence," said Corny.

"And hopefully my boy!" exclaimed Teddy, who was pacing back and forth.

Detectives Kurz and Parlefsky had their communications frequencies coordinated with the techs in the infrared imaging truck. They began to hear a voice coming through with some crackling.

"Okay detectives. Got your report," the tech notified.

"Copy that. Who am I speaking with and what do you have? How many adults do your read?" asked Kurz.

The other detectives made a semi-circle around Kurz and Parlefsky to listen.

"This is Detective Joe Miles. Looks like six adults. Possibly five males and one female. The males are strapped with sub-machine guns, perhaps Uzis," explained the tech.

"Do you detect any children? Any small kids?" asked Kurz.

"Hard to tell. Could be a kid upstairs. We got the woman and a man on the second floor in the south east corner bedroom. The other four males in what looks like the kitchen area."

"Okay. Let me know if anything changes Miles," said Kurz.

"Copy that detective."

Kurz laid out for everyone where the adults are at the moment and hopefully where the child is, if in fact, the child is Micah. Manes finalized the plan for breaching the home and everyone nodded in agreement. They were all experienced and each knew their role.

Del asked, "do we have SWAT support for the breach?"

Manes responded, "unfortunately we do not. They were called to a serious domestic abuse situation in Glen Cove. We should be alright with our tactical gear and the eight of us."

"Copy that." They all nodded in agreement.

Trunks opened, bullet-proof vests fitted, assault rifles and hand guns checked and loaded. Manes gave the signal and they started a slow trot around the corner to Deepdale Drive. Several uniformed cops were instructed to close the street with their vehicles and stand guard. As they approached the property, a Nassau County Police helicopter circled the area giving the detectives communications support. In two minutes they reached the house. Corny, Del, and Parlefsky went around the left side to the rear door in the backyard. Teddy, Joey, Kurz, and

Manes approached the front door, with Johnson taking the lead carrying the battering ram.

All coms were coordinated and Manes would give the signal to breach at the same time.

Johnson hefted the battering ram and was ready to swing upon command. Everyone had eyes on the windows, looking for movement.

One of the drapes suddenly swayed in the bow window of the living room at the front of the house. Someone saw them coming. Corny noticed and nodded to Manes. She nodded and they all knew the element of surprise was lost.

"Rear and front units. They know we're here. Saw us in front. Heads on a swivel and watch your sixes. Respond."

Corny responded, "Copy that. Ready."

Johnson swung the battering ram behind his shoulder and...

CHAPTER 43

The large wooden door creaked open one last time. The only teens left were the twin sisters, Jordan and Emma. They were sitting on one of the mattresses. Emma was humming and Jordan was whispering to her. The same two men, Leonid's bodyguards, entered. Pavel dangled two jet black zip ties from his thick fingers.

"Okay. Stand up! Both of you. Last trip we make to the farm. Hurry up. Let's go," ordered Mikhail.

The two girls reluctantly stood up and gazed at each other. "Where are the others?" asked Emma.

"Farmhouse. All cleaned up. Nice new clothes. You next," said Mikhail.

Pavel walked behind the girls and gently grabbed Jordan's wrists and curled them behind her back. In two seconds he placed one of the zip ties around her hands and zipped it closed, leaving a bit of wiggle room. Then he did the same to Emma, who wriggled her shoulders back and forth.

"You're hurting me. Ouch! Hey," Emma complained.

"Don't get your panties in a twist little girl. For your own safety," Pavel smirked. A hearty chuckle escaped from Mikhail's throat.

"These two aren't little girls. They are beautiful young women, Pavel," laughed Mikhail.

Both Pavel and Mikhail leered at each one. Pavel moved inches from Jordan and stared into her hazel eyes. His gaze slowly shifted down to her ample breasts beneath her white tee shirt. Mikhail's eyes studied Emma's rear end in her tight yellow shorts. They each grunted and became aroused.

Jordan spit a wad of saliva into Pavel's face. The spittle

dripped down his cheek to his angular chin. He immediately saw red and raised his muscular arm to slap her. Instantly, Mikhail blocked Pavel's response and pulled him away.

"Hey. The boss gave strict orders. We don't touch or harm these kids. We're not getting millions for damaged goods," scolded Mikhail.

Pavel snarled and wiped this face with his left forearm. He stared at Jordan with evil dark eyes.

After ushering the two teens into the back seat of the SUV, they arrived at the farm fifteen minutes later. The girls slid out of the SUV and purposefully noticed as many details as possible about the house, the barn and the property. They each were hopeful they might need to describe it to their uncle Corny. As with the others, Anika met them at the front door. They slowly walked into the house and committed to memory the house layout, as well.

"Let's go upstairs. The showers are up there and so are the others," explained Anika.

Emma and Jordan were directed to shower together in the same bathroom that the others cleaned up in. In 3 minutes they were done. Emma stepped out of the modernized walk-in shower naked onto a green mat first. She grabbed a white towel from the hook on the back of the closed door. Jordan was next. She snatched the other towel. Suddenly the door opened slowly. A puff of cigar smoke entered first.

"How are we doing ladies? All cleaned up?" asked Leonid. He continued to puff on his cigar as he, too, leered at these young women.

Emma and Jordan quickly wrapped their towels around their shapely frames tightly and turned away from him. They remained quiet. Emma began to tremble. Jordan pulled Emma closer to her.

"We have nice new clothing for you after your warm showers. Anika will take you to the dressing bedroom," explained Leonid. He clutched the half-smoked cigar between two chubby fingers and smiled. Then he turned around and walked out the door and down the stairs.

Leonid re-entered the kitchen in the back of the house. There were soiled dishes partially filled with leftover food scraps. Dirty silverware was strewn about on the table. Empty green beer bottles dotted the tableau next to a few filled ash trays. Some of the men were seated at the table, some were chewing on sandwiches while standing at the granite countertop near the sink.

"Okay. The last two are almost ready. We're just waiting for Victor and Stanislov," announced Leonid. He blew a few smoke rings toward the ceiling and tapped some ash into a tray.

"And Dmitry, right boss," added Mikhail.

"Well, we got a new big problem with Dmitry," whispered Leonid.

"What?"

"Another fucking undercover cop! That fuck was good. But thanks to Sophia, we found out he was talking bullshit!" Leonid spit in the sink and screwed up his fleshy face.

"Holy shit! No kidding!" exclaimed Pavel.

"That's right. Unfortunately he won't be able to attend our little party here. He will be permanently tied up, as they say."

Leonid walked over to the large bay window and stared out at the wide open field behind the house. He took another long drag from his cigar expelling the smoke through the window. He watched the cool breeze playing with the branches of a tall cedar tree.

CHAPTER 44

Just before the end of the Long Island Expressway, Victor sent a brief text to Stanislav. The phone dinged in his left pocket and he retrieved his iPhone to look. While keeping his eye on the road, he scanned the text from Victor. It said: *'After LIE, find a secluded spot on 25 to pull over. Some problem with a tire. Dmitry's a cop!'*. Stan's took a deep breath and gazed into the rear view mirror. He made eye contact with Victor and noticed a slight nod of Victor's head. Dmitry was watching the forested area alongside the L.I.E. and hadn't noticed the exchange of communication.

Route 25 was wide open from the L.I.E. for a few miles and then narrowed to one lane each way. Stan was searching for a secluded spot on either side of the road. Then he had a thought.

"Did you guys feel that?" asked Stan.

"Feel what?" asked Victor, who knew what his intent was.

"I felt a blip, blip. Must be a tire. Gotta check it out. Gonna pull off 25." Stan replied.

"I didn't feel anything," said Dmitry.

"Yeah, well, your hands are not on the wheel. Take a minute."

Stan spotted a narrow road on the left. He waited for traffic to ease and made a left onto a wooded lane. He drove about a half mile and came upon a dirt driveway. He pulled the SUV over and got out. He pretended to check each tire and looked at the under body of the vehicle. Dmitry and Victor joined Stan in his search for the 'problem 'with the SUV. Victor eyeballed the entire area and saw no pedestrians on the road. There was no traffic either.

"Dmitry, get down to check the under carriage. There may be something loose. Maybe a shock or a strut," commanded Victor. "Leonid will go batshit crazy if we show up with a fucked up vehicle. We need to be able to deliver the goods. Come on, check."

Dmitry glanced at Stan and Victor, searching for a 'tell' that indicated that the stop along the road was bullshit. Neither men showed any sign of anxiety or anger. They stood with poker faces. Dmitry dropped to his knees in the front of the SUV. Holding onto the front bumper, he tilted his head to see under the engine. Stan wasted no time. Victor gave him the signal and Stan swiftly removed his Glock from the holster under his left armpit. He viciously swung it directly against Dmitry's right temple three times in rapid succession. Blood gushed from the blow and Dmitry collapsed into the dirt in front of the dark SUV. A dark red puddle swirled in the dirt around Dmitry's head. Victor bent down to check his pulse, but quickly stood back up hearing the loud blare of an approaching ambulance.

"Shit we need to get out of here. Stan, let's pull his body into the woods. We cover him with leaves," said Victor.

They each took a shoulder and dragged his 200 lb. dead weight about 10 yards into the small stand of trees. Within a minute they completely covered his body with dead autumn leaves.

"Move. Let's go."

Stan ran back to the driver's seat and waited for Victor to hop into the passenger's spot. Stan slowly backed the SUV up and made a U-turn to head back to route 25.

"What the fuck, Victor? Thought you guys checked him out. What went wrong?" asked Stan.

"His cover story was solid with proof of who he was and where he came from. But Sophia did a deeper dive into his past and found that his story was all bullshit. Leonid told me to take him out before we got to the farmhouse. Now we have to worry about being tracked by the cops or the FBI," said Victor.

"Yeah, but if they were tracking him, this is the end of the line. No way they'll find the farmhouse. No way," said Stan.

"Let's fucking hope, for all our sakes."

Stan made a left turn back onto route 25 and continued driving east. Victor took out his phone to make a call.

CHAPTER 45

Special Agents Belman and Myers pulled into the Melville FBI office parking lot a little after noon. Myers parked the black Ford sedan in the second row of spots across from the rear entrance.

"I don't like what I see on the tracking program, Bruce," said Belman.

"What's wrong?"

"I can understand the 10-minute stop on the L.I.E. There is a large rest top near Dix Hills. A piss and snack stop," said Belman.

"Yeah, so?"

"But a half-hour later, another stop on Route 25 and no further movement since," explained Belman.

"Okay, maybe that's the spot where they're holding the kids," suggested Myers.

"Doesn't feel right, Bruce. Not really the North Fork yet," Belman pointed to the computer screen.

Myers leaned over to take a look. "Right Jack. Only a few miles from the end of the L.I.E. Think they made Dmitry?" Asked Myers.

"I certainly hope the fuck not!" Belman spit out. "Dmitry's our best shot at finding the kids. Let's get up to the office and figure this out with Curlee."

Both agents got out of the sedan and entered the F.B.I. building. SAC Masters greeted them at the elevator bank.

"Hi John, good to see you again. This is my partner, Bruce Myers. Bruce, meet SAC John Masters. We worked together a long time ago in the Philadelphia office," explained Belman.

"Special Agent Myers, good to meet you. You're partnered

with a good man. Belman's as solid as they come." Looking at Belman, "so what do we have at this point? I know you've been tracking Dmitry. Come on back to meet the rest of the Task Force team," said Masters.

They all walked back to the large squad room filled with desktop computers manned with a cadre of analysts. There were several computer screens mounted on the walls and the members of the team were loosely huddled in conversation with each other and the techs. Masters conducted quick introductions as Agent Curlee stepped forward.

"So, Agent Belman, where is your undercover man now?" Asked Curlee.

Belman opened his laptop on the edge of one of the desks so one of the tech analysts could plug it into the office system. The tracking program opened up on the central wall screen and Belman pointed to a spot on Route 25.

"Agent Curlee, no movement for over a half hour at this spot. According to my contact with Agent Kussov, he was going to the North Fork, which would be way past this point on 25. It doesn't feel right. I pray he's alright and wasn't made," said Belman. "We got to get out there, now!"

"I agree. Finding him gives us our best lead for getting to the Russians and those kidnapped kids," said Curlee.

Agent Winchester suggested, "I would not send up a chopper at this point. Wouldn't want to spook the Russians into hiding the kids any deeper. What do you think Agent Curlee?"

Curlee thought for a moment and glanced at SAC Masters. They both nodded in agreement.

Benitez jumped into the conversation. "We need to alert the Coast Guard and harbor patrol units for outgoing yachts, boats, fishing charters, etc. They may be shipping the kids out across the Sound or down the east coast or even to the Caribbean."

Curlee commanded, "Carlos, make those calls now. We need to keep those kids on the Fork before they end up God-Knows-Where."

"Any luck with your teenage hackers getting info from abroad?" Asked Detective Morris.

Curlee strode over to the small conference room in the left corner of the bullpen. Three Gen Z's, two guys and one girl, all in jeans and T-shirts, were feverishly working their keyboards in deep concentration. The tall one with a sandy colored mop on his head raised his eyes to Curlee. "Getting closer. We need a bit more time, boss," said Jason.

"Call me ASAP, Jason. Got it?" Asked Curlee.

"You bet, boss." He went back to typing and Curlee frowned as she joined the others. She wasn't used to being informally addressed, but recognized where it came from. It was definitely a generational thing.

"Okay, we're moving out in five. Got to call my SWAT team to meet us in the parking lot," said Curlee.

The agents and detectives got their gear ready as Detective Morris's phone buzzed in his pocket. He took a look and walked over to the window to take the call. Detective Winchester's eyebrows arched and her neck stiffened instinctively. That was the third suspicious phone call Morris got in two days. Normally he would share his business and even personal life with her. These calls were strictly private. After partnering with him for five years, the mutual trust had been established a long time ago. However, something told her she needed to keep a close eye on his actions. Maybe he was more focused on his impending retirement than on this extremely intricate and important case.

In two minutes he caught up to her at the elevator banks. "Everything okay, Sid?" Asked Winchester.

"Oh, yeah. Fine. My son decided to come to us for Thanksgiving this year. We're good, Lakesha."

Lakesha Winchester gave Morris a sideways glance with her piercing dark brown eyes. She knew he was giving her BS, but left it alone.

In 5 minutes they were all in their vehicles, anxious to

find Dmitry Kussov and those scared kids. Agents Belman and Myers took the lead out of the lot, heading east.

CHAPTER 46

Johnson's mighty swing resulted in an explosive sound of metal on wood as Manes and Teddy charged through the doorway first.

Shards of wood splintered and flew from the frame around the thick hardwood front door. Kurz and Joey were on their heels, hands on the shoulders of Manes and Teddy. No immediate resistance as they all spread out from the foyer. Manes and Teddy went left, heading for the stairs; Kurz and Joey went right.

Corny kicked in the rear door within seconds of the front door breach. Parlefsky entered the modern kitchen first, followed by Del and then Corny. White cabinetry around the perimeter, under a vertical black-white-gray design of small glass subway tiles complimented the high-end stainless-steel appliances. A large island of slate blue cabinet draws topped with gray streaked marble countertop stood in the center of the kitchen. Sitting atop of the marble was a scarred butcher block cutting board with remnants of tomato, red onion, feta cheese and Genoa salami under two paring knives. Sandwich plates were strewn in the stainless steel country sink and empty Heineken bottles were on the counter in random display. Parlefsky gazed around the rectangular room and checked a small pantry closet. Del and Corny were right behind him eyeballing the archway leading out of the kitchen.

"Clear." Said Parlefsky.

Just as he was about to walk through a wide butler's pantry, a shot rang out and Parlefsky was hit in the upper thigh of his right leg. He immediately went down onto the bleached oak floor with a thud and a groan. Del and Corny backed up, taking either side of the doorway. They returned rapid fire with their Glocks. Then more rounds shot through the pantry, embedding the doorframe and the kitchen cabinets. Corny bent down and grabbed Parlefsky under his arms. He pulled him back into the kitchen while Del continued to deliver return fire after she replaced a full magazine from her belt.

Corny grabbed a dish towel from the dishwasher handle and placed it with force on Parlefsky's wound. Simultaneously, Corny moved his head left to his communication mike.

"Officer down! Parlefsky took a round to his thigh. Heavy bleeding. We need a bus to our location ASAP. Officer down! Taking fire from what appears to be an office through the butler's pantry," Corny explained.

"On our way from the front foyer. Gonna box them in. Hold tight!" Kurz responded. "We're coming to you. Johnson called Great Neck dispatch. Ambo on the way."

Corny took the leather belt off his pants and tied a makeshift tourniquet around Parlefsky's upper thigh. A high-pitched yelp escaped from Parlefsky's throat when Corny tightened the belt to try to stop the bleed.

Three gunman were taking cover in the center of the first floor, spread out between an office and the expansive den. Two large hunter green sofas and two upholstered easy chairs surrounded a huge glass coffee table. Each man carried Kalashnikov Light Machine Guns and semi-automatic hand guns. One gunman was hit immediately by Johnson who was the last one inside but rushed into the doorway of the den. He managed to hit a tall assailant in the neck with his assault rifle. Luckily he had been a skilled sniper in Afghanistan for two years prior to joining the police force. Joey and Kurz joined Johnson with return fire from the living room and Del crouched down zigzagging through the butler's pantry. When the two assailants tried to back into the pantry, she fired two rounds into the shoulder of one of them. The other guy dropped his weapon and raised his hands in the air.

Kurz ordered, "hands behind your head and down on your knees. Don't move!"

Johnson ran over to him and cuffed the assailant's hands behind his back. Joey checked on both of the injured men. The one shot in the neck was dead. He cuffed the man who was shot in the shoulder. Joey shouted, "where's the little boy?"

The injured man looked up at the staircase.

Teddy and Manes were upstairs already. Manes kept her left hand on Teddy's shoulder. "Now keep your head, Teddy. We need to get your boy out safely," said Manes.

"I'm good." He briefly turned his head to her. "Copy that Sergeant."

They quietly reached the second floor. Both of them got a message in their ear pods that the three men on the first floor were down. A slight smile formed on Manes's lips. She thought they now had some leverage. A wide hallway with four doors, two on each side, was in front of them. Two doors were open and two closed. Teddy ran to the first opened door and placed his back against the wall and doorframe. He whipped his body into the room with arms extended and Glock pointed. No one there. Manes made the same move into the second opened door. Again, empty.

Teddy led the way to one of the closed doors. He and Manes took either side of the doorway. With his Glock, Teddy knocked on the door gently. No answer. He knocked. Again, no answer. Manes nodded to Teddy to take the lead.

"You're men are down. It's over now. I am Detective Ted Huong, NYPD. That's my little boy in there. His name is Micah. I just want my boy back. You have nowhere to go. We have five detectives downstairs with plenty more on the way. Give yourselves up and no one else needs to get hurt."

Manes and Teddy just listened for any noise or response. Nothing. No sounds of movement, no crying from Micah, nothing. Sweat covered Teddy's face and his neck was tight. Manes remained calm, but worried about what was behind both doors. Supposedly there were two assailants on this floor. But where? And where was Micah?

Teddy tried calling out to Micah. "Micah, Micah. It's

daddy. Micah!"

Suddenly they heard a muffled cry. It came from the door on the left. Maybe they kept Micah in a closet. They both listened carefully. Again, the muffled cry came louder.

"Micah, daddy's coming. Micah..." called Teddy.

A second later, two shots blasted through the other closed door. Manes swiveled to her right and took a huge chance. She plugged three low shots through the same door. They both heard a loud thud. All of sudden, Corny appeared in the hallway and ran to Teddy with his Glock in his right hand. He assessed the situation and watched Manes kick the door in on the right. Corny and Manes trained their guns on the inside of the bedroom. One of the gunmen was laying on the floor with two bullet wounds in the gut. Corny cleared the rest of the bedroom while Manes checked the assailant for a pulse. A moment later they heard a loud smash of wood.

Teddy shouldered the bedroom door on the left and bulldozed his way inside. The room had a queen sized bed between two large windows. Under each window was a small cherrywood table. There were six high hats on the 8-foot ceiling and a cherrywood triple dresser on the left wall. A 60-inch Samsung television was mounted over the dresser. Teddy scanned the room and bounded toward the closet across the room.

"Micah, Micah!"

Teddy turned the brushed chrome door knob slowly, yanked the door open and aimed his Glock. He saw a cavernous walk-in space with two high hats in the ceiling and wood shelves on both sides. A terrified woman stood with Micah wrapped in a light-weight yellow blanket in her arms. Micah was crying and red-faced. Tears and mucous dripped down to his chin and chest. When he saw Teddy, Micah reached out to him, but the woman retreated a few feet. When she backed up out of the shadow, Teddy was able to see her holding a six-inch carving knife in her right fist.

CHAPTER 47

A loose mixture of dried copper and red leaves shuffled randomly under a stiff autumn breeze. A trace of undulating ripples underneath could be spotted if someone was looking at this patch of ground within a copse of tall maples surrounded by thick yews. No one was nearby when what appeared to be three stiff fingers poking through the blanket of leaves. Those fingers desperately reached up into the air revealing a long, weak arm shaking to and fro with jerky movements. Finally finding his buried face, this one hand clawed at the leaves to allow him to breathe in some fresh air. This poor man had been buried alive after he'd been viciously beaten. Confusion and jack-hammer pain rattled the inside of his head. His eyes remained closed. He tried calling out for help, but no sound emerged from his dry throat. His lips were cracked.

Twenty minutes later, four dark vehicles pulled to the side of the road. Doors opened and slammed.

"This is where the signal ends. It's been over an hour already. I suggest we spread out carefully to look for him. He could be in a house, garage, buried in the woods somewhere," explained Agent Belman.

Curlee shouted, "houses are far apart. Let's walk a grid of approximately 50 yards. Benitez and I will take the houses up the hill. Detectives Morris and Winchester take the woods up ahead on the right. Agents Belman and Myers take the woods across the road up to and including that stream. Agent Bolton, spread your men out across the road as well as up to those condos on the left."

Each team moved out quietly and efficiently. Fifteen minutes later Morris communicated to everyone on the search that he had found Agent Kussov. Morris's foot got snagged on the man's boot as he and Winchester shuffled through the bed of leaves between some tall trees. Before anyone else arrived, Winchester moved all of the earth and leaves off of his body with her gloved hands.

"Got him. Buried in the woods. He's alive but in bad shape. Head trauma. Winchester called 911. Ambo should be on the scene in 10."

Everyone rushed to the wooded burial spot. The FBI SWAT officers side-stepped down the slope on the opposite side of the road. Curlee and Benitez left a card with the homeowner of the first house they reached and ran down their pebbled driveway to the scene. Curlee and Belman bent over Dmitry, looking for signs of consciousness. His eyelids fluttered when they tried to talk to him. The fingers on his right hand flexed open and close. He growled in a low tone and opened his jaw.

Winchester yelled to the SWAT members that she needed a bottle of water. One female uniformed member rushed to her with an unopened bottle from their truck. Winchester twisted the cap and gently held the bottle to Dmitry's lips while Morris propped his shoulders up a bit.
Dmitry felt the cool wetness of the water and licked with his swollen tongue.

Suddenly a siren bleated it's tune loud and clear. "Okay, let the EMS guys do their thing. Let them through," yelled Curlee.

"I'm going with him to the hospital," exclaimed Belman.

"Good deal, Belman. We'll follow after we get forensics to analyze this scene," said Curlee.

Within minutes Dmitry was on a gurney and in the ambulance. Belman hopped up inside and closed the rear doors. The siren engaged once again. They transported him to Peconic Bay Medical Center. Their trauma center was top notch and hopefully Dmitry was a fighter. Curlee called Masters requesting a forensics team to their location ASAP.

All the agents and detectives gathered around SAC

Curlee and waited for instructions. There was a feeling of disappointment and hopelessness in the air. Even some of their exhaustion was evident in some body slouching and foot shuffling. Curlee exhaled slowly and dramatically. She looked up at the tree canopy on the edge of the woods and pondered their next steps. Dmitry had been their best lead and advantage in finding this cell of criminals.

"Okay. Benitez, call the office. See what Jason and his team had uncovered so far. We need a fucking break for God's sake. I am not letting those kids leave this island." Curlee looked around the circle at every member of her task force. "We got any coffee in that van?"

"Yes we do, SAC. Give me a minute," responded Watkins, a young SWAT officer.

Just then Curlee's iPhone buzzed in her pants pocket. She scooped it out and placed it quickly to her left ear. "Curlee," she barked.

CHAPTER 48

Corny ran into the second bedroom and found Teddy at the mouth of the walk-in closet. He placed his hand on Teddy's shoulder. "Easy, Ted, easy."

"Lady, I'm Teddy and I'm the boy's father. Put the knife down and give Micah to me. Nice and easy. Come on."

"If I do that, you gonna shoot me. No way. No way," said the woman.

"Look, I told you my name is Teddy and I'm not going to shoot you. I'm a NYPD detective. What is your name, ma'am?"

Teddy kept his eyes rotating between the knife in her hand and the woman's eyes. He noticed her light blue eyes began to water. He figured she was forced into this situation by the criminals.

"I'm Gina. Don't hurt me. They make me take care of this child. They force me. They said if I don't work for them, they kill my family back home."

Gina began to sob. Teddy moved two steps closer and tried to concentrate on talking her down. Micah was crying and screaming. He was squirming in the woman's arms.

"Gina, please. Give me the boy. Please. Your arms are probably getting sore holding Micah. Please, Gina, drop the knife."

Gina's shoulders suddenly drooped and she pleaded with Teddy, "but my family. You save my family back in Russia. You bring them to America. You bring them." Gina implored.

"We will see what we can do. I will speak with the district attorney and the State Department. Please, Gina. Drop the knife and give me my son."

Gina made eye contact with Teddy and then with Corny.

She finally understood that her situation was hopeless. She opened her fist and dropped the knife. Teddy rushed over to her and grabbed Micah and held him tight.

"Micah, it's Daddy. Micah, are you okay?"

Teddy backed out of the closet and snatched a few Kleenex from a square box on a shelf. He wiped Micah's nose and face. Corny rushed into the closet and grabbed Gina by the arm. He placed her hands behind her back and placed handcuffs on them while reading her Miranda rights. He had a brief thought about her family abroad and certainly believed her story about the threat on their lives.

"I'm gonna take Micah to the hospital, boss. Gotta call Maggie, too. She must be a wreck between her parents' attack and Micah being abducted."

"Of course, Teddy. Go! I'll call Woods and explain everything. Go be with your family."

Manes met Corny at the doorway of the bedroom. She shook her head which meant the other assailant was dead from her gunshots through the door. They both walked Gina out and down the stairs.

Two ambulances had arrived. One for Parlefsky. EMT's worked on him in the kitchen and took him out on a collapsible gurney. Another team of EMT's worked in the den on the assailant who was shot in the shoulder. Minutes later they got him into the second ambulance and took off. Kurz and Johnson took the third assailant outside after they read him his rights. They put him in the back of Johnson's cruiser. A few minutes later the coroner showed up for the first guy who was shot and killed as well as the dead assailant on the second floor. A Nassau County forensics van had parked in the driveway to process the entire house. Despite the drizzle, some of the neighbors and assorted onlookers began to gather behind the police tape. A few were shaking their heads, whispering to each other and craning they necks to see what was going on inside the front door.

Del walked up to Corny and laced her arm around his back. Corny gazed down at her pretty face and asked, "you okay?

No injuries or bullet holes?"

"No, I'm good. And you?"

Corny smiled. "Wow, you were a tiger in there with that Glock of yours. You saved my butt, Babe."

Del's grin widened.

"Just another reason why you're a keeper," whispered Corny.

"You know you saved Parlefsky's life in there. Now you can moonlight as an EMT if you have the time, big guy!" Del's eyes sparkled whenever she looked at Corny.

They were both exhausted. Corny had blood stains all over his white shirt and blue blazer. But they knew they needed to get back in the hunt for the kids, and especially for his nieces.

"Del, please call Woods and fill him in. I'll call my sister and Curlee."

"Copy that, chief."

Each of them retrieved their iPhones from their pockets and they walked to two separate areas on the front lawn to engage in their conversations.

Del and Corny met back in her canary yellow Hummer. She grabbed two bottles of Poland Spring and some power bars from the trunk. She got into the driver's seat because she knew Corny had almost no sleep in the past few days. She thought he'd take a cat nap for an hour or so on their way to the North Fork.

"How'd it go with Lieu?"

"He was happy to hear that Teddy rescued Micah. He also understands that we need to rejoin the task force out east. He had spoken with your sister yesterday when she called the office. She couldn't get you on the cell, but she left you a few messages," explained Del.

"Well, she's still frantic about the girls. I told her we're closing in, but Cara and Doug are beside themselves, especially with no news. She was crying and sobbing. I swore to her that I'd find them, Del."

Del looked directly into his bloodshot eyes and shook her head. She wrapped her slender yet muscular hands around

Corny's thick left wrist. "Honey, you know you cannot promise Cara and Doug that you'll bring the girls back. We're gonna try like hell, but you know in our business there are no promises."

"Del, what else can I say to her? How else can I comfort her? I know we're gonna get them back. I won't stop until I get them back from those Russian pigs!"

Del turned the key in the ignition and looked straight ahead. She initiated the navigation in the console and asked, "okay, where are we headed, boss? I know you spoke with Curlee. What's our status? Where are we at?"

"I'll fill you in on the way. Take the LIE to Riverhead. We'll meet up with the task force at Peconic Bay Medical Center."

"Why the medical center?"

"The FBI's second undercover agent nearly got killed today."

"Oh God. We need some solid leads for a change. Try to get some sleep, big guy."

Del gunned the engine and maneuvered out of the parking spot toward the highway.

CHAPTER 49

Leonid's cell phone buzzed. When he saw the caller, he uttered a few curses in Russian. He dreaded speaking to his boss. Leonid let it ring several times. He definitely needed to light a fresh Cuban cigar for this conversation. After biting off the tip and spitting it into the sink, Leonid held his gold plated lighter to the end as he rapidly sucked on the Cuban.

Curlicues of smoke escaped into the air above the kitchen counter.

"Aleksandr, I was just about to call you to keep you informed. How is everything in St. Petersburg, my friend?"

"Vasiliev, we are not friends," his boss responded sourly. "Get to the point. When will the goods be delivered? I need to see my funds deposited in my accounts. I know the FBI is on your tail and closing in fast. You'd better make those deliveries quickly. Once the jobs are done, we need to move in another direction."

"Aleksandr, we are working as fast as we can and as safely as we can. We already flushed out two undercover FBI agents, so there is no way they know where the farm is. I'm also sure that your Sophia has smartly covered her digital tracks so that our clients remain anonymous. No trace of delivery locations. Don't worry. The jobs are almost complete, Aleksandr," explained Leonid.

He took four or five quick puffs on his cigar and stared out the window.

"But, my dear Vasiliev, I do worry. My livelihood is at stake. And, if my operation takes a hit due to your incompetence, your remaining Russian relatives will unfortunately take a hit," said Aleksandr Kuznetsov, the Russian oligarch who created an entire global criminal enterprise.

"Aleksandr, there's no need for that kind of talk. I promise to get the jobs done and you'll get your funds deposited. I assure you. We are just now getting ready to make the deliveries as per your specifications. Everything is under control," explained Leonid.

Mikhail and Pavel walked into the kitchen and overheard some of the phone conversation. They knew who was on the other side of the phone. They stood silently and just watched their boss, acknowledging his anxiety.

"By the way my dear Vasiliev, how is your lovely family? I heard your opulent home in Bayside, Queens is most luxurious."

"Aleksandr, there is no need for any kind of threats, please. I guarantee that I will deliver."

Vasiliev, the next time we speak, I expect to see my bank balances upgraded. Period."

Leonid's boss hung up the phone and Leonid took more nervous puffs. Then he turned to his men and said, "I assume the kids are ready. Get the men assembled in the kitchen. It's time for all of you to get your delivery assignments, yeah?"

Pavel nodded, "you got it boss."

As Pavel and Mikhail walked out of the kitchen, Leonid's phone buzzed again. This time he was hoping for some positive news.

CHAPTER 50

Del's yellow Hummer rolled up to the main car port of the hospital. Corny was still asleep and slumped over to his left side. His cheek was slightly wet from dripped saliva. Del hopped out and met the parking attendant at the curb. She showed him her ID and asked him to park her ride in one of the reserved spots to the right of the front door. She briefly explained who they were and why they were at the hospital. She left the key fob in the cup between the two seats and opened the passenger side door.

"Hey, big guy. Wake up. We're here, boss. Come on."

Corny opened his eyes and stared at her pretty face but didn't move. His eyes had trouble focusing.

"Come on. We're at the Peconic Bay Med Center."

He rubbed his eyes and took a swig of tepid water from the bottle in the slot on his door. "Okay, okay. I'm coming, I'm coming." He swung his long legs out of the vehicle and stepped down on the sidewalk.

Del explained, "Curlee, Benitez, Morris, Winchester, and Belman are waiting for us on the third floor. Agent Dmitry Kussov is being treated in the trauma center.

"What are we waiting for? Let's go." Said Corny, who was now wide awake.

He led the way into the hospital and they both approached the information desk with ID wallets opened in their hands.

"We need to meet with the FBI agents and Suffolk County detectives on the third floor. We were told that would be on the trauma floor," explained Del.

A round-faced brunette in her mid-thirties was on the landline and raised one red nail-polished finger as she tried to finish her phone conversation. Five seconds later she hung up the receiver and partially stood to study their IDs. She wore a chrome name tag that read: *A. Malten* pinned to her beige sweater.

"Yes, of course, detectives. Take a left at the end of the counter and halfway down the hallway, you'll see a bank of elevators. Third floor."

"Thank you," responded Corny.

They followed the instructions and stepped off the elevator on the third floor. Del looked left and right. Corny spotted Agent Belman pacing back and forth down the hallway on the right. They approached as a few hospital workers eyeballed them with keen interest. Corny thought they weren't used to much police presence in this kind of local facility, especially on the North Fork.

"Sorry to hear about your man, Belman. How's he doing?" Asked Corny.

"Thanks. He's in critical condition. Medically induced coma." Belman's glassy eyes shot to the white speckled ceiling tiles. "He's a good man; balls of steel! It's hell going undercover like he did. One of the many honest Russian emigres who came to America to work hard to serve the public," said Belman. "It's bad enough I lost one undercover, Nikita Sidorov. She was 'made' at the Russian club, *Spasibo,* in Brooklyn. She was always in danger, but was able to get some solid intel for us. Both dedicated agents who put their lives on the line...to save others.

Corny placed his arm around Belman's shoulders and gave him a slight hug. "Any news yet about Dmitry from the doctors?"

"No, much too early to tell if he's gonna make it," replied Belman.

Del asked, "how the hell did they make Dmitry? He was on his way out here with members of the Russian cell. I don't get it."

"His back story was well-established...or so we thought. Unless they did a deep dive into his profile. These Russians have tremendous digital prowess. They're known for their hacking abilities." Belman shook his head.

"Where are the others? We need to keep moving before those kids disappear." claimed Del.

"One of the hospital administrators temporarily surrendered his office for us to coordinate our efforts. Come on, it's around the corner," said Belman.

As they turned the corner, they spotted Detective Morris in the hallway, facing a small window overlooking a garden courtyard, whispering on his cell. They walked into a corner office, small but private.

Winchester greeted them at the doorway. Her ramrod physique was worn and weary, but she managed a smile.

"How did it go with your Detective Huong? Did you guys get his kid back?" Asked Lakesha Winchester. She had a sculptured ebony face with sharp edges, but a soft heart, especially for children.

"Thanks for asking. Yes, we recovered Micah and he's safe and sound with his mom and dad. We had quite a fire fight at the north shore mansion where the kidnappers were holding him. But we took them down hard. One of our guys, Parlefsky from Nassau County, was shot in the thigh. Not life threatening," explained Corny.

"So where do we go from here," asked Del. "Any solid leads on the kids?"

Curlee hung up her iPhone and a small smile began to etch across her lips. "Good to see you guys. I heard you got the boy back alright."

"Yup, Teddy and his son were reunited. Thanks. What do we have, Agent Curlee?"

"Finally a lead. Remember the Estonian criminal, Egor Kukk, who was shot in the leg and then interviewed by Belman and Hernandez? Well he decided to sing like a bird. Very pissed that his boss shot him. Wants revenge and, of course, witness protection, which we promised him if his info panned out," explained Curlee.

Everyone in the room leaned in to listen to what Curlee had to say.

"We have a name and an address where we think they're keeping the kids. Take your phones out. A farmhouse at 412 Anchor Way, Southhold.

"Who's the boss of this operation?" Asked Corny.

"Leonid Vasiliev. We've liked him for prostitution, gun-running, extortion, and now for trafficking youngsters for sex," explained Benitez.

"Saddle up, boys and girls! Benitez, alert Agent Bolton to get his SWAT team in gear. They're in the parking lot downstairs.

"Copy that SAC," said Benitez.

Curlee shuffled her feet to be the first one out of the tiny office. Everyone else was on her heels. Winchester met up with Morris in the hallway and gave him an inquisitive look. She was mentally counting the number of phone calls and texts he was on today. Morris nodded, starred straight ahead and joined the group. They all rushed into one elevator.

CHAPTER 51

Some of the men stood. Others parked their butts on the hardwood stools that surrounded the center island. The dishes, bottles, and debris from their meal had been cleaned off the countertop. Leonid rested a manilla file folder   in front of him to the left of the custom Viking stovetop. And then he lit another Cuban, blowing rings at the ceiling.

"All of you will have your delivery assignments with specific details, yeah. Remember, if you do not deliver, none of us get paid. Gonna repeat. If you DO NOT DELIVER, none of us get paid. But more important is that, Aleksandr Kuznetsov will not get paid if you fuck up? Who knows what that means, yeah?" Questioned Leonid.

More smoke rings circled their heads like buzzards. None of the men answered his question. Why? Because they knew the consequences. They always lived in fear, whether they accepted it or not. They feared for their lives. They feared for their families, girlfriends or boyfriends, relatives. They were all locked into a serious risk/reward lifestyle. However, they felt their chances were much better in the criminal cell than working a nine-to-five or in a small business trying to make ends meet. Each of them swore allegiance to their bosses and knew that they could not escape the life once they committed to it.

"Do we understand each other? Yeah?" Asked Leonid. "And we know the Feds and detectives are coming for us. So we need to get our merchandise delivered fast. Okay?"

All of the men nodded or whispered, 'da'. Each of them gazed around the circle of men with intensity. Each wondered which ones would succeed or fail. But, each man worked with the members of the cell before and knew that they were tough and determined.

Leonid opened the folder and passed out the assignments. The men read their delivery specifications carefully and completely. Names, addresses, delivery routes, transportation details, etc. Of course, at the top of each document was the name(s) of the person(s) to be delivered. Leonid carefully matched the kid to the deliverer to minimize any problem that might arrive during the trip. Leonid felt it necessary to read aloud the assignments.

"Alexey and Boris you have the twins, Emma & Jordan Brady. Watch them very carefully. They might have the confidence to plan an escape since there are two of them and they are very close. Plus we all know who their uncle is. NYPD Detective Cornelius Prince. No doubt he'll be coming for them. Be careful and smart."

"Victor, you have Kimberly Weinstein. She's the oldest and seems to have much common sense. Watch her like a hawk. Stanislav, your delivery is Wesley McArthur. He's the youngest and very vulnerable. Make sure he doesn't attract attention by crying or screaming to people along the route. Mikhail, yours is the toughest kid. She takes no shit from anyone. Carmen Rodriguez needs to be drugged for the entire trip. Make sure, yeah? And Pavel, you got Brianna Park. She should be easy, but be careful too. Yeah?"

"Any questions about the delivery routes? Any questions about anything else?"

No one challenged Leonid.

Mikhail asked, "who's gonna watch your back, boss?"

"Don't worry about me. I got two more guys coming to help me get out of the North Fork. I'll see you guys at *Spasibo* after your jobs are done."

"Okay. Study your sheets again and let's get moving, yeah? Make sure to zip tie their hands behind their backs and bring bottles of water."

Leonid puffed on the remnants of the Cuban and looked nervously around the kitchen. He was thinking of how this was the second hardest part of the job. Delivery. After studying their directions, the men stood and took the ties and water and began to walk out of the kitchen into the living room. The kids were all cleaned, dressed nicely and waiting nervously for the inevitable. A few were crying and some were trying to comfort those who were losing it.

Leonid followed the men into the living room and watched them secure their deliveries with the black plastic zip ties. He wasn't a religious man at all, but he said his own little prayer, of course, in Russian. The kids were herded out to the vehicles and into back seats. Leonid smiled and waved to them as if they were all going to a Broadway show.

CHAPTER 52

Two dark blue sedans, one bright yellow Hummer and two black SUV's sped along Sound Avenue to Middle Road straight into Southhold, sirens blaring and lights flashing. The main road, Route 25, was too heavily trafficked and shot through too many small towns. According to the Agent Curlee's lead vehicle's navigation, they should make it to the Anchor Way address in twenty six minutes. Benitez was at the wheel.

Del was driving her Hummer behind Morris and Winchester. Corny's phone buzzed. He answered immediately. "Cara?"

"Corny, it's Doug. What's going on, bro? Cara and I are out of our heads. Getting any closer to getting our girls back?" Asked Doug.

"We're on our way to Southhold. We believe one of the criminal bosses has the girls stowed away in a house near the bay. How is Cara holding up?" Asked Corny.

"Not good, Corny. She's out back with your parents, chain-smoking. She's a wreck and so am I. How can I help?"

"God she hasn't smoked since she had a miscarriage years ago."

"What can I do? I'm sitting on my hands here. Going crazy."

"Doug, we got a solid lead and we have the FBI agents, SWAT and other detectives all speeding to the location as we speak," Corny explained.

"Are the girls still on the island, Corny? Tell me the truth!" Demanded Doug.

"I am telling you the truth. We aren't sure, Doug. But we won't stop 'til we find them. That I can promise you."

Cara came into the house from the yard. She grabbed the phone. "Corny, where are my girls? You promised me…". Tears welled up in her dark brown eyes. "Corny, what's going on. How close are you?" Pleaded Cara.

"Cara, hang on. We are ten minutes from Southold. We believe they're keeping the girls there. I promise, we will not stop until we find them. Promise, honey, promise."

"You call me as soon as you see my girls, you hear me?"

"Yeah. I hear you."

Cara hung up. Corny looked straight ahead and his eyes watered, too.

"Okay, boys and girls. We're five miles out. Everyone kill the lights and sirens. We go in hot and quiet," instructed Agent Curlee.

"Copy that," said Winchester.

Corny and the SWAT commanders echoed agreement.

Agent Benitez followed the navigation instructions off the main road onto secondary and tertiary roads. There were some sedans, a few SUV's and one bakery truck that passed them going the other way. He turned left onto Anchor Way and spotted an old brown farmhouse with several trees around it. There was some acreage behind the house with small pine trees in neat rows. Each vehicle skidded to a halt on the gravel front yard behind three assorted sedans. A few lights were on in the two story building.

The SWAT officers were out of their SUV's first and approached the front door and the rear of the building. Curlee and Benitez ran up onto the porch behind the SWAT assault team. Corny and Del joined them. Winchester and Morris were ordered to the rear. All wore bullet proof vests and carried assault rifles in their hands, which were, no doubt, slick with sweat.

"On my go, copy?" Asked Curlee into the comms.

All agreed and responded.

"Three, two, one, GO!"

CHAPTER 53

Sweat covered Corny's forehead and beaded the small of his back. Del's heart fluttered like a humming bird's wings. They both silently prayed that this was the moment of successful rescue. Instantaneously, upon Curlee's 'Go' command, SWAT officers swung their battering rams into the front and rear wooden doors, sending splinters into the air. The SWAT guys charged in first yelling "FBI, drop your weapon!"

Curlee and Benitez took the first floor and Corny and Del slowly took the steps to the second level. All of them trained their rifles along their lines of sight and each had a high beam flashlight adjacent to their guns.

On the main level, Curlee called out loud, "FBI. Drop your weapon!" They met the rear door assault team in the large kitchen area after checking each room and behind every door. SWAT agents ran down the basement stairs. After searching every nook and cranny, each of them called out, 'clear'!

On the second level, Del and Corny called out, 'clear'! After searching, they trotted down the steps and met the rest of the assault team in the kitchen area.

"Fuck, they're gone. This was their staging area, but we're too late again. Every God damn time, they're one step ahead of us! Fuck!" Exclaimed Curlee.

Winchester piped up, "I certainly hope the Russians don't have someone on the take inside the FBI or within our departments, feeding them info." She shot a glance at Morris. The others turned their heads toward Morris with acute interest.

Morris scowled, "Winchester, if you have something to say to me, bring it on. I got years and years of dedicated service on the 'Job' with a sparkling record. Shit, I taught you plenty on how to be a freakin' detective. Now you're questioning me? Pointing in my direction?" His face turned crimson from a pop in his blood pressure.

"Sid, just saying you've been on your phone texting quite a bit without a good explanation," Winchester responded.

Curlee rushed over to Morris and placed her face 6 inches from Morris's. Eye-to-eye she challenged him. "Detective, do you have something to tell me that I need to know?"

Sid Morris stared back into her grey eyes. He said nothing for quite a few seconds. And then, he said, "No, Special Agent in Charge. I'm good."

"Are you sure? 'Cause I know you're about to retire and maybe you see something coming your way to make your pension a little bit fatter?"

"Bullshit, Special Agent Curlee. You want to inspect my phone?" He scooped it out of his pocket and shoved it into her chest.

"Agent Benitez, take the detective's phone and check the call record." She continued to lock in his gaze. "Just to be totally clear and transparent."

Benitez took his phone, asked for the code and ran his finger over the keys to check the call record of the past three days. After a few minutes, Benitez said, "looks clean. But we all know texts can be erased."

Curlee said, "give the phone back to him. Trusting you, Detective. Remember we have a sacred job to do. If I find out you're lying, you'll never see the light of day, and you can forget about a comfortable retirement on some lake somewhere."

"Copy that Special Agent," retorted Morris.

Everyone in the room made a skeptical sigh of relief.

"Now we gotta find out where the kids are going. They must be in transit as we speak," said Corny. "Any luck getting info from the young genius techs your office hired, Curlee?"

"Nothing yet. Calling Majors now. Let's see if they made any headway." She walked over to the window and dialed Majors directly. After a brief dialogue, she shook her head and pocketed her phone.

The detectives quickly rummaged through the kitchen and the other rooms for any trace of documents or scraps of paper with information indicating where they were taking the kids. Unfortunately they found nothing. The criminals were smart and careful. They knew how to cover their tracks.

Two phones buzzed. Winchester and Morris dug out their iPhones. Winchester answered first. "Winchester." She listened to the caller. "Yeah, got it. Place a BOLO (Be On the Look Out) on the van. It definitely could be related to our case. Let us know ASAP if you find it. Okay."

Morris asked, "What was that about?"

"A report about a stolen bakery van, New York tags. Didn't we see a bakery truck going in the opposite direction on our way here?" Winchester asked.

Agent Curlee said, "I bet we missed them by only minutes. Shit, they could have had all of the kids in that truck."

Benitez said, "should we call for a chopper, boss?"

"Do it, Benitez. Do it now! We gotta find that truck. And Benitez, get a forensic team over here to process the house and the three vehicles outside."

CHAPTER 54

An FBI's CIRG (Critical Incident Response Group) helicopter got permission to land on the helipad of the Peconic Bay Medical Center. Agents Belman and Myers walked toward the landing site, keeping their heads down. The experienced pilot set it down slowly without incident as the agents climbed aboard. Myers took a back seat and Belman leapt in the front seat. Both adjusted their headsets and tested their mikes.

"Welcome aboard, Agents. I'm Agent Scott Levy. Glad to have you fellas."

Belman responded, "Agent Bruce Myers in the back and I'm Jack Belman. Any sightings yet of the bakery truck?"

"Just before I landed, I got a report from the office. Surveillance cameras caught sight of the stolen truck heading toward the bay. Our people think they're headed for Brick Cove Marina."

"Scott, was the Coast Guard alerted? We don't want to lose them out at sea," said Belman.

"Yes, the Coast Guard are en route. We can box them in at the marina. Agent Curlee and her crew are on their way as well. We'll get 'em."

"I sure as hell hope those kids are in that truck. I figure their most likely plan is to traffic them to their destinations by boat. We gotta get ahead of them this time."

Myers asked, "how long to the marina, Scott?"

"Figure about 5-10 minutes."

"Do we know the boat they're taking?"

"I spoke with SAC Masters. His people are trying to nail it down. They're getting information from the harbor master of Brick Cove as we speak."

"Okay. Hopefully we'll know more once we get there. Anyplace to land this bird nearby?"

"Doubtful, but we'll eyeball it once we approach."

"Copy that."

CHAPTER 55

The driver of the bakery truck parked across two spots in the parking lot. Leonid climbed down from the front passenger seat and craned his neck, searching for the Feds. He thought, '*so far so good*'. He and his two men calmly walked to the pier. He searched the slips with his eagle eyes for the cabin cruiser that was purchased last year by a phony holding company. Within a few minutes he spotted it. It was a navy blue and white Intrepid 409 Valor with a length of 40 feet, beam of 11'1" and 3 outboard motors. It was built for performance with loads of comfort and space accommodating a large group of people.

As the men approached the cruiser, Leonid called out loud, "Hey Benny!"

As soon as Benny heard his boss's foghorn voice, he ducked out from below decks and appeared on the aft deck. Benny had three or four days of a salt and pepper scruff on his face and wore a green tattered captain's hat. His average height and weight was loosely contained in a plum-colored Long Island sweat shirt and black sweat pants. A thin cheroot was hanging from his thin lips.

Leonid and his men came aboard and continued looking for the Feds in the parking lot and at the road beyond.

"Welcome aboard boss. We're just about ready to cast off. My guys are finishing below and will be up in a jiffy, as the Americans say."

"Are the young ladies down below as I requested, Benny?"

"You bet they are. A fine looking group of sweeties, Leonid. Just the way you like 'em."

"Were they loud enough for them to be noticed by other boaters as they came aboard?"

"Of course, boss. Their mini-dresses and high heels got the attention of several dirty old men and some dirty old ladies on the dock. Made sure of it."

"That's my man, Benny."

Leonid helped himself to four fingers of Grey Goose vodka over ice in a large tumbler that was sitting on a small glass table on the rear deck. Then he took a seat in one of the captain's chairs under the canopy. He removed a Cuban from his shirt pocket and cut the tip with his teeth. While lighting his cigar, he was thinking of how he would play this next scene with the Feds, who, no doubt, would catch up to him. His men kept watching the dock area.

"Benny, where is my caviar? I need caviar with my vodka, Benny. And it's time to shove off. We need to get ahead of these bastards. Come on, Benny."

Smoke rings hit the inside of the navy blue canopy and dissipated. And then Leonid heard it. The whirring noise of a helicopter engine.

CHAPTER 56

"There's the bakery truck! Sitting in the parking lot across two and half regular spots," said Belman.

"Yeah, I see it. Now the question is, did they leave the marina already or not? It would help if we knew the name of the boat or had a description," replied Levy.

Belman ordered, "Bruce, get on the line with SAC Masters. Find out if they discovered what boat belongs to these guys."

Agent Myers punched in a speed dial number on his iPhone. After two rings, Masters picked up himself. They had a brief exchange. Bruce hung up.

"The harbor master found that one cabin cruiser was listed as belonging to Superior Financial Corporation, a holding company created in Talinn, Estonia. Get this, Jack. The boat's handle is: *One Step Ahead.*"

"Bingo! Freakin' bingo!"

"What's the slip number where it docks?" Asked Levy.

"The harbor master said it rests at aisle three, spot 12," responded Myers.

Belman asked, "anywhere we can land, Scott?"

"Afraid not. We need to wait for Agent Curlee and her people to search the marina. In the meantime, let's circle the marina and then the bay."

"Copy that. Let's go. Gonna call Curlee to see how close she is."

"Agent Curlee, Belman here. We're circling the marina, but haven't spotted their cruiser as of yet. How close are you?"

"Pulling in now, Belman. We have the aisle and slip number. About to approach on foot. Looking for a navy blue and white 40-foot cabin cruiser with the name: *One Step Ahead.* Isn't that a fucking hoot?"

"So these Russians have a sense of humor, huh?"

"Keep circling. Could be they're still in the bay. Be in touch." Curlee hung up.

The FBI tactical team took point. Assault rifles at the ready, they crabbed-walked to aisle three and cautiously approached slip number 12. As they got closer, they slowed down. Slips number 12 and 13 were both empty. They lowered their rifles and turned to Agent Curlee.

Agent Bolton, commander of the tactical team, shouted, "They are gone, Agent Curlee. We need the Coast Guard here, now!"

Curlee immediately called the Coast Guard commander. Fortunately they had a coastal patrol boat, the U.S.S. Ridley (WPB 87328), patrolling close by, out of the Montauk Station. The commander assured Curlee that they'd be able to pick up her and her agents in 10-20 minutes at the east end of the marina.

"Okay. Agent Bolton, have your people canvas the entire dock. Someone had to know who boarded that cruiser and when. Also find out when the boat left the pier."

"Copy that, Agent Curlee."

"We need to get to the east end of the marina for the Coast Guard pick up in 10. Let's mount up, people."

By the time they parked at the east end, U.S.S. Ridley was slowly coming into view and heading toward the marina. Curlee, Benitez, Corny, Del, Morris and Winchester boarded the Coast Guard patrol boat. The FBI tactical team would be overkill since there were a good number of armed Coast Guardsmen on board already. Commander Bolton and his tactical team remained on the dock. After brief introductions, Agent Curlee explained who they were looking for and why. It didn't take long for the patrol boat to cast off. They were also in communication with Agent Levy in the chopper, searching in 10-mile semi-circles from the marina.

Agent Curlee's phone buzzed and she picked up. "Go for Curlee."

"We got two witnesses on the dock that saw three men and presumably a captain usher 5 or 6 young women dressed… uh, provocatively, I guess, onto the boat approximately an hour ago. Then three more men boarded about a half hour ago. The boat left the pier soon after that."

"Good work, Bolton. Please wait for further instructions."

Agent Curlee reentered a chamber behind the bridge where Benitez and the four detectives were waiting.

"I got a report from Commander Bolton. There are several young ladies in 'evening wear' aboard the cruiser along with seven men, presumably armed. They could be the kids they're trafficking. I hope to God we can catch them and put an end to this nightmare."

Winchester said, "Where the hell are they taking them? Caribbean? Around Montauk Point?"

No one ventured a guess and only hoped they could put a stop to this Russian crew.

Del exclaimed, "I can only imagine what their parents are going through."

Within 30 plus minutes, the surveillance and radar systems on the patrol boat picked up a few boats within 20-40 miles of the marina. One was a small boat and one was, by estimate, close to a very fast 40-foot cabin cruiser. At one point, radar indicated the two cruisers may have crossed paths. The Coast Guard patrol boat headed for the latter at full speed and caught sight of the 40-footer, 35 miles southeast of the marina. Even though they had partial sun mixed with some cloud cover, the waters were extremely choppy due to a 30 mph wind.

"Corny, how much longer do you think it will take to overcome their cruiser?"

"I don't know. What's wrong, Del?"

Del's face lost all color. She grasped the gun-metal gray handrail with both fists. She stretched her neck to gaze at the high puffs in the sky. The salt air streamed into her nostrils, but her stomach did tumbles reminding her of the clunky clothes dryer in their apartment.

"Del, are you okay?"

"No, no."

Del leaned over the handrail and vomited into the undulating waters. Then she wretched several more times and managed to expel spittle from her sour mouth. Corny rushed over to support her and grabbed her shoulders.

"It's alright. Let it go. It's alright."

The patrol boat kept its fast pace and cut a swath through the waves' crests and troughs, heading toward its target. Corny plucked a partially filled water bottle from his back pocket and offered it to Del. After a few minutes of shaking while keeping her eyes shut, she took the water bottle and unscrewed the cap. She took small sips and spit overboard. Then she took a long drag and swallowed. She turned to Corny, revealing teardrops streaming down her cheeks. Del stared into his eyes.

"Is this what I think it is, Del?"

"Don't know yet. But, could be."

"Have you had other moments of sickness?"

"This is the first one. Maybe time to take the test, Corny."

Corny cradled her face in his hands and smiled.

Once the commander saw he was closing in on the rogue cruiser, he took the mike from its mounting on the bridge. His men were already on deck with assault rifles and Kevlar vests. The agents and detectives were behind his men.

In a firm voice, the commander spoke. "This is the United States Coast Guard! Cut your engine immediately and be prepared for us to board!"

CHAPTER 57

Four Coast Guardsmen, Curlee and Benitez, as well as the four detectives boarded the Intrepid 409 Valor cabin cruiser on the edge of the large, open stern. They were greeted by three men whose hands were in the air, indicating they had no intention of an armed conflict. The second in command of the U.S.S. Riley, Lieutenant Briggs, took the lead.

"Are there any weapons on board?" Asked Lieutenant Briggs. He directed his question to the scrappy man wearing a green captain's cap, who stood in front of the other two beefy guys.

"Good afternoon officer. I'm Bennie Crafton, captain of this fine cruiser. What can I do for you?"

"Mr. Crafton, we boarded your cruiser because the FBI has a search warrant to inspect your vessel. And I repeat, are there any weapons on board?" Asked Briggs.

Two of the guardsmen took positions behind the other two men standing with Bennie. The third guardsman, Agent's Curlee and Benitez, along with Corny and Del, guns at the ready, ducked their heads and entered the lower cabin down a short flight of steps.

Bennie explained, "my guys always carry, to make sure our boss's investment is safe and secure." He turned around to his two bodyguards and nodded. Each of them removed their semi-automatic hand guns and placed them on the table in the corner. The two guardsmen retrieved the weapons and patted down the two guys as well as Bennie.

Briggs asked, "who is below decks and what is the purpose for your cruise Mr. Crafton?"

Bennie replied, "Just a party boat, officer. We have a few

guys who paid big bucks to have some fun with a few party girls. We're not breaking any laws here. Your people went down to check and they can search the entire boat."

"Drugs or booze below decks?"

"No drugs, just booze, officer. And the girls are all of legal age. Promise." When Bennie smiled he revealed a missing incisor in his upper jaw. The rest of his teeth were yellowed, presumably from smoking.

The large lounge area below was well appointed. A lavish, mirrored bar, stocked with top shelf liquors and liqueurs extended twenty feet across the cruiser. Sky blue silk curtains framed each rectangular window on each side of the room. Navy blue plush sofas and chairs were strategically affixed to the stained oak floor boards. Four of the party girls were standing at the bar and two more were huddled in conversation on one of the sofas. A sturdy six-foot handsome man, dressed casually, was serving drinks at the bar. The other two men stood on opposite sides of the room glaring at the girls, who wore mini-skirts or dresses.

Agents Curlee and Benitez relieved the men of their handguns and questioned them individually. Corny and Del briefly interviewed the girls. None of the people below decks revealed anything useful. Benitez and the detectives searched the lounge and only found a few pills and some marijuana.

Del was the first to emerge from below decks. "Lieutenant, the girls down below are not the kids we are looking for. They are, indeed, paid party ladies. We recovered several handguns on the three men and we seem to be missing one other man reported to have boarded the cruiser at the dock. No one admits to knowing anything about this other man."

Briggs moved closer to Bennie and stared into Bennie's rheumy black eyes. "Where is the seventh man, Mr. Crafton?"

"Lieutenant, there are only six men on board and six little ladies. I told you, it's a party cruise. There's nobody else here."

Agents Curlee and Benitez stepped back up to the stern of

One Step Ahead.

"Well, Mr. Crafton, the party is over. You and your vessel will need to return to the marina. The FBI will need to question all of you more thoroughly. Is that clear?" Asked Curlee.

"Well that's a crying shame since these guys paid good money to have this little soiree with these pretty little girls," said Bennie. He cleared his throat of some mucus and spit overboard.

Lieutenant Briggs explained, "All of you will be restricted to the cabin below and one of my guardsman will pilot your vessel back to the marina."

Bennie raised his hands high, shook his head, and nodded for his bodyguards to follow him down below.

Sergeant Mendelson and Lieutenant Briggs accessed the bridge and Mendelson began to become familiar with all of the systems on the bridge console. Briggs radioed the Commander of the patrol boat and explained what the search uncovered and did not uncover. They both knew that they needed to return the cruiser to shore, since Agent Curlee needed to interview the men and women sailing aboard. She hoped that they could attain some leads in order to find Leonid Vasiliev and the abducted youngsters.

When Mendelson was ready, he cranked the engines and followed the patrol boat back to Brick Cove.

CHAPTER 58

The smaller yacht sailed through Shelter Island Sound and into Noyack Bay, rocking and bouncing in ten to twelve foot swells. It took a good hour to finally dock at Sag Harbor Cove Yacht Club on Water Street.

A burly man with a bowling ball gut, curly black hair and a cigar stub protruding from his fleshy lips stepped onto the pier. A wide, muscular man was a few yards behind him with his head on a swivel. Both men slowly walked along the wooden walkway to the concrete parking lot. A navy blue SUV was supposed to meet them, but did not arrive yet. Leonid lit another Cuban cigar and took his phone out.

"Victor, where the fuck are you? Did you deliver the goods? If not, you're behind schedule, yeah."

"Boss, I'm on my way. I had some traffic before, but no problem with the delivery, boss. Give me about 10 minutes."

"I need to grab a bite, Victor. Move your ass."

Leonid hung up the phone. His bodyguard, Aleks, looked at Leonid and shrugged his shoulders. He took a cigarette from the pack in his shirt pocket and lit the end, drawing in the smoke.

"Don't worry, boss. Victor's a good man. He'll be here. At least we know he made his delivery."

"Yeah, yeah. I'm worried about the others."

Leonid puffed several times and blew the smoke into the air.

"Hey, Aleks, I fooled those fucking Feds, yeah? I got them following the other boat. They'll never find me or those kids. Never. Yeah?"

"There's no one smarter than you, boss. You're still

getting away with shit and they can't touch you."

The two of them paced back and forth for another 5-10 minutes. And then the SUV pulled up. Leonid took the passenger seat and Aleks took a back seat.

"Victor, about fucking time. You know of a good Italian place we can eat? I'm starved."

"Yeah. I know a place. You can get whatever you want. Great food, boss."

"Let's go. By the way, was the client happy with the goods?"

"Boss, the client was very happy. As soon as I took her out of the SUV and handed her over, I saw the client developing a huge boner in his pants. He definitely liked what he saw."

"Did you watch the money transfer, Victor?"

"Of course, boss. Right into our company account. Easy peasy!"

"That's a good boy, Victor. Fuck, let's eat."

CHAPTER 59

Two large FBI vans met the agents and detectives at the marina. One accommodated the party girls and one carried the six men back to the FBI office in Melville. Agent Curlee and her agents needed to question all of them in detail in hopes of getting a real lead to find the abducted young people and Leonid Vasiliev.

Corny owed his sister a call to let her know the progress of the case. She was beside herself, trying to envision where her two girls had been trafficked and if they would ever be returned to her. Doug was hopeful and tried to be positive, as were Corny's parents, who stayed over in Cara's house for the duration of this horrendous episode in their lives.

Del made some phone calls as well. First, she called Lieutenant Woods to catch him up to speed. It turned out that he had been continuously informed of what transpired by SAC Masters. The two of them briefly worked on a previous case several years ago, so they had history together. Del also called Teddy to find out how his son was, as well as his in-laws. Teddy reported that Micah was doing exceptionally well, not really remembering what had happened during the kidnapping. He was just happy to be back with his parents. Teddy's father-in-law suffered severe head trauma that resulted in an acute concussion. He remained in the hospital for a few days for observation. Maggie's mom was treated and released to go home late in the day of the attack.

The party girls revealed that they truthfully had been working for an escort service and all they knew was that for a thousand dollars each, they were to provide company for some men on a party boat for a few hours. Agent Benitez contacted the woman who supposedly owned the service, a Sheila Barrett. She claimed that her service was hired by a wealthy investment banker from Ottawa for some clients. The banker chose to remain nameless. She said she had no knowledge of the name, Leonid Vasiliev. The computer analysts in the FBI bullpen did a deep dive into the escort service and discovered that the company that funded the escort service was Superior Financial Corporation. This was the same company that owned and operated the 40-foot cabin cruiser, *One Step Ahead.* And coincidentally, this was the same company that bought the smaller boat in slip number 13, the other empty slip at the pier.

"Well now we know where the seventh man disappeared to. The two cruisers met at a predetermined spot miles from the marina and 'Mr. Seventh Man' transferred to the smaller vessel, knowing full well that we'd be following the 40-footer," explained Detective Morris.

His partner, Lakesha Winchester looked at Morris with renewed admiration when he posed that theory.

"Good point detective. I remember from watching the radar on the bridge that at one point the cruisers' paths crossed. And that seventh man is Leonid Vasiliev, I bet," responded Agent Curlee.

"What is the name of the smaller cruiser? Anyone know the name and where it may be now?" Asked Corny.

Agent Benitez turned to one of their computer analysts for assistance. "David, please call the Coast Guard station in Montauk and see if you can get that information. They know that the U.S.S. Ridley was out with us tracking these cruisers from Brick Cove Marina."

"Copy that Agent Benitez."

"What did you get from interviewing the men, Agent Curlee?" Asked Corny.

"Nothing. Mouths shut. They claimed not to recognize Leonid Vasiliev and claimed no knowledge of any Russian criminal cell. They also claimed no knowledge of any kids being abducted," explained Agent Curlee.

"They are much more afraid of the Russian big shots, here and in Russia, than anything we can throw at them. Threats to family abroad and threats to their own lives in America trump any prison time or worse. It's a closed coven, so to speak. They pledge allegiance to the crime syndicate just like any other criminal group. The same as the Albanians, the Italians, the Chinese, etc.," said Agent Benitez.

Corny said, "so even if we catch up to Vasiliev and capture him, we may never get any information regarding where the kids are being trafficked."

"Our best bet is to either keep pressuring the cell members we have in custody or hope that your wunderkinds in that back room can find the source of the cell from Russia," said Detective Winchester.

Corny jumped in. "There is another avenue we have not explored as of yet."

Everyone in the room gazed at Corny with patient interest.

"I hinted at this road before. Why don't we sit on Vasiliev's wife and kids with our surveillance equipment. At some point one of them, either the wife, son or daughter may try to contact him via text, email or phone. Then of course we can try to triangulate and find his position."

Agent Curlee raised her eyebrows and agreed. "Let's set up that surveillance immediately. Benitez, contact Agent Belman and assign him and Myers to that stakeout. We need to move on this fast. Time is running out for those kids."

"Copy that. I'll get Levy to pilot them back to Queens to get started."

Agent Curlee turned to the kitchen area and poured herself a cup of black coffee. She faced the detectives in the room. "It's time to kick some ass. I want to know what those three computer geeks have come up with!"

CHAPTER 60

Cornbluth, Steinberger, Levine, Block were some of the names on the elaborately engraved headstones that could be seen from the narrow road. The dark blue SUV slowly made its way down aisle five and made a left at row H. The driver pulled over after coasting for two and half short blocks. He got out of the vehicle and walked toward the rear. It took a few seconds to spot the man he was due to meet. The description he was given was that of a slightly rotund 30-ish guy, average height with short dirty blond hair.

A light drizzle dotted the windshield and Victor's black leather bomber jacket. He walked over to the man facing a large granite headstone that had the name Warren etched in black letters. This man had just placed three large stones on the top of the headstone which was typical of Jewish tradition marking a visit to a deceased loved one or friend.

"What do you got for my boss, Bradley? We need to keep ahead of your guys," said Victor.

Bradley Warren turned to meet Victor's gray-eyed stare. He regretted his business arrangement with Leonid and his cronies. He absolutely hated himself for getting roped in with these Russian mobsters, but at the time he felt he had no choice. A ferocious gambling habit consumed his life. His wife eventually divorced him and he was only allowed to see his two young kids only once a month. When Leonid and his organization discovered that Bradley worked for the FBI as a computer intelligence analyst, they seriously 'had him by the balls'. The deal was that as long as he supplied Leonid with pertinent information about the FBI's progress, they would reduce his debt by a substantial percentage.

"Well, Leonid did fool them by his cabin cruiser stunt. They were convinced that the abducted kids would be on that boat. They also couldn't figure out to where the hell he had disappeared. By the time they realized that he may have transferred to the smaller cruiser out in the bay, they lost track of the second vessel," explained Bradley.

"Excellent. The boss still has a few tricks up his sleeve. What else should we be aware of? I know you owe 14 or 15K, my friend, and I'd love to help you with that. But you have to give us something really good."

"Victor, the FBI brought in three young hackers who excel at finding information on the dark web. They seem to have the know-how that our experienced analysts do not," said Bradley.

"What did they find out? Have they tracked the global communications from Eastern Europe?" Asked Victor.

"I really don't know. They work in a separate room from the bullpen. Everything is hush, hush regarding their work."

"Shit. This can fuck up our whole operation."

"I have absolutely no control over their involvement. I can only try to find out what they know already," explained Bradley.

"Do not fuck us, Bradley. This is what we pay you for. Understand?"

Bradley stared over Victor's shoulder. He watched the tiny raindrops plop onto his father's headstone. He tried to figure out a way to get the information from those young super hackers.

Bradley responded, "I know, I know. I'll do my best."

"Fuck your best. Just fucking do it. We need to stay ahead of them."

Victor turned away from Bradley and walked back to the SUV. The rain was coming down at a nice clip now as the SUV's wheels kicked up some of the gray gravel on the road.

A black sedan with the motor running sat outside of the cemetery entrance. Two agents watched the discussion between the two men in the rain in row H. The agent in the passenger seat held a powerful set of Bushnell Rangefinder binoculars to his eyes. The driver hefted a Nikon SLR with a long range zoom lens. He snapped several shots of each guy separately, as well as together. After a few minutes, they recognized one of the men.

"Now we know who the leak is, Sam."

"SAC Masters had been suspicious of our man Warren for about a week, Joseph."

"The guy in the leather jacket must be one of Vasiliev's men, Sam."

"Once we pull the photos, we can identify him through facial rec."

"Yeah and he's awfully friendly with our very own Bradley Warren."

"How did Masters spot Warren as the mole?" Asked Joseph.

"He noticed Bradley texting during work and his short lunch trips out of the building, Joseph. You know most of us stay put during the day. We all use the cafeteria most of the time," explained Sam.

"And Curlee and Benitez thought that Detective Morris was the weak link. I could definitely imagine the aging detective seeing the need for some extra cash for his retirement," said Joseph.

"And now, Bradley will be facing Federal charges. I wonder what his motivation was for sleeping with the Russians."

"We will soon find out. Okay, time to report to Masters. Let's go."

CHAPTER 61

Curlee and Benitez led the detectives into the small, stark conference room where six laptops were set up at random locations on the glass-topped conference table. The room had four large windows with brown slatted metal blinds, drawn. Ten high hats spread energy-efficient illuminance across the rectangular surface, giving the three young computer geeks more than enough light for their work. Most of their time was spent on each of their two laptops. Yellow legal pads were provided for taking occasional notes. A large coffee urn with plenty of cups sat on a table near the windows. A host of sandwiches, danish, fresh fruit and water bottles encouraged Jason, Molly and Holden to remain in the room to work on their time-sensitive project. Their work was crucial to finding the abducted teens sooner than later.

"Okay, boys and girls. We need information and we need it now! What have you got?" Asked Agent Curley.

Molly and Holden looked at Jason to speak for the team. "I think we may have nailed down the source of communication to the Russian-American criminal cell. We had some possibilities, but nothing concrete...until twenty minutes ago."

Beads of perspiration were slowly dripping from Jason's forehead, even though the room temperature was 71 degrees. He held Molly's and Holden's gaze for a moment before he committed to their findings. The importance of their search overwhelmed all three of them.

"Okay, let's have the info. What? Come on," said Curley impatiently as she took a long breath.

"We searched all over the dark web where we know that illegal purchases are negotiated for and finalized. We focused on Eastern Europe—Russia, Albania, Estonia, Czech Republic, Bulgaria, Ukraine, Romania, etc. Nothing came up...until there was a wire transfer of 3 million euros to a computer server in St. Petersburg, Russia. Molly knows how to follow the money trail and back track to the source. She found an IP address that had trolled the dark web many times before with contacts within America, specifically, New York and the tri-state area," explained Jason in layman's terms.

Jason continued. "This particular dark web site is flooded with pornographic connections and sex trafficking."

"Did you find a name or company associated with the IP address?" Asked Curlee.

"She goes by the moniker, 'Whiplash', but we think we have her real name from somewhere else. Too complicated to explain. Her name is Sophia Lebedev and she is using a computer terminal in St. Petersburg."

"Anything else, Jason? Time is crucial here!" Said Benitez.

"She has been associated with a Russian oligarch named Aleksandr Kuznetsov," said Jason. He spelled both names on his legal pad for the agents.

Jason looked over at Holden for an additional part of the story. Holden cleared his throat and took a gulp from his water bottle.

"Here's the connection. We found several communications between Kuznetsov, Lebedev and Leonid Vasiliev. He's the guy you're looking for here, correct? He's the criminal boss who abducted the kids, right?" Asked Holden.

A slight smile formed on Agent Curlee's lips. "That's good work, boys and girls. This info could provide us with a solid lead."

Benitez, Curlee and the detectives all stared with admiration at the three young geeks, when SAC Masters walked into the conference room.

Curlee grilled them again. "What else? You've got to have more."

"Yes, yes. Because Molly followed the 3 million, we found

out the address of the first delivery, as they call it. One teen (we don't know which one) was recently delivered to a Sag Harbor address."

Jason used the legal pad to write the address and passed it to Agent Curlee.

"We do not know the name of the buyer, unfortunately."

"That's okay. The address will do for now. What about the others who were kidnapped? Any info on them?" Asked SAC Masters.

Jason cranked his body around to address SAC Masters. "We are reasonably sure that as soon as the money is exchanged, we can get those addresses as well. Just like the first one."

Masters nodded and finally felt some hope for the poor parents who were insane with fright, anxiety and dread. "Great work you three. Please keep going and give us the intel as soon as you discover more addresses. Understand?"

Jason sat erect in his swivel chair and almost shouted, "Yes, sir. For sure."

Agent Curlee turned to lead the detectives out of the small conference room, but SAC Masters gently grabbed her elbow and drew her back toward him. He made eye contact with Detective Morris and grinned. And then he made a brief announcement.

"By the way, and this is no small victory, we found our mole. One of our computer analysts in the bull pen was feeding Vasiliev whatever intel we had discovered along the way. It was Bradley Warren. We now have him in Interrogation #1."

"No kidding. How long has he been working for us?" Asked Curlee.

"About five years. Don't have the motive yet, but I will be doing his interview ASAP," responded Masters.

SAC Masters and everyone else looked over at Sid Morris. Detective Winchester took a few steps closer to Morris with a questioning demeanor. "I'm so sorry I doubted you, Sid. But why all the texts and phone calls? And what's with all the secrecy?"

Detective Morris finally had to come clean. A very private man with a stoic personality. He never felt the need to advertise his life story.

"Look, I needed for everyone to focus on this case. My wife of 43 years, Shelly, has pancreatic cancer. We've been battling it for a good couple of months now. I've been communicating with the oncologist and speaking with her to keep her spirits up. Sorry to lead all of you astray."

Lakesha wrapped her arms around Sid and gave him a tight hug. The others placed a caring hand on his back and wished him well.

"Okay, we need a team of detectives and agents to head to Sag Harbor. I will text everyone the address." Curlee studied Winchester and Morris. "Are you guys up for the first team to go? I'll send you with a tactical unit."

Detective Morris called out, "We're on it. Let's go Winchester."

CHAPTER 62

The dark blue sedan sat crouched under the shadows of the tall elm trees. An elongated scrape snaked along the center of the two doors on the driver's side. A light breeze whispered between entwined leafy boughs and limbs. The half moon played peek-a-boo with battleship-gray cloud puffs. A slim man dressed in dark jeans, white sneakers and a burgundy windbreaker walked a dark brown Doberman on the other side of the street. He seemed oblivious to the two men in the sedan. The driver picked up a half-filled 12 ounce cup and sipped on lukewarm black coffee. The passenger munched on a Nature Valley chocolate-nut bar. A few cars and trucks bounced by the address they were watching in Bayside, Queens.

"I called the hospital this morning, Jack."

"How's Dmitry doing, Bruce?" Agent Belman kept his eye on the laptop computer that sat on the fold-out stand that was custom built between the passenger seat and the center console. Bluetooth earbuds plugged his ears.

"His doctors said he's conscious and responsive. He suffered a sizable concussion and a jaw fracture. Thank God no apparent brain damage, as of yet."

"Bruce, that's great news. I assume we have an agent or two keeping watch over him?"

"Of course, Jack. A few Suffolk uniforms are also on duty."

"Wait…" Belman put up his left arm to pause what Myers was saying. He studied the computer screen. His program was tracking the incoming and outgoing phone calls made by Irina, Nick, and Julie Ventura (aka Vasiliev), Leonid's wife, son, and daughter. Each had a cell phone and there was a landline in the house, as well.

"Nick's dialing a new number. Let's see where this call leads. Maybe we'll get lucky. Kids don't think before they do."

Agent Myers placed his buds in his ears to listen in also on the call, which would be recorded on the computer program.

"Listen, dad. You gotta be kidding me. We can't just pick up and leave! Dad, I've got commitments, school, friends. Dad, why now?"

"Nicky, it cannot be helped, Nicky. I know what you got, yeah. But I need to get out now. Just did big business and they need me and my family to go back…for a short time."

"I don't believe it. This is shit! Julie can't go either, now. She's applying to colleges and she'll have interviews and…"

"Nicky, just for a short while. Think of it as a vacation. I've got the feds up my ass." Leonid could be heard puffing and sighing loudly. "Put your mother on. We've got final arrangements."

"I'm here honey. Not over the phone. You know how to send the details."

"Yeah, will send them. Get ready today. They're on my ass, yeah?"

"Okay, will take care of everything. Kids won't like it, but they have no other choice. I'll talk with them."

"Okay, sweetheart. See you then." Leonid hung up and so did Irina.

"Jack, are we taking them into custody?"

"No, sounds like they'll be on the move either tonight or tomorrow. We need to continue the stake out and follow them. My guess will be LaGuardia or perhaps JFK. I'm bettin' on LaGuardia. It's closer."

"We're gonna need at least another four agents to surveil them also. We need at least two or three cars to follow them to the airport, or wherever they leave from. We need to capture the big fish—Leonid Vasiliev!" Exclaimed Myers.

"Bruce, call the New York office. Get us more manpower, ASAP."

If we can arrest Leonid and place his family in custody. Use them as leverage for Leonid to give us the information we need to find those poor kids," said Belman.

"Jack do you actually think Vasiliev will talk? Giving up his bosses in Russia will be the same as a death sentence."

"It all depends upon whether or not he values his wife and kids. We need to threaten him with charges of obstruction and collusion for his wife, Irina. He can go to prison for life and she can get 15-20 years," said Belman.

"Yes, then what happens to the son and daughter?"

"Exactly!"

CHAPTER 63

Before they got on the elevator, Morris scanned the office for the Men's Room. He stopped a tall employee wearing a striped dress shirt and solid blue tie. "Hey buddy, the Men's Room?"

"End of the hall on the left," pointed the young man.

"Winchester, give me 3 minutes." Morris jogged down the hall.

Winchester frowned, turned her eyes toward the ceiling and nodded. She smirked and thought about older guys and their prostates.

Through the door and into a stall, Morris took out his phone. He texted as quickly as his stubby fingers could move while he listened for any sounds of other bathroom occupants. He heard none and was relieved.
Within 5-10 seconds he received a response in one sentence. He replaced his phone in his front pants pocket and then took a well-deserved piss.

Back at the elevator bank he was breathing heavy. "Thanks, Winchester." He glanced at his partner for a second and then faced the elevator doors. "It's an old man thing." She snickered and waited for them to open. "Let's do this!"

Winchester drove their SUV and the FBI tactical team followed. It took a little over an hour to reach the Cypress Terrace address. The expansive two-story mansion was bathed in cream colored stucco and dotted with floor-to-ceiling vinyl windows framed in chestnut brown. The lavish landscaping was creatively sculptured and manicured in front and around the home. Thick charcoal steel security fencing blocked the driveway entrance and surrounded the entire property. A call box with a chrome number pad was installed on the driver's side left brick pillar. The owner of record was Roger Collings, a hedge fund executive in his mid 40's.

After eyeballing the property through the security gate, Winchester drove up to the call box and pressed the call button. Several seconds later, no answer. Two security guards stepped down from the porch and approached the gate. Winchester pressed the call button once again.

One of the guards shouted through the slats in the gate.

"Private property. What do you want?"

Morris took his badge wallet out of this suit pocket and flipped it open. "FBI, pal. We have a warrant to search the premises."

"Let's see the warrant," said the guard.

"We need to speak with the owner, Mr. Roger Collings."

Morris held the folded warrant out of the SUV window and waved it. "We need the owner, pal."

Both guards looked at each other and the second one punched the open lever from the inside. The gate slid horizontally to the right through the carved hedges with more than a few audible squeaks. The guards turned on their heels and led the two vehicles up the driveway to the huge house. Before they reached the the front double doors, one of the guards spoke into a shoulder mike, alerting Mr. Collings. Winchester and the tactical team brought their cars to a sliding stop on the beige and brown pebbled surface. The detectives and the officers jumped out and approached the front entrance with guns drawn, but pointed toward the ground. Before they could knock, a 6'2" slim man with sandy colored straight hair stepped out onto the porch. He wore pressed lime green slacks, a white custom-tailored shirt with two buttons undone at the top and a pair of Brunello Cucinelli brown leather penny loafers without socks. A yellow cashmere sweater was tied around his neck.

"Good morning. How can I help you?"

"We have a warrant to search your premises and your vehicles, Mr. Collings."

"Why on Earth would you want to search my house? I've done nothing criminal. I'm merely a businessman."

"We have reason to believe that you are harboring an underage girl against her will," said Winchester in a soft voice.

"Oh, my. That's nonsense. Where's the warrant?" Roger Collings offered a smooth open hand with clear polished nails to receive the folded paper in Winchester's grip. He turned to one of his guards. "Bobby, ask Mr. Ward to step out here please. You'll find him on the veranda in the rear."

"My attorney will take care of this. Just a moment."

"We need to enter the premises now, Mr. Collings. Please step aside."

As the detectives were about to enter, with the tactical team on their heels, the front door opened wide. A sturdy man, sporting a barrel chest, in his 60's with a trimmed salt and pepper beard, stepped outside. He snatched the warrant out of his client's hand and perused details. "I am Joseph Ward, Esq. I am Mr. Collings's counsel. What is the legal basis for this warrant, detective…?"

"I am Detective Morris and this is my partner, Detective Winchester, Suffolk County Police Department. We are searching for kidnapped youngsters who we believe have been trafficked and sold to certain individuals. Your client's name and address came to our attention after some rather deep investigation by the FBI. We need to search the premises and your client's vehicles."

"Roger, I'm afraid this is legitimate. Allow them in. Not that they'll find anyone or anything."

Roger Collings etched a crooked smirk on his handsome sun-tanned face and stepped aside. "If you must."

The detectives and six tactical officers rushed in and began their extensive search. Mr. Collings and his attorney slowly walked through the main level and out onto the veranda to continue drinking their Bloody Marys.

The leader of the tactical unit, Sergeant Wills and one of his men searched the huge basement level. After walking through a stark empty foyer, they came upon a steel enforced door, secured with a large padlock.

"Agent Shavers, did you bring your clippers?"

"On on it, Sergeant. Give me a minute."

Shavers removed a rather large set of lock clippers from his belt housing and muscled the padlock until the steel snapped. Inside was an extravagantly decorated room containing a kingsize poster bed with a silk comforter and a huge mirror on the ceiling above. A wrought iron rack was installed on the cement wall with leather whips, collars and other sex paraphernalia hanging neatly from it. There was also a black leather swing hanging from the ceiling from thick black ropes.

Sergeant Wills activated his shoulder mike. "Detectives, we're in the basement level. You gotta see this ASAP."

CHAPTER 64

Holden opened the door to the small office and signaled Agent Benitez with a beaconing hand. Benitez tilted his head toward Curlee and they both made a beeline for the back office.

"Tell us you have other addresses," Curlee blurted out.

Jason took the lead again. "Yes, agents. We have good news and bad news."

"What? God damn it," Curlee spit out of her thin lips. Her body stood erect. "Okay, let's have it."

"Good news is that we have two new addresses on Long Island. One in East Hampton and one in Wainscott. I'll write them down."

"How much money was exchanged for each?

"Same as the first one—3 million euros."

"Yeah, okay. And the bad news?"

"The back door channels we were tapping into…are now unfortunately closed!"

"What the hell happened? Are you sure?"

"Yes. They must have gotten word that we were on to them and they shut everything down."

"Is there any other way of getting this intel?"

Jason explained, "we'll try, but we don't know yet. Sorry." Jason shrugged his shoulders. Molly's eyes were moist. Holden had a terrified look on his face and lost color.

"Okay guys." Curlee tried to calm herself. She took a few deep breaths. She whispered, "great work. Please keep at it, alright?"

Each of the three hackers nodded and went back to their screens.

Both agents walked out of the office with renewed focus, even after the bad news. Curlee called out to the SWAT commander, who was pouring a cup of black coffee. He placed the half-filled cup down on the counter and strode over to Curlee.

"Agent Bolton, we need you to lead one of your tactical units to this address in East Hampton, ASAP. We will email you a warrant to search the house and property. We believe one of our abductees is being held there. Is your unit ready?"

"Yes, Agent Curlee. They're on standby. Leaving now."

"Benitez, I want you to take another SWAT unit to this address in Wainscott. Same applies. I'll ask SAC Masters to obtain a warrant and it will be emailed to you before you reach the premises. Let's get these kids back, pronto."

Benitez activated his handheld mike and contacted the sergeant of SWAT unit #3, which was waiting in the ground floor bullpen. As he walked to the elevator banks, he received a positive response within seconds. "On our way, Curlee. Will keep you informed."

SAC Masters called out to Curlee. "My office, Agent."

Curlee sidestepped a row of computer desks and breezed into Masters' corner office.

"What's the latest intel Sam?"

"The hackers got us two more addresses and I assigned Bolton and Benitez to lead the searches. One in East Hampton and one in Wainscott. They will need warrants. Could you please make that happen?"

"Of course. I'll call Judge Casey again. What else?"

Curlee's eyes rolled and her gaze landed on the ceiling tiles. "We got some bad news. The back channels that the kids were utilizing to extract the addresses were shut down. They're probably on to us. It all comes from St. Petersburg. Someone warned them."

"Oh, Christ. So we're closing in on the whereabouts of 3 kids, but we have no clue about the rest. Does that kind of sum up where we are at present, Curlee?"

"Yes, sir."

"Well, I also heard from the detectives in Sag Harbor. No

abductee was found as of yet, but we are sending a forensic team to scour that mansion. They found a sex den in the lower level of the house. Whips, swings, other sex paraphernalia. We need to collect and identify DNA samples ASAP and compare them with the samples surrendered by the parents, in order to bring Mr. Collings in for questioning. Most likely he had the girl removed to another location because someone clued him in that we were coming."

"Again, one step ahead of us. Bastards!" Exclaimed Curlee. "I put a rush on that DNA. At least a few hours in our lab."

SAC Masters said, "We got the mole from our office. Bradley Warren. But I get the feeling there is someone else who's feeding them intel. These criminals have money to burn. They intimidate and buy as many informants as they can. Are we sure that Detective Morris is clean?"

Curlee shrugged her shoulders and suggested, "we need to have Jamie run the financials on each of the detectives on the task force, starting with Morris."

"Sam, get Jamie to run 'em ASAP and report to me."

"Copy that, boss."

"We have one more possible ace in the hole, Sam. Vasiliev and family are on the move. Belman and his agents have them in their sights. We desperately need to snatch them up before they escape," said Masters.

"Any other leads, boss, at all?"

"I'm going to place a call to a contact that I have in 'the company'."

"You have someone on speed dial at C.I.A.?"

"Curlee, we did not have this conversation." His eyebrows arched. "It may or may not work. Worth a try. My dad used to say: 'if you don't ask, you don't get'."

CHAPTER 65

"It appears you were right on the money, Jack. LaGuardia it is."

"Bruce, makes sense since Bayside is the closest airport. And don't think they're flying directly to the motherland. There will be at least two or three flights to make it more difficult to follow them."

The dark blue Uber SUV glided to the edge of the sidewalk of Terminal B. It services Air Canada, American, Southwest, United and JetBlue. At 8:00 AM it was anyone's guess. Vasiliev and family needed to be closely followed on foot.

"Bruce, do you have the passenger manifests for all of the morning flights out of Terminal B?"

"Got 'em right here." He lifted a thin leather briefcase to eye level. "I printed them out early this morning, Jack."

"I doubt very highly that we have any passengers with the surname of Vasiliev or Ventura, correct?"

"Correct again, Jack. This guy Leonid has false identities for himself and his family up the kazoo. With the money they rake in, they can have anything custom made."

"Do any of the names stand out? Or were you able to isolate families of two adults and two teenagers?"

"Jack, I did that with a simple algorithm. There are 34 such families on all of the airlines departing before noon. None stood out, Jack."

The driver of the Uber jumped to the wet asphalt and ran around the hood to open the front and rear passenger doors. A large middle aged man wearing a dark blazer, blue dress shirt and dark fedora, low on his brow, slipped off his seat onto the sidewalk. A pretty redheaded woman, wearing a fashionable crimson pantsuit and black high heel pumps emerged from the rear door. A tall, lanky young man wearing a solid navy blue sweatshirt, jeans and Nike Air Flight Lite Mid-Basketball sneakers jumped out after his mom. Last to emerge from the car was a stunning raven-haired beauty in a pink Vineyard Vines shirt pullover atop white skin-tight slacks and low sandals. The driver dug into the rear cargo hold and handed each of the four their own small carry-on suitcase.

All of the agents had ear buds and mikes for communication. Each of the three cars of agents pulled up to separate doors of the terminal. Agent Belman gave his instructions via his mouth mike.

"Myers and I will enter the center set of doors. Follow discreetly so we can box them in before boarding."

"#2—Copy."

"#3—Copy."

The family of four began to walk, searching for their airline. They dodged slow walkers, young families with children and several wheelchairs accommodating those with mobility issues. The airport was busy as usual. Myers and Belman were craning their necks trying to keep the Vasilievs in sight.

"Looks like American. Converge from left and right flanks. We will approach from behind," said Belman into his mike.

Once they reached the American Airlines desks, there was no need to stand in line to check in. All they had to do was utilize the kiosks to print out their boarding passes. No luggage needed to be checked. They had to wait several minutes to access a free kiosk. Belman and Myers hung back while the four of them printed out the passes. Once they were finished, all of the agents surrounded the family.

Myers unfolded his ID wallet and displayed his shield and ID card. "FBI, FBI! You all need to come with us." The six agents surrounded them and ushered them to a small area beyond the airline desks. They had arranged to commandeer a small security office between a tour desk and the lost luggage room.

The red headed woman protested very loudly. "Where are you taking us? We have a flight to catch. What's the meaning of this?"

Once in the office, Belman asked them to be seated. They reluctantly occupied four plastic seats against a gray wall, leaving their luggage at their feet.

"We need to see your passports, please," said Belman.

Each of them had their own that cradled a boarding pass. Myers collected them.

Belman and another agent studied them at the security desk. The middle-aged man remained silent, but his dark eyes darted from agent to agent and then to the door of the office. His hat was dipped below his forehead. The boy squirmed in his chair and the girl sucked her teeth and ran her slender fingers through her long shimmering hair.

"What the hell?" The girl whispered to her brother. "What time do we board the plane? This is shit."

"Calm down. This won't take long," whispered the boy.

Myers removed a small iPad from his briefcase and started to hunt and peck. An image appeared of a man in custody who was approximately 50-55 years old. It was an image of Leonid Vasiliev as a younger man who had been arrested years ago for other charges that had been ultimately dropped. Belman held the older man's passport photo next to the image on the screen. Similar, but not quite a match.

"So this is the Bennett family? Living in Bayside, Queens?"

Mr. Bennett said, "yes, sir."

"Mr. Bennett, please remove your hat."

Mr. Bennett slowly removed his fedora from his head and revealed a thin crop of grayish hair that surrounded a bald pate. All of the agents stared at him. The man stared back up at Belman, keeping eye contact.

"I know this is the Vasiliev family," snarled Belman. He

pointed, "Irina, Nick, Julie. But, you sir, are not Leonid!!" Belman froze for a few seconds. He snatched one of the boarding passes with the gate number scrawled on it. Ramirez, Forbes, stay here and Do Not Allow Them to Leave! Bruce grab your manifests and come with us. Chan, Williams, let's go. Gate 43."

The four agents shuffled out the office and ran to the security line with ID's in hand.

"Boarding in 5 minutes, shit. Myers, call the Director of Operations and tell him to hold flight #415 to Toronto, now!"

"Jack, how sure are you that he would be on the same flight?"

"I'm not, but my gut tells me he will be. And disguised as someone else with another phony passport."

Once through security, they trotted down the causeway to Gate 43, sidestepping a host of slow-moving passengers, their trailing luggage and a prancing maltipoo at the end of a thin blue lead.

CHAPTER 66

Judy Gomez, a 9-year veteran American Airline agent, was standing guard in front of the door leading to the jet bridge at Gate 43. Her body was erect and her dark brown eyes were hyper alert. She was expecting the FBI agents and had the manifest in her hand ready to help. Within two minutes of communicating with her supervisor, she spotted four men in suits jogging up to the counter. One of them took the lead.

"Agent Gomez, we're the FBI agents looking for a passenger. I assume your supervisor gave you the heads-up? I'm Special Agent Belman."

Belman and the other agents had their ID's in hand to show her. She nodded, admittedly a bit stunned. This was the first time she had the FBI at her counter. NYPD needed her help from time to time, but this was a federal issue and she was ready to cooperate.

"How can I help?"

"We know all of the passengers boarded already and we know that the pilots were given orders to stay put for now. We need to identify one passenger, also possibly an accomplice."

Myers took his phone out of his jacket pocket and scrolled for the photo of Leonid Vasiliev. He showed it to Agent Gomez.

"Do you recognize this man? Did he board the plane?"

She leaned forward and studied the pic. The tip of her tongue licked the corner of her mouth briefly as she looked closely at the man's features.   "I can't be sure. Maybe." She took two steps to her computer monitor and punched a few keys. "One hundred and fourteen people boarded. And we have sixteen empty seats."

"Bruce, compare your manifest with Agent Gomez's. See if anyone jumps out at you."

Myers laid the copy of his manifest on the counter and followed the names on both lists. He went down the rows of names on each of the three pages.

"No one stands out, Jack. We need to board the plane."

"Before we do...Agent Gomez, were there any folks who looked nervous or particularly sweaty? Or anyone in wheelchairs or with walkers? Anyone who looked elderly or sick with an aide or companion?"

Agent Gomez thought for a second and met Belman's gaze.

"Actually there was a gray-haired old woman in a wheelchair with a female nurse helping her. There was something about the woman that seemed a little off."

"What do you mean?"

"Well her hair looked like a wig, but not a good one. You could tell it was fake hair. Also she had a thin tartan blanket over her legs and a thin scarf around her mouth and chin. She also had a square portable oxygen device on her lap with the tubes leading to her nostrils."

"Remember her name or the name of the nurse?"

"As a matter of fact, yes. Her name was Lilian Vance. I took note since she was a bit odd."

"Bruce, hear that? Lilian Vance. L.V. What seats were she and the nurse assigned?"

She pecked a few more keystrokes. "Seats 24 A & B."

"Ok, Agent Gomez. Inform the pilot that we do not want any announcements other than the fact that there will be a short delay due to runway backup. Open the door please. Let's go men. Check everyone as we go up the aisle. Myers and Chan take the left side. Williams, you're with me on the right. Heads on the swivel."

A short but stout, dark-haired flight attendant stood at the end of the jet bridge that abutted the opened cabin door. She had been briefed and expected them to board. A pleasant smile was plastered on her pretty face and her ice blue eyes darted from one agent's face to another as they stepped into the cabin. "Seats 24 A & B, right side, half way up the aisle."

Belman nodded. "Thanks."

Belman and Williams entered first and slowly began walking up the aisle. The chief flight attendant was told to announce that there may have been someone on board who was on the wrong flight and airline personnel needed to check into the error. More than a few passengers knew something important was happening since the men in suits did not look like personnel from the airport. Only a few people were obstructing the aisle space, still adjusting their overhead luggage and getting last minute items for their flight.

Myers and Chan studied the faces on the left side of the plane. No red flags. Upon reaching row 24, Belman found the suspicious old woman with her face covered and the oxygen tubes in her nose. He looked at Williams and raised his bushy eyebrows. The nurse sat in the aisle seat and averted her eyes. She wore a powder blue set of scrubs and white sneakers. She pretended not to notice the men studying her and her 'elderly companion'.

Belman had his ID wallet out and unfolded. "Passports please."

"Sir, this is America. We don't need to show you our passports. I'm escorting this old woman, who is unfortunately gravely ill, to her relatives in Toronto."

"Either you show us your passports or you come with us for questioning to the FBI office in Manhattan. And, ma'am, I need you to unravel that scarf around your face, to compare with your picture on your passport."

The woman began grunting and coughing. She seemed to be in some kind of respiratory distress.

"Agent, you're agitating this poor sick woman. Please! We just want to get to Toronto to her relatives."

"Passports, now!"

All of the passengers in the vicinity of seats 24 were

staring at the agents and at the nurse and her patient. The old woman began mumbling and coughing. One man and a child stood up to see what was happening.

Belman raised his voice once again. "Leonid. The ruse is up! I know it's you. Both of you, out of your seats. You're both under arrest."

Agent Williams grabbed the nurse by crook of the arm and dragged her up and out after disconnecting her seat belt. Then Leonid finally relented and unraveled his scarf revealing his jowly face coated with a day-old coating of gray stubble. He got out of his seat and put his hands behind his back.

"Wow, Agent Belman. I applaud how smart you are. Very clever, yeah. But you know my attorney will have me out of these bracelets within hours."

"Not this time, Leonid. Not this time. Let's go."

Belman reached up and snatched the woman's gray wig from Leonid's head and tossed it back onto the seat. "You won't need this where you're going, pal."

Myers and Chan retreated out of the aisle and exited the plane. Willams and Belman followed with Vasiliev and his 'nurse' in cuffs. As Belman walked back onto the sky bridge, he smiled at the pretty flight attendant. He said, "so sorry for the delay. We needed to take this excess baggage off the plane so you could take off now."

"Thank you, Agent. I will inform the pilot."

She ducked into the cabin and secured the door behind her.

CHAPTER 67

Del poured a cup of hot water over an English Breakfast teabag as Corny paced back and forth with dread. Curlee approached him with sympathetic eyes. "Hey, hey. We'll get them. We will. Have faith, okay?"

"My sister just called and I let it go to voicemail. Don't have the heart to tell her that her babies are still out there... somewhere."

Del offered Corny a half a cup of coffee and he gripped it with his large left hand. "Thanks. Cara just called. Didn't pick up." A few tear drops escaped from his eyes and slowly rolled down his bronze cheeks.

"Want me to call her back?" Asked Del.

Corny took a few sips and swallowed. "No, I'll call her. Or maybe I should call Doug instead. He seems to be holding it together better than her."

Curlee's phone buzzed and she immediately took the call. "Go for Curlee."

"Belman here. Good news. We captured Leonid Vasiliev and family at LaGuardia before they were able to make their escape. We are bringing them all back to your office ASAP."

"God we need some good news. Now we need leverage to make him talk. Won't be easy. Good work."

Corny leaned in and asked, "who was that? What's the good news?"

"We stopped Vasiliev and his family at LaGuardia and they're in custody. They are on their way back here."

"No shit. Now we need to figure out how we're gonna make that low- -life criminal talk," Corny exclaimed. "I want to be in on the interview, Curlee. My nieces are still out in the wind.

Another one is out there, too!"

Curlee was contemplative for a few moments. "Corny, I'll agree as long as you let me take the lead. You're too emotionally involved. You'll need to control your urge to wrap your hands around his neck. Let me finesse him."

"Yeah, alright."

"I'm serious. You understand? The moment you go apeshit on this guy, you're out of the room?"

"Copy that, Curlee. I got it." Corny used both hands to push his sparse hair back on his head. Then he used a napkin to wipe the beads of sweat from his forehead.

Del had walked back to the kitchen area to call Lieutenant Woods to bring him up to speed. She came back to where Corny and Curlee were standing. "Just spoke with Lieu. He knows what you and your sister are going through. He said that Joey and Teddy insisted on helping us find Emma and Jordan. They should be here within the half hour."

Corny nodded and took his phone out of his pocket. He walked out into the corridor to call Cara and Doug. The phone rang only once.

"What the hell is going on, Corny? Oh my God. They say that if a kidnapped victim is not found within 24 hours, the chances are slim to none that they'll never be found. Corny... please. What do you know?"

He knew she'd be frantic. "First of all, try to calm down. Second of all, this is not your average kidnapping where they want to abuse and then kill. These scumbags paid large sums of money for these kids and they don't want them hurt or damaged in any way."

Doug grabbed the phone from his wife while Corny and Cara's parents listened in on speaker. "Okay, brother. What leads do you have at this point?"

"Hey Doug. We have some solid leads and we were able to get three addresses of where we think three of the kids are being held by wealthy buyers. We also have young super hackers tracking down intel from the Russian oligarch who is at the head of the criminal organization. We even know who his computer geek in St. Petersburg is."

"Okay. So where are Emma and Jordan?"

Corny hesitated and licked his dry lips. "That, we still don't know yet. But the good news is that FBI agents recently arrested the head of the Russian cell and he's in custody. We're gonna smoke him for the intel. We even have his wife and kids for leverage."

Corny's father interjected into the conversation. "Son, how much longer until you find our girls? Corny we're on pins and needles here. Corny…"

"I know Dad, I know. But we're working on it 24/7…"

Del took the phone from Corny. "Mr. Prince, we promise you we will bring the girls home. We need a bit more time. Hang in, please. We have our entire squad and the FBI on this case. Top priority."

"I hear you, Kristina. I thank you…Be careful and keep us informed."

"We will, sir."

Wendell Prince gave the phone back to his daughter. She pleaded with Corny. "Please Corny. Please…"

"I know, I know."

She hung up the phone, crying.

CHAPTER 68

SAC Masters burst from his office. He got Curlee's attention and waved her over to him. Del and Corny followed, alert to Masters' body language and facial gestures. They detected a slight smile and a head roll.

"Great news, thank God. Agent Benitez called me twenty minutes ago. He and SWAT successfully recovered Wesley McArthur from the Wainscott mansion. Thankfully, there was no armed confrontation.

Benitez and his men, with the warrant, got the drop on the few private security men who were goofing off behind the house at the pool. Our guys arrested the owner, a wealthy real estate investor with ties to the Albanian mafia. They found Wesley in an upstairs bedroom, sitting in a corner on the floor. He had a blanket wrapped around himself and was rocking back and forth," explained Masters.

"I also got a call from Commander Bolton who raided the East Hampton estate. They safely recovered Carmen Rodriguez after a fierce, but brief firefight with private security men. Two of our SWAT officers were injured. One suffered a leg wound and one got a round through the fleshy part of the upper arm. None life-threatening."

"How did they find Carmen?" Asked Del.

Masters said, "Bolton and his men found her nude in a fetal position under the covers in the master bedroom. The fucking pedophile who purchased her, like one would buy a racehorse, was in bed with her, smoking a cigar with a shit-eating grin on his face."

"Who was that scumbag?" Asked Del.

"Maurice   Latterice,   the   richest   pharmaceutical distributor in the country," said Masters.

"What's the condition of the kids?" Asked Curlee.

"From their outward appearance they look unharmed, except for a few bruises. However, Wesley is still in shock and Carmen couldn't stop crying. Our people rushed them to Peconic Bay Medical Center. I immediately called their parents and instructed them to meet their youngsters at the hospital. Benitez reported back to me that the press began to swarm the hospital's front entrance soon after our people arrived with the abductees."

"Just what they need now. A media circus," said Corny.

"Yeah, but none of the reporters were allowed in the building. Probably waiting for the parents to arrive so they could hound them. Huge story for Suffolk County."

Del shook her head. "Those poor innocent kids, for God sakes."

Curlee responded, "The doctors will examine them fully, do rape kits, and provide psychological services for them. They're in good hands in Peconic Bay's trauma unit."

Corny said, "Okay, so we got two of them back. What about Sag Harbor. Did they find Kimberly Weinstein yet? Were they able to get a DNA match from the basement sex den?"

"Our guys put a rush on the DNA analysis and we decided to bring Collings in for questioning despite his attorney's protests. Without a doubt, he's got the resources to flee the country in a heartbeat. Right now he's downstairs in one of the interview rooms, sweating. We offered him a deal before we find a DNA match. I know he's considering revealing whereabouts of the girl. The most important thing is to recover Kimberly, even if he gets a lesser sentence," explained Masters.

Corny began to pace back and forth again. Del walked with him staring up into his scowl. He was fuming and snorting and twisting his neck. He desperately needed to find his two nieces and was running out of patience. He approached SAC Masters and in a low voice through gritted teeth, spit out, "John, what do you hear from your man in 'the company?'

"Detective, I know you're in a pressure cooker. We all are, until we get all of these kids back home. Working on it. Trust me." Masters met Corny's gaze with steely gray eyes. "The moment I know, you'll know."

"What about Vasiliev? Is he back here yet?"

"En route. We'll grill him and use his wife and kids to smoke him. This is not our first rodeo. Takes time."

Corny walked away and wandered to the kitchen area. He poured himself another cup of black coffee. Del watched him from a distance.

"Agent Curlee. Agent. I think I got something," called Jamie, one of the financial analysts.

"What do you got?"

"I ran a deep dive on the financials of the detectives, like you asked. Detective Morris has tremendous medical bills from his wife's cancer treatments."

"Yes, and..."

"He seems to be paying them off on a regular basis. Can he do that on a detective's salary?"

"How much are we talking?"

"Roughly $65,000 and he doesn't seem to be in debt."

"Well, that seems very odd. Does he have investments with dividends or any family money socked away?"

"None that I can trace. The strange thing is, looks like he's making cash deposits every two weeks into his checking account at Citibank."

Curlee turned her head to Del and said to her, "take a walk with me into the SAC's office."

"John, I think Jamie found our second mole..."

CHAPTER 69

She followed Sophia Lebedev from a distance for a dozen blocks through a foggy mist. It was a Friday night and many of the clubs in St. Petersburg celebrated Ladies Night—drinks were two for the price of one. The click-clack of high heels against the cobble stones echoed off the exterior walls of stucco buildings and shops. Wisps of cigarette smoke billowed into the air from solitary walkers, as well as couples, rushing to undetermined destinations.

She noticed from a half block away that her mark was headed for Maximus, a nightclub at Bol'shaya Morskaya Ulitsa, 15. Perfect place to approach her prey. The 35-year old zaftig blonde took a last puff of her cigarette, tossed it into the street and winked at the muscular bouncer outside the club. She walked in without hesitation, her generous hips swaying to the beat of the techno music from within. Five minutes later, a gorgeous tall brunette approached the bouncer, too, and was waved into Maximus with a flick of his meaty hand and a lustful smile. She turned her head and smiled back at him, admiring his handsome face and strong physique. He was about to flirt with her, but she swiftly shuffled into the warmth of the establishment. Other young ladies in mini-tube dresses and high heels waited to be admitted.

The main room was bathed in reds, purples, blues and blacks. Velour sofas stuffed with plush pillows hugged the carpeted walls. Circular chandeliers hovered over several empty tables opposite the well-stocked bar. An elevated dance platform containing shiny silver poles took center stage. It was too early for the erotic dancers to climb the steps to perform their gyrations and pole acrobatics. Ladies Night began at 8pm, but the real action began after 10:00.

When she walked in, Anya Baranov, the tall brunette, scanned the room and bar area. There were several women in the club already. A half dozen were clumped at the far end of the bar. All had drinks in their hands and apparently knew each other. They were carbon copies—high heels, tight mini skirts or dresses and heavily made-up. Two other women sat by themselves. One, a shapely blonde, was in the midst of ordering a Greek salad and a tray of cheeses. After ordering her food and an apple martini, Sophia swiveled her stool to face the loud group toward the back. The stool to her right was free.

Anya removed her black leather jacket and slipped onto the free stool. Only Russian was spoken. "Is this seat taken, hon?"

Sophia spun around to face the newcomer. She almost gasped at the sight of the gorgeous brunette next to her. At first her mouth went dry as she stared at Anya. "Uh, uh, no. Sit, sit. I'm not expecting anyone."

Anya combed her dark brown pixie cut with her slender fingers, tipped with lacquered pink nails. Her tight scarlet dress offered a V-shaped view of plump milky breasts that warmly nestled an onyx and gold pendant. Anya's wide lips were covered with a nude satin shimmer lipstick that Sophia could not stop staring at. It did not take long at all for Sophia to feel a burning heat within her body.

"I'm Sophia. Hello."

"Hi, I'm Anya. Nice to meet you. First time for me here."

"Oh, okay. I generally come here to unwind at the end of the week. Ladies Night. Drinks are two for one. The food isn't too bad either."

"Good to hear. I'm starving. What's good?" Anya reached for one of the menus on the side of the bar. She took a peek and scanned the items.

"Sophia, what did you order other than that martini? First one, hon?"

"Yes, first drink. Just got here 10 minutes ago. I asked

the bartender for a Greek salad and a cheese tray," she said awkwardly.

"Don't tell me you eat salads all the time. You have a very sexy figure, hon. Do you eat meat, potatoes, and…"

"Oh sure I do. Just want to lose a few pounds here and there." She blushed and pushed her blonde tresses behind her ears.

"Honey, I wish I had your generous figure. You don't need to lose any weight. And your hair is gorgeous." Anya placed a warm hand on Sophia's bare arm and rubbed gently. Sophia immediately felt an electric charge up and down her spine. Her mouth went dry again. She took a sizable gulp from the martini glass. Before she was able to ask for a second, the bartender placed another one on the bar.

"Hey babe. What can I get you?" Asked the bartender.

Anya smiled coyly and said, "I'll have what she's having. Oh and also a meat platter and a small plate of the least expensive caviar, please."

Sophia's raised her eyebrows. "Wow, caviar. You must earn a nice living or perhaps a rich husband."

"Honey, first of all, we're gonna share this food. Second, I'm not married. In fact, I'll tell you honestly." She gazed into Sophia's ice blue eyes and smiled broadly. "I like women. I really like women." Anya's eyebrows arched.

Sophia's heart pounded in her chest. Tiny beads of perspiration dotted her forehead under her straight bangs. She needed to break the spell so she turned her head toward the back of the bar, thinking that maybe she would get lucky tonight.

Anya moved closer to Sophia and she cupped Sophia's chin with her smooth graceful hand. They were inches apart and Sophia's lips parted. Anya leaned in and kissed her lips softly and tenderly. Suddenly, each tongue slithered out, searching to explore each other for a few heavenly seconds.

CHAPTER 70

Leonid Vasiliev and his family were squirreled away within two small, but separate interrogation rooms. His wife and two teenagers were bitterly complaining about being held against their will and proclaiming that they absolutely knew nothing about Leonid's business dealings or criminal activities. Leonid refused to say a word to the FBI interrogators until his attorney arrived. He was certainly concerned about his wife and kids, but he was really dying for a Cuban cigar, of which he was denied.

Agent Curlee was the primary interrogator, with secondary support from Corny and Del, who were both outside the room, pacing back and forth. They, of course, could stare at Leonid through the 36 X 50 inch one-way mirror. They watched his dark, beady eyes continually scanning the sound-proof room which was painted a dark green and beige. He twisted his thick neck several times and stopped more than once gazing up at the corner cameras that pulsed tiny green flashes. Both of his wrists were handcuffed to the heavy steel desk legs. He had just enough room to flex his arms. Leonid's body tick was licking his lips continuously, again, imagining the aromatic smoke of his precious cigars.

Suddenly the heavy metal door opened and an FBI agent ushered counselors-at-law, Maxim Popov, and Galina Volkova into the narrow hallway. Agent Curlee greeted them politely and each of the attorneys produced their business cards for her.

"We need to see our clients immediately," exclaimed Popov. He wore a navy blue Tom Ford, custom-fitted two-piece sharkskin suit. His posture was starkly erect and his eyes were crystal blue. Gray-tipped straight hair suggested a professional and expensive styling. No smile and all business. Ms. Volkova sported an expensive woolen black business suit, cut low at the bust line. Her Christian Louboutin hot chick patent leather pumps clacked a rhythmic tune on the ceramic tile floor. Her eagle eyes were emerald green and sat above a sharp, thin nose. Ms. Volkova's thin lips drew a crooked line.

Curlee met them eye-to-eye within six to eight inches and replied,"that is your right as counselors and their right as individuals under arrest. However, we do not have time on our side. Three more young girls are still out there somewhere, kidnapped by your Mr. Vasiliev, held against their will, sold to God knows who, for God knows what purposes…"

Mr. Popov interrupted her, "allegedly, Agent Curlee."

"Look, both of you. Quite frankly, we are not interested in Leonid's wife and kids. She may or may not be privy to Leonid's criminal activities. However, the District Attorney may file charges against them, none the less. We need the information about those three poor girls, now! We need Leonid to start talking."

Mr. Popov said, "and what may I tell my client, as you Americans say, is 'on the table,' Agent Curlee?"

SAC Masters entered the hallway at this point. He introduced himself and spoke with both counselors directly.

"I just spoke with the District Attorney. We need to get those girls back, unharmed, to their families. The DA is willing to deal for information leading to the recovery of those kids. Time is of the essence."

"What are you offering my client, Special Agent Masters?"

Masters glanced at Corny and Curlee. He once again addressed Mr. Popov.

"Agent Curlee and I would like to propose a deal directly to your client with you present." He turned to Del and Corny. "Detectives, please wait out here in the hall. You may listen in, of course."

Mr. Popov nodded and said, "please give us ten minutes to discuss a few thinks with our clients. I will wave you in when you may enter. Agreeable?"

"Okay. Time is running out, Mr. Popov."

Each attorney entered their respective interrogation rooms and immediately sat in the empty gun-metal chair. Each attorney initiated a dialogue with their clients in private. In about 10-15 minutes, Mr. Popov stood up and waved the agents inside. Simultaneously an analyst from the 'bullpen' stepped into the corridor and whispered something in Curlee's ear. She cocked her head in the direction of the door and Masters nodded. Curlee walked out to interrogate Mr. Collings who had been brought in an hour ago by Detectives Morris and Winchester. SAC Masters opened the door to the room where Vasiliev was sweating.

"Alright, Special Agent in Charge Masters. Let's talk."

CHAPTER 71

Detective Morris approached Curlee as she walked to Interrogation Room #3. "Agent Curlee, Winchester and I want to be present for Collings's interview. We know he's hiding Kimberly Weinstein at a secret location. Collings was tipped off before we showed up."

Curlee shot him a cold deadpan look without a word. She peeked over his shoulder. Agent Stu Barnes was leading Captain Michael Brenner, Morris's superior at the 3rd Police Precinct, to where Curlee and Morris were standing. Detective Winchester looked perplexed to see her boss striding with purpose in the FBI office.

"Captain. Surprised to see you, sir," said Winchester.

Morris whipped his head and shoulders around swiftly and his jaw dropped. "Captain. I was going to call you with an update. You didn't have to come all the way..."

"Save it, Morris." Captain Brenner put up his left hand as a stop sign. "You had a few months to retire. Sid, after a long and distinguished career...What were you thinking?"

Agent Barnes circled around Morris and said, "Detective Morris, you're under arrest for suspicion of aiding and abetting a criminal conspiracy. Put your hands behind your back."

Agent Barnes cuffed him and read him his rights in front of the entire 'bullpen' of agents and analysts.

Morris's cheeks turned red and at first looked toward the light streaming through the windows. "Michael, I, I... it's Shelley. The cancer came back with a vengeance." He had tears in his eyes. "The Russians contacted me with a very sweet offer." Captain Brenner shook his head and stared at Morris who, suddenly looked like a pathetic old man. His once broad shoulders drooped. "I'm sorry, Michael. I needed the money for her treatment. Only chance I had to keep her going."

Morris wept openly and Winchester was kind enough to use a Kleenex to wipes some of the tears from his cheek.

"I'm so sorry, Lakesha. I had no other choice..."

Captain Brenner plucked Morris's gun and shield from his holster and pocket and Agent Barnes led Morris away to one of the cells in the basement level.

"Agent Curlee, I'll be in touch," Captain Brenner said sadly. He ambled toward the elevator bank.

"Two moles so far. Any other surprises Detectives?" Asked Curlee rhetorically. She was addressing Del and Winchester. Corny was still watching Masters interrogating Vasiliev. A pang of nausea gripped Del and she trotted toward the ladies room. Winchester followed Del with inquisitive eyes.

"Okay, time to talk with Mr. Collings. We did get a DNA match for Kimberly Weinstein in that slime-ball's sex den. You're both invited in. But, I'm the primary."

Winchester said, "Copy that Agent. Del needed a few minutes."

They walked into Interrogation Room #3 where Mr. Collings and his attorney were whispering to each other. Winchester took a standing
position against the wall. Curlee sat in the empty chair and wasted no time.
Del joined them after a few minutes. She had a wad of Kleenex in her fist.

"Mr. Collings, the way I see it, you can walk through one of two doors. Door #1: You can deny you have any knowledge of Kimberly Weinstein again or any knowledge of her whereabouts and spend the rest of your miserable life in prison. Door #2: You can tell us immediately where you have Ms. Weinstein hidden so we can bring her back to her frantic family. Thus we can tell the District Attorney that you cooperated with us and perhaps you can receive a reduced sentence by accepting a deal from the D.A. And before you answer, I must inform you and your attorney that we now have a DNA match!"

Mr. Collings's face lost all color and urine began to drip from his sporty slacks onto the tile floor. His attorney pulled his client closer to him and whispered yet again in his ear. Mr. Collings nodded woodenly and turned to Agent Curlee.

His attorney spoke briefly. "Mr. Collings has important information regarding the girl. But before his talks, he would like to know what deal is on the table."

"After speaking with the D.A., Mr. Collings could expect to get a reduction of 5-10 years, depending upon whether or not we recover Ms. Weinstein and what her condition is."

His attorney agreed. "Tell them where she is and do not leave out any detail."

Mr. Collings gave specific directions to his other property in Sag Harbor and asked for a phone so he could tell his security people, who are guarding the girl, to surrender.

CHAPTER 72

It was after midnight when the two women emerged from Maximus. It was colder since the wind picked up. Sophia and Anya were both pleasantly drunk and walked arm-in-arm for warmth in a dizzy zig-zag down the street. After a half block, Anya stopped and turned to face Sophia. She bent down a few inches and leaned in to kiss Sophia. In spite of the cold, Anya's glossy lips were warm and tender. Sophia hungrily kissed back. Anya's leather jacket was open so that Sophia could snake her plump arm around Anya's waist.

Sophia whispered, "come back to my apartment. Only a few blocks."

They exchanged breathless kisses again, both feeling electric pulses. Anya placed her arms around Sophia's neck and nodded. "Thought you'd never ask, hon. Let's go."

Sophia placed her hand up Anya's skirt and squeezed her muscular ass.

Anya smiled and said, "wait, baby. Let's hurry to your place. It's cold out here."

Sophia's apartment was in an old red-brick building in the Petrogradskij district. It had a small elevator that rattled as it climbed to the third floor. Her apartment was clean and stylish. Minimalist wood furniture, an upholstered gray sofa and two ornate easy chairs filled half of the large living room. On one wall, between the curtained windows, was a wide cherry wood desk with two large iMacs resting side-by-side. There was a gold-plated pole lamp in one corner and a crystal chandelier hanging from the ceiling. A fresh coat of pale yellow paint with soft green highlights coated all three rooms: living room, bedroom, kitchen. The small bathroom was black and white tile.

Obviously, Sophia was paid well for her savvy computer skills.

Both women threw their coats on one of the chairs. Anya pushed Sophia up against the wall that separated the kitchen and living room. She raised Sophia's skirt and felt between her legs. Sophia's knees trembled and she began to slip down the wall.

"Sophia, do you have some cold vodka? I could use one more drink."

Sophia stood erect and moved aside. Her face was flushed as she pulled her skirt down.

"Sure. It's in the fridge. Be right back." She giggled and slid into the kitchen.

Anya took that opportunity to switch the radio on. It was already tuned to a classical station. She turned up the volume. Tchaikovsky, Serenade for Strings in C Major. Quickly, she reached for the left pocket in her leather jacket. Anya wrapped her strong hand around the cold Makarov PM pistol. It was small enough for a woman to shoot with accuracy at close range. This weapon had saved Anya's life more than once. She withdrew it from her jacket and held it behind her back. Two minutes later Sophia walked in with two tumblers of vodka.

"Okay, Anya. Only one more drink for us. Then, I need to get into bed...with you." Sophia licked her lips.

"Yes, baby. I can't wait either. Let's drink to us!"

Anya took the glass in her left hand and moved close to Sophia. She took a gulp of vodka and swallowed. She pushed her lips onto Sophia's mouth one last time, while using her hips to grind Sophia's body against the wall. And then she took the pistol from behind her back and placed it firmly into Sophia's left temple.

"Don't move. Don't you move or I'll blow a hole in your head."

"Who are you? What are you doing?" Sophia's eyes bulged and tears trickled down her fleshy cheeks.

"You are going to fire up your computers because I need some information from you."

"Who the fuck are you?"

"Don't worry about who I am. Just do as you're told. Get over to the desk. Now!"

"Okay, okay. But I don't have any information that you would want. I am a software engineer for a company that makes health care products."

"Shut up and get those computers up and running. Yeah, I know that you work for Align Technology. That's your day job. But I want crucial information that you obtain for Kuznetsov!"

Sophia's face became flushed with a deep crimson at the mention of the name Kuznetsov. But she tried to calm herself by slowing her breathing. She turned on the computers. She turned to Anya, thinking that just minutes ago how she was fantasizing about making love with her all night long.

"I don't know what you're talking about. I don't know anybody by that name? I am a simple engineer. Please, Anya. You must have the wrong person. Please, put the gun away."

"I'm going to count to three. If you don't hurry up and get to the dark web pages with the information you sent to Leonid Vasiliev for that bastard Kuznetsov, I will put a hole in your kneecap."

"Okay, okay. You have to give me more time. It takes a few minutes to access the dark web. But I still don't know what you're looking for. I don't know Kuznetsov or Vasiliev," feigning ignorance.

Anya got closer to Sophia and pointed the pistol at her left knee. "One, two,…last warning, Sophia. I need the addresses of those scumbags who bought those young ladies from Vasiliev. I need them right now."

Terror was etched on Sophia's face. She turned to Anya and cried, "if I give you that information, I will be executed by tomorrow. No one betrays Aleksandr Kuznetsov. I will not!"

"If you don't tell me what I need to know, I will cause you a lot of agony. But if you give me the information I need, I will let you live and get you out of St. Petersburg. I have resources to bring you to America to start a new life. No one will know your past."

Sophia began to type to access certain pages. Then she stopped suddenly and turned in her chair. "How do I know I can trust you? Kuznetsov is a very powerful man. He has tentacles that reach very far."

"I need those addresses, Sophia. Believe me, you can trust me."

Sophia's fingers lingered over the keyboard, not moving. She was terrified.

"Too bad, hon. I warned you."

Anya fired one bullet into the fleshy portion of Sophia's thigh. After a few moments of shock, she began to howl and scream. She became a wounded animal. She fell off the chair onto the living room rug. Sophia grasped her leg with both hands and writhed in pain. Rivulets of blood seeped out of the bullet hole and pooled on the flowered woolen rug. Anya ran into the kitchen for a towel. She grabbed two and hurried back to place them tightly on Sophia's wound.

"Put pressure on the wound. Press hard. I need to get something to wrap around your leg to stop the bleeding."

She scanned the room and her gaze rested on the drapes. There were draw cords. She lunged for one of them and yanked the drapes from the window frame. She extracted a small folded knife from a tiny sheath in the small of her back underneath her skirt. She cut an ample length and quickly tied a tourniquet. Sophia screamed even louder.

"Shut the fuck up or I'll put a bullet in your head. Now, get the fuck back on the chair and get me those addresses. Do what I say and I will not only let you live, but we'll extract you out of Russia."

Anya grabbed her under her arm and pulled her off the floor and onto the chair. Sophia's face was ashen and beads of perspiration dotted her forehead. Her bangs were partially plastered to her forehead. She began typing even though she hung her head in pain. Sophia gritted her teeth.

"Come on, come on. Addresses. Get them and I'll write

them down. Give me a pen and paper."

Sophia opened the top pencil draw and took out a pen and a pad. She finished typing and reached the page with the addresses.

"Here they are. Write them down. I need a doctor. Does your CIA people have doctors. I need medical care before we leave Russia. See, I gave you what you wanted. But I need protection."

Anya wrote down six addresses, folded the paper she wrote on and wedged it in her right shoe.

"You won't have to worry about Kuznetsov any more. I'll take care of you, hon."

In one smooth motion, Anya removed the Makarov from the small of her back and shot Sophia in the back of the head.

"Now, hon, you have no worries. And by the way, you do need to lose a few pounds."

Anya found another clean dish towel in a draw under the sink. She wiped down all the things she remembered touching in the apartment. Then she sat on the sofa and made a quick call. It took about 30 seconds to read off the 6 addresses she had written on the note paper. Upon hanging up she went back into the kitchen, using the dish towel, she searched for a book of matches. Finding a half book, she lit a match and burned the paper she plucked from her shoe to ashes in the sink. Anya ran the cold water, washing away any remnants of ash and bits of paper. She then turned off all of the lights except the pole lamp and rushed to the door. Anya slipped out of the apartment and hurried down the three flights.   When she emerged from the front door, the cold air swirled around her pretty face. A sense of satisfaction filled her heart and mind knowing she did her part to help get those kids back with their parents. Anya swiveled her head in all directions before she began walking. Confident no one was observing her, she walked left toward her rented apartment, steeling herself from the cold.

CHAPTER 73

Corny watched Leonid Vasiliev very intently as SAC Masters took his seat across the table from the Russian mobster and his smartly dressed attorney. He reached for the knob in the corridor and raised the volume. He did not want to miss any conversation. His stomach was churning and his head was throbbing. Corny was desperate for any information about his nieces.

"Leonid, it is all over. We have you. We have your wife and kids. We tracked down some of the kids you 'allegedly kidnapped' within the past week. We need to get the rest of the kids back with their families. Families just like your own. We need to know where those kids are and you have that information."

"Yeah, yeah," said Leonid. He stared at SAC Masters for a good few minutes. He turned to his attorney and raised his eyebrows. He continued to lick his thick lips. No smile. No emotion.

"Look, Leonid. I spoke with the District Attorney. We are willing to offer some kind of deal for the information leading to the recovery of those kids. But we need you to talk now."

"SAC Masters, my family should not be under arrest. They have no idea about my business dealings. They have no information. I wasn't even living at home in Bayside for the past three weeks. However, I work for an extremely dangerous and vindictive man. I need for my family to get protection. FBI protection, yeah?"

"Give me the location of those kids and we'll consider the Witness Protection Program for your wife and kids."

Leonid turned to his attorney and whispered in his ear. "I

can give you all of the names of my men and where you can find them. You can press all of them for where they took those kids. I cannot give you that information. If I do, I will be dead within hours. That's for sure, yeah. My boss has his people all over and they will get to me."

"You will definitely stand trial and the FBI will protect you during that process. After your sentencing, I can arrange for you to be incarcerated in a highly secure facility somewhere in the western U.S. They will never get to you there. You'll live out your days in safety."

Corny began pacing again in the corridor. He ran his hands through his hair and he had a lump in his gut. He began spitting out expletives in the empty hallway.

"Masters, give me a pen and that pad and I'll give you all of my men and their addresses. Most of them go all the time to a bar in Brooklyn. *Spasibo*, yeah. You know it, yeah. But I need my family protected. You have to promise."

Masters pushed the pad across the table and said, "start writing. But, I need the guys who transported the sisters and Brianna Park at the top. Let's go. We're running out of time."

"What about my family? You have to promise."

"If we recover those three kids and they are safe, I promise to relocate your family," claimed SAC Masters.

Maxim Popov nodded and Leonid began to write his list. Masters watched him closely and shook his head. He was not getting the information he needed...until he got a brief message in his earbud from Curlee. He immediately stood up, his chair overturned backward and he rushed out of the interrogation room.

Corny asked, "what? Did you get new info? What?"

SAC Masters smiled and said, "our CIA contact came through. Come, let's go into the bullpen."

They rushed inside the large bullpen area and walked over to one of the intelligence analysts. Agent Curlee was bending over her shoulder, scanning the computer screen. Del was in the kitchen area already talking with Teddy and Joey who had arrived about twenty minutes ago. The three of them were anxious to find out what the new intel was.

"SAC Masters, I just received all of the addresses from a CIA communique through back channels. Printing them out now."

Agents Belman and Myers were in the room as well. They, too, crowded around Masters, who grasped the page as it came through the printer. He and Corny studied the sheet and identified those addresses that they had not had before. One was in Bridgehampton and one was in Amagansett. The second location had an asterisk attached to it and a notation of the enormous payment.

"Amagansett is the one my team and I will take. I know my girls are there. I fucking feel it." Corny was jumping out of his skin and his eyes were gleaming.

"Belman, you and Myers take Sergeant Bolton and his team to Bridgehampton. I'll email you the address and I'll get the warrant from the judge. Go downstairs and mount up," ordered SAC Masters.

Masters picked up the nearest phone. "Agent Levy, I want the SWAT chopper ready to take off from the roof. I want four SWAT officers with extra firepower loaded on board. Sending up four NYPD detectives. And you'll be flying to Amagansett. The detectives have the address."

"Del, maybe you should sit this one out. I've got Teddy and Joey. You know, if you don't feel well," said Corny.

"What's the problem? Afraid of flying, Del?" Asked Joey.

Teddy was curious, too, but he kept his mouth shut.

"No, Corny. I'm good to go. I'm not standing down...not when it comes to Jordan and Emma."

Corny shook his head and pursed his lips.

"Masters, my team is ready to go. Thanks."

Masters nodded and patted him on the back.

"Good luck.

"One thing, John. Where the hell is the staircase to the roof?"

CHAPTER 74

Corny and his team boarded the chopper, staying low beneath the beating blades. Each detective immediately reached for their seatbelts. They were unaccustomed to the odor of engine oil that swirled through the open cabin on the stiff breeze. The four-man SWAT team was already inside, with extra assault rifles, bullet-proof vests, battering rams, and mouth mikes with ear buds. First, Corporal Kathy Bender distributed state-of-the-art headphones so they could communicate with each other in the helicopter. Once the detectives were ready for communication, she gave out mouth mikes and vests to the detectives for the assault. Corporal Ken Barry distributed the large hardware. He gave Joey and Del MP5/10 submachine guns with extra clips. He offered Corny and Teddy, Remington 870 12-gage shotguns, each with extra ammo.

Slowly the chopper rose from the landing pad as SAC Masters stood watching with thumbs up. His hair and trousers were flapping in the updraft of the large aircraft. Agent Levy guided his Bell 407 up and away from the building and headed east.

"Agent Levy, this is Detective Corny Prince. I have the exact address in Amagansett for you. The target is at 133 Bluff Rd," said Corny.

"Copy that, Detective."

"Call me Corny. And with me are three other detectives on my team. Joey, Teddy and Del. We have reason to believe that my two teenage nieces are being held against their will at that location," explained Corny.

Suddenly, all of them heard a retching sound. The SWAT team, as well as the detectives, spied Del suffering from nausea.

One of the SWAT guys grabbed a paper barf bag and shoved it into Del's hand. Her breakfast violently came up, mostly into the bag. Corny quickly scooped up the hair around her slender face, which was stark white, so that the vomitus did not get entangled. Once he thought she was finished, he grabbed the filled bag, closed the top and gave it to the SWAT officer to dispose of. Corny placed his arm gently around Del's shoulders. Teddy offered Del a half bottle of cool water. She nodded and took a few swigs.

Joey asked, "what the hell? I never knew you to get motion sickness."

Teddy responded, "dude, this looks more like morning sickness."

They both looked at Corny with questioning looks. Corny's mouth formed a huge shit-eating grin. Del took a few deep breaths and the color in her cheeks began to resume its normal blush.

"Is she okay?" Asked Levy.

"Yeah, I think so."

"As I was saying, first thing is, Corny, we need to determine an area to land this baby. No pun intended."

Everyone in the cabin chuckled.

Corporal Bender, who was sitting up front next to pilot Levy, jumped into the conversation.

"I was tasked to set up communication with SAC Masters at FBI headquarters. His people will research the best place to land and arrange for local law enforcement to set up a perimeter."

"Go ahead Corporal. We have them on speed dial," joked Levy.

"Chopper 1 for SAC Masters. This is Corporal Bender."

"Go for Masters, Bender."

"We need a place we can set the aircraft down in Amagansett, sir."

"Already ahead of you, Corporal. There is a small section of Amagansett National Wildlife Refuge just east of the main section. You can set her down there and I will alert local law enforcement to assist you once on the ground."

"Thank you sir."

"Sending you the coordinates, Agent Levy."

"Copy that, sir. How far will we be from the target address, sir?"

"Approximately 100 yards. You'll need to make a path between a few estates to the south. Local police will provide access."

"Do we have a green light to breach the target, sir?"

"Your warrant from the judge just came through. I will send it to Detective Prince's phone," said SAC Masters.

"Copy that."

"How many minutes to your target, Levy?"

"Fifteen to twenty."

"Good luck."

"Any intel regarding private security at the estate."

"Unfortunately, no. But you'll have the support of the local people."

"Got it."

"One more thing, Corporal. Make sure all of your body cameras are turned on. I want video coverage in real time."

Bender replied, "Of course, sir. Over and out."

CHAPTER 75

Several East Hampton Town Police vehicles were aligned in a wide circle on the eastern portion of the wildlife refuge, indicating the target landing site for the FBI chopper. The members of the SWAT team were the first to emerge from the Bell 407, followed by the four detectives. Quick introductions were made with Lieutenant Kohl and his officers on the ground. They explained what path they intended to lead the assault teams between two estates up to the target address.

"I, of course, had a lengthly debrief over the phone with SAC Masters. He explained the gravity of the situation and assured me that he obtained a search warrant of the property at 133 Bluff Rd. I explained to him that our entire law enforcement resources would be at your disposal. We will assist in any way we can," said Lieutenant Kohl.

"Good to hear Lieutenant. Do you have any intel about the house and the owner?" Asked Corny.

"Yes. The owner is Joseph Carrington. He is a luxury real estate investor on Long Island and Connecticut. The house is a sprawling modern three-story estate on approximately ten acres of prime land. We had no time to get a floor plan as of yet. I have some of my people working on that as we speak."

Corny opened the page on his phone with the warrant and showed it to the Lieutenant. Kohl nodded and asked if there were any other questions.

Del piped up. "Are you aware if Carrington has security forces on the property?"

"We are not aware, but I can guarantee he has people. Most of the well-to-do in this neck of the woods hire private security firms to protect their property and valuables. If this guy is holding abducted youngsters, you can take it to the bank he has plenty of security agents. And as you may know, most of those agents have had plenty of military experience and combat skills."

Corny and his team listened to and observed Lieutenant Kohl very carefully, assessing his ability to lead them safely to Carrington's estate and supporting their efforts once on the property. Kohl was approximately 50 years old, tall and lanky. He sported a dirty blond crew cut. He was most likely a product of the Army or the Marines. Kohl seemed like he had a no-nonsense approach to this situation and quite a bit of experience. His demeanor suggested that he was not at all protective of his Amagansett resident owners, in view of the fact that the FBI wanted Carrington for harboring children against their will.

All law enforcement teams aligned their communication devices and laid a plan they would follow to approach the property, surround the estate and breach when they were able. Corporal Ken Barry was senior SWAT in charge. Corny was second in command. Within twenty minutes they were ready to approach. The lieutenant's officers formed a chain between two houses so that the assault teams could proceed.

When they all reached the blond wood fence that surrounded the estate, they used cameras in different locations around the perimeter to scope out the grounds. They spied four armed security men stationed around the building. Corporal Barry needed to inform them of the search warrant and ask to see the owner. Before he did that, he asked Lieutenant Kohl to place his snipers at various points around the perimeter of the property high in the trees. Once they were in position Barry approached the front gate. It had wrought iron spikes with two-inch spaces between each rod.

He shouted, "FBI. We have a warrant to search the premises. We need to speak with the owner, now."

No immediate response to Barry. One security guy began speaking on his shoulder mike. The one-sided conversation was inaudible to the assault members. They waited.

"FBI! We have a search warrant for the premises. We need to speak with Mr. Carrington, now! Open the gate or we will breach the property with force!"

A baritone voice from inside the compound shouted, "Okay, wait a minute. Getting the owner to speak with you. Hold on."

Corporal Barry and Corny scanned the estate through the bars and watched the security team scramble to take positions in front of two apparent entry doors with AK-15 assault rifles strapped around their bodies and ready to fire. A huge steel door motored across the iron gates from left to right, obstructing the view of the house.

"They are getting ready for a fight. Obviously this Carrington character is guilty as hell. As planned, Corny, Del, Willams, Douglass, take positions at the rear wall. Lieutenant Kohl—send four men with them.
My team, Ted and Joe, get ready to breach on either side of the steel door."

A chain of 'copy' responses filled Barry's headgear.

"Corporal Bender, on my signal, launch the tear gas canisters and flash bangs toward the building."

"Copy that, Corporal."

After 5 minutes, "Corny, is your assault team in place?"

"Copy that. Our sniper is setting up in a pine tree with a sight line to the top two floors of the house. Give us a few more minutes."

"Our sniper is nesting in a tree south west of the home also with a clear view. We'll give it another five minutes. I got your man Ted setting a small C-4 charge at the front gate."

"Teddy was a marine and an explosives expert in Afghanistan."

"Let me know when your rear team is ready, Corny."

"Copy."

CHAPTER 76

"Corporal Barry, I now have the owner's land line number. I think it best that we try to establish a dialogue with Mr. Joseph Carrington. What do you think?" Asked Lieutenant Kohl.

"Good idea. If we can gain access to the estate and rescue these young ladies without a massive gun fight, all the better. Please give me the number. I've had experience with hostage negotiations."

Kohl gave Barry the phone number and he dialed. One ring. Two rings. Three rings. Four rings. And then someone picked up.

"Yes, who is this?" Asked a woman who sounded mature. Sixties, maybe.

"This is Corporal Barry with the FBI. We have a warrant to search the premises of your home and the property. All vehicles included. To whom I am I speaking with?"

"This is Mrs. Carrington. Why on earth would you have a need to search my house?"

"Mrs. Carrington, we have good reason to believe that Joseph Carrington allegedly purchased two young ladies from a criminal entity on the dark web. He is wanted by the FBI in relation to human trafficking."

"Corporal Barry, that is absurd. My son is a very successful and influential real estate developer. He has no problem getting a date. Perhaps the girls you speak of wandered through our gates last night. My son threw quite a lavish party with so many guests, of all ages. I'm sure he didn't even know half of the people who wanted to hobnob with the rich and famous."

"Ma'am, we need you to order your men to open this gate

immediately."

"Well, if you must enter...just a moment."

In about three minutes, the steel door began to move laterally. Two of the security men, still armed with AK-15's, moved forward to the iron gate. These two men were devoid of any facial expressions that could indicate anxiety or nervousness. Their eyes remained sharp and steady. However, all of a sudden a thunderous explosion of metal against splintered wood erupted at the west side of the huge estate. A black Cadillac Escalade with darkened windows shot through the wooden fence like a rocket.

The assault teams and the police were caught off guard. The only one who reacted immediately was Corny. He backed away from the rear assault position and sped around to the front. Del was on his heels in a flash.

"Lieutenant, I need one of your cruisers!"

Kohl recognized that Corny had skin in the game and had to follow that Escalade.

"Take my vehicle. Fast mother."

Kohl tossed him the keys.

Before Corny could say another word, Teddy and Joey jumped in the back seat behind Corny and Del. Corny gunned the engine. The police SUV clawed the asphalt attempting to catch the escaping vehicle shooting west on Bluff Road.

Simultaneously, Corporal Barry gave the order to breach the property. Both teams breached and immediately were met with heavy fire power. Those AK-15s sprayed their rounds left to right and back again. The snipers were able to pick off three of the security forces before they did much damage to the police or the SWAT officers. The fourth defender was down with leg wounds. One police officer was shot in the shoulder and was on the ground. Within 30 seconds both teams were entering the huge modern estate. Glass shattered and doors battered in shreds, the SWAT team, two in front and two in the rear, were the first inside. The East Hampton police officers were right behind them. They obviously were well-trained and skilled at clearing room-to-room. The first floor seemed cleared. Once the SWAT officers climbed the stairs, they faced trouble.

CHAPTER 77

"Corny, do you see the Escalade?" Asked Del.

"They were in front of about half dozen vehicles. Weaving back and forth. It's only a two-lane road. Luckily not much traffic," explained Corny.

Joey said, "we have to stick with 'em. We have no idea where they're headed. Whether they have a boat, or a warehouse, or another hidden property in the woods."

"Bottom line is, even if we catch up to them, we cannot shoot. If the girls are in that vehicle, they could be harmed," shouted Teddy.

"And that is a big 'if' boys," suggested Del. "Maybe we're following Joseph Carrington and not Emma and Jordan. Maybe they're still holed up in the estate behind several highly paid goons."

Corny said, "I had to make a split second decision based on gut instinct. We need to box them in somehow or run them off the road so that the Escalade stays intact."

"I see the vehicle. It fell in behind the red pick-up truck from the opposing lane. Step on it Corny," ordered Joey.

Corny gunned the engine and swung into the eastbound lane while no cars were coming. He sped up again, until he spotted a white delivery truck up ahead. He needed to swing back into the westbound lane, but two sedans and one SUV were keeping a tight line. He flipped the switch for the cruiser's flashing lights only. The SUV held back so that Corny could sneak in. The delivery truck slowed as the police cruiser lunged ahead.

"They are making a quick left," cried Del. A wave of

nausea was creeping up from her stomach. She groaned and bent over.

"Fuck, Del. You should have stayed behind," said Corny.

"It will pass, I'm fine."

Joey asked, "Teddy, did your wife have morning sickness with Micah?"

"I'm afraid almost every day for a few months in the beginning."

"Hold on, making a sharp left. Hold onto to your cookies, boys and girls."

The police cruiser took the quick turn with the rear tires spinning out a bit. The Escalade was now thundering down a rutted road, part gray gravel and part wet earth. The trees were thick on both sides of the thin path. They were definitely in the woods now, probably the wildlife preserve. Maybe this was a service road for employees and delivery trucks. Corny kept the cruiser on track, bouncing and rolling. And Del was groaning again. For some reason, Corny shouted out, "Oy vey!" Joey and Teddy looked at each other quizzically.

Suddenly, the Escalade made a sharp right into the thick of the woods. There was a rougher path with tree roots and muddy dips. Corny stayed right on him, about 50 yards behind. The Escalade came to an abrupt halt behind a stand of 5 or 6 thick cranberry and red oak trees. All the doors flung open and four burly security men in sport jackets spread out in a semi-circle and pointed their submachine guns in the direction of the cruiser that came to a stop and slid in the mud several feet.

The humid air could no longer hold the rain. It came down in plump drops that bounced off the windshield of Kohl's SUV. Lightening lit up cracks in the gun-metal sky followed by sharp thunder claps. Corny found a few flares under the driver's seat and stuffed them in his back pocket. The four detectives took their assault rifles and jumped down silently into the soft earth.

CHAPTER 78

Machine gun rounds pock-mocked the slate gray wall, lining the staircase. Plaster spit in all directions. The SWAT officers wore clear eye goggles and kept low, avoiding the attack. They returned fire straight up to the second floor. At one point they heard a loud thud. Corporal Bender was thinking that one of the security guys was down. The four SWAT officers pushed their way up to the second level using short bursts of 5-10 rounds at a time. They heard shouting and movement. The security men seemed to retreat into another section as Barry and Bender reached the top step. The others followed with assault rifles at the ready.

Now the SWAT team and four police officers, including Lieutenant Kohl were searching the vast second floor. There were six bedrooms and six bathrooms, another living room, a library and a glass-enclosed Florida room. Two outdoor decks, one on the east and one on the west were accessible from the the Florida room and the master bedroom. All clear. The defenders and the owner had to be on the third level, which could be reached by a spiral staircase and another straight staircase hidden in a corner closet off the library. Half of the assault team took the spiral stairs and the other half climbed the hidden one in the closet.

Bender poked her head over the last step of the metal spiral staircase. Shots rang out and she ducked down. Barry was able to get to the top of the hidden staircase and climb onto one of the outdoor decks where lime green lounge furniture sat under a huge white pergola topped with lush ivy and pink roses. His men followed him silently. For some reason, the security men were not stationed at this section of the third level. They approached the east side by spreading out cautiously. They had the advantage, since this section was higher than the west rooftop level. When they reached the glass half-wall, they were able to see four security men aiming their guns at the top of the spiral staircase. An elderly woman was sitting on a red leather loveseat 40-50 feet behind a corner of a chimney. She was oddly thumbing through a magazine.

Corporal Barry gave the order over the com set and his entire team hopped over the glass partition and aimed their weapons at the defenders.

"FBI! Put down your weapons! You are surrounded!" Barry bellowed.

Two of the men spun around and fired. Barry and his men shot them both, one in center mass and one in the head. Intense training was the key. The other two threw down their guns and dropped to their knees. Barry's men cuffed the remaining two security men with black zip ties.

"All clear, Bender. Suspects are in custody."

Corporal Bender and her team climbed up to the roof sections and they all did a thorough search of the third level. Barry approached Mrs. Carrington first.

"Mrs. Carrington, please stand up and put your hands behind your back."

"Why officer? What did I do?"

"Stand up now."

He placed a black plastic zip tie around her wrists after shifting her arms behind her. He read her her rights, of course.

"Where is your son, Joseph Carrington?"

"Oh, he's not home. And I don't know where he is."

Corporal Barry gave the order to search every nook and cranny of the huge estate. He wondered if Joseph was indeed home, but in a secret hiding place. Money can buy any contractor to build a safe room or a secret man cave.

In the meantime, Corporal Bender contacted Agent Levy in the chopper. "Agent Levy. We need you to head west over Bluff Road. Try to find the four detectives who commandeered, with permission, Lieutenant Kohl's police cruiser. Two police snipers are now heading in your direction to accompany you. And try to reach Detective Prince on the com so he can guide you to his position. They may need help."

"Copy that Corporal."

One of the other SWAT officers gave a shout out to Corporal Bender. "Corporal, we found our suspect down on the second floor!"

Bender walked over to the top of the straight staircase and gazed down at one of her men. She climbed down and joined the officer at the rear wall of the library. He had found a lever that opened a bookcase into a 12'X12' safe room. And there was Joseph Carrington, in a fetal position on a leather sofa. There was a horrid odor of fecal matter, since he had obviously lost control of his bowels. He was sucking his thumb and hiding his face in the corner of the sofa.

"Cuff him and get him out of here. Don't forget to read him his rights."

Bender chuckled under her breath.

CHAPTER 79

In a low voice Corny gave a command to his team. "Spread out now. We don't want them to attack from the left and right flanks. Keep your heads on a swivel. Remember, do not fire at their vehicle. The girls could be locked in the rear. I hope for God sakes."

Teddy crabbed-walked left and Joey did the same on the right side. They kept keen eyes on their adversaries hopping from tree to tree. Corny and Del took positions in front of the police cruiser, behind trees with wide trunks. The ground was uneven and slippery from the rain. Suddenly the woods came alive with multiple rounds whizzing around their heads. Splintered bark and hunks of tree pulp shot in every direction. Corny and his team fired back with equal force.

Three of the security men attempted to close the circle around Corny's team. They obviously had military training and experience. Joey and Teddy continued to jump from tree to tree firing short bursts at chest level. The firefight continued for several minutes. Then, a message came through the com from Agent Levy in the chopper.

"Corny, I'm in the air heading west. Could you identify your location?"

"Levy, we headed west on Bluff Road and followed left on a dirt road into the wildlife preserve. Heavily wooded."

"Headed there now. Will try to locate."

"Let me pop back into the cruiser to put lights and sirens on."

"Copy that."

Just then, several rounds exploded the windshield of the

cruiser. Corny ducked down low across the seats. Sharp pain lit his ear and cheek on fire. He either sustained gunshot wounds or glass splinters from the windshield. He gingerly felt his cheek with his left hand which got sticky-wet with streaks of blood. He searched for a towel or cloth in the glove box to apply to the bloody areas. No luck.

"Corny, you okay? Corny," shouted a panicked Del.

"Del watch your six. I'm okay. A bullet grazed me."

Del moved closer to the cruiser to aide Corny while firing burst after burst at their attackers. One guy moved in closer and landed a round into the side of Del's chest, two inches left of the edge of the vest. Del slumped down into the muddy forest floor. She used her powerful legs to push herself closer to the rear tire of the cruiser.

"Del, Del. Are you hit?"

"Got clipped Corny. Got clipped."

It was hard for Corny to hear her over the loud sirens. He opened the driver side door and slipped out of the seat. Simultaneously he fired two shotgun shells at the closer assailant. The man's head exploded in a bloody mess. His lifeless body did a strange float dance to the ground. The second security guy kept firing, making a Swiss cheese design on the side of the cruiser. All of a sudden, that guy dropped to his knees with a crimson hole in the top of this head. The chopper hung overhead and one of the police snipers expertly found his mark.

Corny ran to assist Del at the rear of Kohl's vehicle. She was on her back holding her hand on her bloody wound and wheezing.

"We need medical attention immediately to our location. Officer down, officer down. We need an ambulance now!" Corny screamed into his com.

Joey ran back to the cruiser and squatted down to offer help to Corny. He found gauze pads in his own gear and ripped open the package. He immediately applied a wad of them to Del's wound.

"Del, help is on the way. Stay with me. Stay with me,"

pleaded Corny.

Del whispered, "not going anywhere big guy. I'm fine. Don't worry."

Teddy joined them. "Two assailants are down."

"Teddy, open the back of the Escalade. Look for my girls. Teddy."

Joey and Teddy ran around the cruiser and over to the black vehicle. They called for Emma and Jordan. They heard no response. Joey hit the trunk release and Teddy rushed to open the rear cargo door.

Inside they found Emma and Jordan in spooning positions, both unconscious and shackled with leg restraints that led to steel rings embedded in the sides of the cargo cavity.

"Emma, Jordan, do you hear me?" Asked Joey. "Emma, Jordan, wake up!"

He gently shook both of them. They slowly stirred and appeared groggy. Thankfully, they were both alive. Teddy searched the dead bodies for a key to unlock the leg restraints and found one on the guy whose head was blown to bits. As soon as he unlocked the chains, he heard the ambulance sirens approaching. Meanwhile, Corny was leaning over Del, holding her hand and her head on an angle. He kissed her forehead, but ignored the blood dripping from his own head onto Del's face. Hot tears streamed down his tired face.

CHAPTER 80

Agent Levy expertly set the FBI chopper on the helipad atop the Peconic Bay Medical Center. A trauma physician, two nurses guiding two wheelchairs and two orderlies ran under the swirling blades with a gurney in tow. As soon as the door opened they immediately hoisted Del onto the gurney and wheeled her quickly to the roof elevator. Joey and Teddy assisted Emma and Jordan off the chopper and each into a wheelchair. The nurses followed the doctor, wheeling the girls, who were still very groggy. Lastly, Corny managed to hop off the edge of the chopper while holding a bloodied compress to the side of his head. Joey and Teddy walked him to the elevator, making sure he didn't keel over from the loss of blood.

"Man, she lost an awful lot of blood," said Corny.

"She will be treated to the best care in the trauma unit, boss," answered Teddy.

"If anyone is a fighter, it's Del. You know that," Joey explained. "Hey, we need to get you in to see a trauma doctor, too. You're bleeding like a pig."

"Oink, oink," grunted Corny. "But don't worry about me. Where are they taking the girls?"

Joey said, "they need to be medically evaluated first. Then, I imagine a psychiatrist will try to talk with them, either together or separately."

"The important thing is that they're safe now. You brought them back like you promised your sister that you would," said Teddy.

Once in the trauma center, a nurse hurried over to Corny and ushered him into an emergency stall and closed the curtain behind her.

"Gentlemen, the waiting room is through those doors. I'll be in touch," commanded the diminutive nurse with curly auburn hair.

Joey and Teddy hesitatingly shuffled to the exit doors.

"What happened to the unconscious detective who was taken off the chopper? Her name is Kristina DelVecchio," explained Corny.

"She was rushed into the OR. She's got one of the best trauma surgeons we have. Hopefully we'll have some information for you in a couple of hours. Meanwhile, I'll get a resident in here to work on you."

The nurse gently pulled the bloody compress away from his head and took a look at his injuries. "Dr. Franken will stop by in a few minutes to take a look."

Corny nodded and leaned back against the angled backrest of the gurney. He was exhausted.

It took Agent Curlee just short of an hour to arrive at the hospital. She strode through the front door and spotted Teddy and Joey, standing in the waiting room sipping cups of vending machine coffee. Joey's mouth was curled up as if he just tasted sour milk. They both spotted Agent Curlee.

"Any news from the surgeon regarding Del's condition?" She asked.

"Still in surgery. Lost a lot of blood. And she's pregnant. The doc knows," said Joey.

"Oh? Wow. How about your boss? Did he take a bullet or was it glass fragments?"

"He's still in a trauma room. They are working on him now. No news," said Teddy. "Want some coffee?"

"Yeah. Would you mind?"

"No. Be right back."

"Agent Curlee, how did it go in Bridgehampton? Did they find the other girl?"

"I'm afraid not. The house was empty. We have a

forensics team there now. The scumbag must have skipped out with Brianna."

"How the hell was he tipped off? You had Leonid in custody way before."

"According to Masters, there was a messy situation in St. Petersburg. The CIA asset had to use force to extract the info we needed. No doubt her associates found her dead in her apartment. They must have gotten word to the last buyer before our agents arrived. Vanished...for now."

Teddy handed Curlee a small cup of coffee, black. "So the task force was able to rescue five out of the six who were abducted."

"Yes. But let's not forget Margot Jeffries, the girl who was murdered before they were able to traffic her."

"Of course." Joey hung his head and rotated his aching neck.

CHAPTER 81

Doug Brady knew he was driving much too fast. His wife, Cara, sat in the passenger seat sobbing the whole way out to Peconic Bay Medical Center. Her parents, Linda and Wendell Prince were in the back seat, trying to console their daughter. They were all so drained from this ordeal, but ecstatic that Corny had fulfilled his promise. Her hero detective, her little brother, rescued her two precious babies. While Doug was bobbing and weaving around the traffic on the LIE, Cara was thinking of the horrors her girls went through.

"Doug, how are Emma and Jordan going to heal? They will never be the same again. They are 17-year old innocent kids. And now, God knows what."

"Listen honey, with a situation like this, it will be one day at a time. They will get all the professional help they need and it will take patience and time. Kids are very resilient," her mother explained.

Wendell, in his baritone voice, said, "we are here for you and for them for as long as you'll have us. You'll see, Cara. They will get past this and move forward. They have their whole lives ahead of them."

"I know Dad. Thank you. But..." Cara began to cry again. She held a wad of Kleenex up to her eyes and blew her nose.

Doug drove around the traffic circle and pulled right up to the front door of the Northwell hospital. A valet walked over to Doug, took his key fob and gave him a parking receipt. They all virtually leapt out of the van and made a mad dash for the double-glass front entrance.

Cara led the group to the information desk. "I'm here to see my girls. They were brought in over an hour ago. Emma and

Jordan Brady. This is my husband and my parents."

Mary wore a beige nameplate over her left breast, pinned to her gray knit sweater. She welcomed them with a warm smile and said, "I need to see everyone's ID please."

They all produced their driver's licenses and placed them on the desk in front of Mary. She studied each one briefly and began typing on her keyboard. In a few moments, four guest passes printed out from the heavy duty HP printer behind her. She passed them and the ID's back to Cara.

"Everyone will need to peel off the back and stick them somewhere on their shirts. It has the patients' names on them. Now let me see if they are in a room or if they are still in the trauma ward."

Mary began typing again. Then she picked up the phone to place a call. She raised the index finger on her left hand as if to say, 'one moment'.
She asked the person on the other end where the patients were currently. And she got her answer. Mary hung up.

"Okay. Your daughters are still in the trauma ward, but a nurse will come out and take you to them. However, only two of you are allowed in at a time."

"Honey, you and Doug go. We'll wait here and see them later," said Linda Prince.

An energetic dark-skinned nurse came through the trauma doors and scanned the waiting room. It wasn't hard to find the anxious parents.

"Mr. and Mrs. Brady. Hi, I'm Jen. I'll take you to Emma and Jordan now. Please follow me."

After Cara and Doug disappeared through the double doors, Joey,
Teddy and Agent Curlee approached Corny's parents. The detectives recognized them as they walked into the lobby and wanted to introduce themselves.

"Mr. and Mrs. Prince. This is Teddy Huong and I'm Joey Hernandez. We are detectives on your son's team and we were with him when he was injured. And allow me to introduce

Special Agent Curlee. She is in charge of the FBI task force."

"So nice to meet you all," said Wendell Prince.

"Mr. and Mrs. Prince, your son is one hell of a detective. He is also a bona fide hero who saved Del's life and along with his team rescued Emma and Jordan. He is a credit to law enforcement," said Agent Curlee.

"Thank you so much for the kind words. He is our next concern. What can you tell us about Cornelius's condition? Was he shot? How bad was it?" Asked his father.

"He was injured and suffered some blood loss and the trauma doctor is working on him as we speak. However, he jumped off the chopper and walked to the elevator and into the trauma section on his own strength," said Joey.

"Well, that's some good news," said his mother.

"And we heard that Kristina was seriously hurt. She was shot and unresponsive?" Asked Wendell.

"Yes sir. She is undergoing surgery now and we have no further information as of yet. Praying for her, sir," said Teddy.

"So the four of you work as a homicide unit in Manhattan?" Asked Wendell.

Teddy raised a soothing hand and guided Corny's parents to some seats in the corner. "Let's sit down and we'll talk. Can I get you some coffee or something?"

Linda said, "no thank you. We're fine." They all sat in a semi-circle on gray and white striped fabric chairs.

"To answer your question, the four of us work in Homicide Midtown Precinct South. Your son and Del were pulled to work on an FBI task force, led by Agent Curlee, investigating human trafficking. They began to work out of the Suffolk County FBI office. Teddy and I joined the unit toward the end of the investigation. All four of us chased down the perpetrators who escaped an Amagansett estate with Emma and Jordan in the rear cargo hold. We were lucky to subdue the bad guys and bring your granddaughters to safety."

"Oh my lord. We don't know how we could ever thank you for what you've done," exclaimed Linda Prince. Hot tears filled her eyes and she grabbed hold of her husband's muscular arm.

Suddenly, the double doors opened and Corny slowly ambled out into the waiting room with a tall, buxom nurse holding onto his right arm. His head was heavily bandaged and his clothes were a muddy mess. Corny looked sweaty and tired, but his lips formed a huge grin when he spotted his mom and dad. Wendell jumped from his seat and he greeted his heroic son with a hearty hug.

"So good to see you son. Your mother and I were sick with worry."

"Dad, it looks worse than it is. Thankfully, we got Emma and Jordan back with us."

The nurse walked Corny to the corner of the waiting room and made sure he made it safely into a chair. "Thanks, I'm fine now."

His mom gave him a hug that could have lasted a half hour. However, she also gave him the evil eye that made him feel guilty for placing himself in danger. They all sat and talked about the terrible ordeal without the gory details. However, they anxiously awaited news about Del. And then he mentioned that Del was pregnant.

CHAPTER 82

Four days later...

The Suffolk County District Attorney's office in Hauppauge was buzzing with television news trucks, reporters and cameramen, tons of equipment, miles of black wires snaking in different directions, and plenty of ordinary pedestrians waiting for the show to begin. The Suffolk County seal was centered in the front panel of the wooden lectern and several microphones were affixed to the slanted top. They were from all of the major networks as well as local News Channel 12. The cacophony that resulted from the news reporters, their staff people, and the excited throng of onlookers began to wane as the Nassau County Executive, the Suffolk County Executive, the District Attorney and two Special Agents from the FBI appeared front and center.

The Executive of Suffolk began. "Thank you all for coming today. It has been quite a tough week since six of our precious, young Long Island people have been abducted. Needless to say, their families were in a continuous state of dreaded terror, anxiety, and exhaustion. Not knowing if and/or when your own child would be coming home is unimaginable. However, our Suffolk FBI field office immediately created a task force that included not only numerous FBI agents and intelligence specialists, but members of an NYPD Homicide detective squad, Nassau detectives, and Suffolk County detectives. They worked night and day in attempts to catch the criminals who abducted these poor youths for purposes of high value trafficking. I will now ask the Special Agent in Charge, John Masters and his top Special Agent Samantha Curlee, who led the task force, to speak to you about the details."

John Masters, wearing an immaculate navy blue Brooks Brothers suit, white shirt and gray tie, was the first to approach the podium after the Executive's initial remarks.

"Thank you sir. I will get right to the point. Human trafficking is not only a local plague, or a nationwide problem, but an international one. As long as there are wealthy individuals who wish to pay huge sums of money to enslave girls, or boys, or young women, it seems as though there are criminal elements who look for opportunities to make lots of money. In this case, there was, and I underline <u>was</u>, a criminal cell of Russian mobsters on Long Island, who, in concert with an overseas Russian oligarch, abducted several teenagers only to sell them to very affluent disturbed individuals. The task force we constructed utilized tremendous resources and talented law enforcement agents to uncover their plans in order to rescue our kids. For more details, I give you, Special Agent Samantha Curlee."

"Thank you SAC Masters." Strands of Agent Curlee's hair danced in the wind around her angular face.

"The facts of this particular case are as follows. One young lady, Margot Jeffries, was snatched out of her own bed by intruders and was unfortunately murdered before she could be delivered to her criminal captors. Six other young people, five young ladies and one young boy were kidnapped and held in two or three locations until the buyers were able to receive them.

Five of the six youngsters were rescued by our FBI agents and detectives, with the help of local law enforcement. They were all reunited with their families. We spared no resources in obtaining information of their whereabouts, utilized undercover FBI agents to gain intelligence and were led on an extensive trail that criss-crossed the Island to recover them. Instituting unorthodox methods, we utilized young and brilliant computer hackers as consultants to gain our information. They were invaluable. And we even enlisted some of our overseas assets, as well, to obtain the addresses we needed to find our kids.

The five alleged pedophiles who purchased these youngsters are in FBI custody awaiting trial. No doubt they will be prosecuted to the full extent of the law.

Unfortunately, one of our young people, Brianna Park, is still unaccounted for. The perpetrators are in the wind. However, we are using every resource at our disposal to find Ms. Park."

SAC Masters moved to the microphones and said, "we will entertain only a few questions at this time."

An NBC reporter was chosen first. "Special Agent Masters, what is the status of the criminal Russian cell at this time?"

"We persuaded the leader of the cell, a Leonid Vasiliev, to cooperate with us in providing addresses and locations of all of his associates. As we speak, agents are in the process of rounding them up and placing them under arrest."

Same reporter asked, "does that mean that Mr. Vasiliev will be extended a deal or receive a lenient sentence if and when convicted?"

The District Attorney slid over to the podium and asked Masters if he could field that question. "Actually with all the charges that Leonid Vasiliev is facing, it is most likely that he will spend the rest of his life in jail. However, we may consider placing him in a prison in a very secluded area of the country. He will most likely serve his time, but not have to worry about his own safety."

The News Channel 12 reporter shot her hand in the air. "What is the physical and emotional condition of the kids who were rescued?"

Masters responded, "Unfortunately, all five of our youngsters suffered sexual abuse and, of course, mental and emotional anguish. Some had bruises, cuts, scrapes and defensive wounds. They are all being treated in one of the best trauma hospitals on Long Island. Each will then undergo psychological evaluations and treatment. That is all I can say."

More hands shot up and shouts were directed toward the officials.

The Nassau County Executive spoke up. "No more questions at this time, thank you. It is truly a time for the kids to reunite with their parents and to begin the healing process. Once again, we owe a great debt of gratitude to our superb law enforcement professionals in the FBI, the Nassau and Suffolk County's police departments and the NYPD. They all did an exemplary job and demonstrated bravery and dedication."

SAC Masters closed with, "Thanks to everyone for their love and support. That's all."

CHAPTER 83

Three Months Later...

The red brick two story building stood on Highway 67 South in front of a dramatic background—a range of snow capped mountains. The stars and stripes flapped violently in the January wind out front. Florence, a high security U.S. Penitentiary was situated in a remote area of Colorado and contained, at the moment, 764 male inmates.

Lunch was daily served at precisely 12 noon. Cliques of inmates gathered at the same tables every day, since humans tended to be territorial, like some animals. The routines were the rule in this facility, as in all penal facilities. The inmates lined up. They picked up their trays and placed them on the rollers in front of the shielded cases of hot food. The servers made no eye contact. They just spooned each portion out—meat, potato, vegetable, dinner roll, dessert, drink—on each tray. Each man picked up the tray and sat with their clique or alone. Each meal, each day, every day.

Many times a particular inmate picked a fight or a dispute with another inmate. Sometimes for a reason. Sometimes for no reason at all. Of course, if your boys had your back, the offender may or may not back off. This was a cloudy Tuesday afternoon and it was in the low 30's.

Three inmates spotted their target and sauntered across the dining room. One 6'3" broad-shouldered man with short blond hair, facial stubble and prison ink on his neck, purposefully knocked into the barrel-chested older inmate who was staring at his food as if he was deciding whether or not to poke his fork in.

The man on the bench turned to the tall guy and stood up.

"Hey, what the fuck? Just trying to eat this shit, yeah. What is your problem?"

This man had a Russian accent.

The other two would-be assailants made a semi circle around the Russian. The first guy with blond hair shoved his muscled arms into the Russian's chest. The Russian lost his footing and fell backwards onto the bench.

"Hey fucker. I guess you don't give a fuck who I am. Yeah? Fucker, I'll knock all your pretty boy teeth out of your mouth. Yeah."

The blond guy moved in closer and blocked the view of the other two. "I'm ready, fat guy. Wanna try it? Come on fat guy. Big guy in here," he said mockingly.

The Russian balled his fists and stood erect. His hard belly extended not more than six inches past his chest. He was ready for a fight.

Meanwhile, one of the other two goons, opened his palm and spilled a small vial of light gray powder over the Russian's mashed potatoes. When the blond guy saw his buddy's signal, he began to back off.

"Okay, big man. You got big balls. Enough now. Maybe some other day. Not in the mood to fuck you up. Let's go boys."

The big Russian sat back down and stuck his fork in the mashed potatoes before they got cold. He also decided to dig into the salisbury steak swimming in mushroom gravy. He washed it down with lemonade. Ready for his raspberry dessert, he suddenly felt his stomach trembling. A minute later he was on the floor of the dining room. His body was in spasm and blood emerged from his eyes, nose, ears and mouth. Tongue bloated and sticking out, he soon lost complete consciousness. His heart exploded within the next thirty seconds. Leonid was dead. And none of the other inmates gave a shit.

<u>Epilogue</u>
February

Tully's Bar was and always will be a cops' hangout. Retired at least five years, Keith Tully served most of his career in the 26th Precinct, which is located on West 126th Street in Manhattan. After several years as a beat cop, he took the sergeant's exam, passed with flying colors, and eventually got promoted to the Intelligence Bureau. He spent his last 20 plus years on the job disrupting criminal and terrorist activity.

Four years prior to retirement (with full pension), his cousin Izzy persuaded him to go 50-50 on purchasing a rundown bar that used to be called **Henry's**, near Midtown South Precinct on West 30th Street. The 52-year old owner, Pete McGill, had trouble getting employees to keep working his old drinking hole. The wooden floors were warped, the mahogany bar had gouges in it from barroom brawls and the furniture was tired and outdated. Pete was barely hanging on; just making his bills with little profit. One night, Pete locked up at 2:00am, brought the iron accordion gate down over the front door and suddenly felt chest pains. Under a dim street lamp, he keeled over and dropped to the pavement. Heart attack took him. The bar was eventually left to his young niece, Wendy, after his estate went to probate. Just to get rid of it, she sold it for a song to Keith and Izzy.

Izzy had some start-up cash from an inheritance and he invested a good $75,000 to fix up the joint. Word spread that a former NYPD sergeant opened a bar that welcomed the boys and girls in blue. Every night it was busy and loud. And Izzy and Tully couldn't be happier. They were surrounded by the New York City's finest and were proud of it.

Lieutenant Woods and his wife, Emily, imagined they were the first to amble into Tully's, since it was early. This was definitely not the first time Jesse Woods spent an evening at Tully's.

"Hey, Lieutenant. Good to see you, pal. And a very good evening to you, Mrs. Woods. Special night for you folks, huh?" Asked Tully.

"Sarge, always a pleasure to see one of our retirees still serving the public. How you feeling, man? How's the Mrs.?" Asked Woods.

"I'm great. Love what I do here. Love being with our own. Know what I mean? And my Iris is just fine. Loves spending more time with our grandkids."

"Good to hear."

"By the way, everything is set up in the back room." Tully nodded.

The lieutenant and his wife followed a path along the huge bar to the spacious back room. Walking through the doorway, they spotted Joey Hernandez and his significant other, Aurora, drinks in hand. They had met each other at a Billy Joel concert in Madison Square Garden last year. Teddy and his lovely wife, Maggie, were getting wine at the bar.

Joey noticed his lieutenant and immediately ushered Aurora to greet them. "Hey Lieu. Emily. This is my girl friend, Aurora. Please meet Emily and Lieutenant Woods."

Aurora's fabulous smile could light up a room. She greeted both of them warmly and shook hands.

"What can I get both of you to drink?"

"Joe, we're good right now. Thanks. But we are definitely looking forward to celebrating the fact that Del has regained her health and was cleared to be back on 'The Job'."

"Not to mention Corny's bravery and key participation in breaking the back of the Russian criminal cell. Recovering five abductees was no easy feat."

"Don't forget, forming a task force means bringing talent and resources from several agencies, working together, Joe," explained the lieutenant.

Teddy and Maggie joined the conversation. The wives had previously met at another occasion. They all exchanged greetings.

And then Mr. and Mrs. Prince arrived, dressed smartly for the occasion. They removed their winter coats and settled into seats at the U-shaped table. Behind them was Corny's sister, Cara, and her husband Doug. Jordan and Emma also shuffled in behind them with matching white Patagonia Puff jackets and stylish boots. Thankfully, they managed smiles and said hello all around.

"So where are the stars of the celebration? Oh, I forgot. My little brother is never on time, right? Doug, I need a martini. Would you get me one please?"

"Sure honey. Be right back."

Emily walked over to Emma and Jordan. She sweetly greeted the girls personally. "Hello ladies. So good to see you both. Love the jackets."

Jordan said, "thanks so much. One of Mom and Dad's gifts to us."

Emma volunteered, "but the real gift will be a family vaca to Hawaii next month for a couple of weeks. After all, we missed the class trip to California."

The lieutenant joined in. "Did I hear Hawaii?"

"Yes, two weeks in the sun…in February," said Jordan.

"And then…"

"We are both enrolled in Hofstra for the first year. After that, who knows. Right now we're staying close to home," explained Emma.

Joey's phone buzzed. He whipped it out of this front

pocket and read the text. "Okay, everyone. Corny just got here. He's right outside. Let's give him and Del a great welcome."

A minute later the back room door opened and Del was the first to appear. Everyone yelled, "Surprise!!"

"Oh my God, what is all of this? Corny, what's going on?"

"Kristina, this is a life celebration for you and me, coordinated by our family and friends. We both survived a pretty tough ordeal, of course, not as tough as my two strong and beautiful nieces."

Del was brave enough to say the obvious. "And they all know how it was for us to lose the baby..." Tears welled up in her eyes. Corny hugged her tightly and then he gallantly dropped to one knee as he slipped his hand into his pocket. You could hear a pin drop. Some mouths were agape.

"Kristina DelVecchio, I could not love you more than I do at this very moment. Let's make it official, please. Will you marry me?"

ACKNOWLEDGEMENT

My lovely wife, Iris, readily agreed to edit One Step Ahead, my second suspense thriller. She spent many hours tirelessly reviewing this project for errors in content and grammar. Iris was extremely competent and enthusiastic in working to help me take this book to fruition. She is the only person who has read the book after I completed the first draft. Thankfully, she was able to confirm that the story arc and flow were appropriately on target.

Thanks Iris! Your confidence in my writing ability continues to give me inspiration.

ABOUT THE AUTHOR

Steve Tullin

Steve Tullin has published numerous short stories and poems. His debut novel, Wound Tight, was published by iUniverse and dropped in August, 2013. He is a retired English teacher and mentor in New York City with an unquenchable thirst for mysteries, thrillers, and crime fiction. He currently lives with his wife in Westbury, New York.

BOOKS BY THIS AUTHOR

Wound Tight

Wound Tight is a cat-and-mouse psychological thriller that primarily unfolds in present day New York City. The antagonist, Herman Girtler, takes center stage as a man consumed by OCPD (Obsessive Compulsive Personality Disorder). He is plagued with obsessive behavior that forces him to strive to control his environment. Unfortunately, Herman is repulsed by the filth of humanity.

Made in the USA
Middletown, DE
20 November 2022

15569799R00166